JU

In her varied career, Juliana Lindsey has run her own hairdressing business, sold clothes from a market stall, worked on a potato harvester, and helped run an antique shop.

Now she writes full time, and is the author of over thirty published novels and many short stories under various names. She writes because the plots won't stop coming, because she loves it, and because it's fun!

Juliana Linden

IN THE NAME
OF HONOUR

The Historical Club
HL.001

Aspire Publishing

An Aspire Publication

First published in Great Britain 1998

ISBN 1 902035 04 6

Printed and bound in Great Britain by
Caledonian International Book Manufacturing Ltd, Glasgow.

Typeset in Palatino by Kestrel Data, Exeter, Devon.

Aspire Publishing – a division of XcentreX Ltd.

Chapter One

'Shall you go to Lucy Thornton's wedding?' Sally
Croxley glanced at the invitation lying on the dressing table. 'It will mean leaving town before the season
is over – earlier than you had planned, I think?'

The girl she was addressing was very beautiful. She
was at that moment in the act of brushing her long
hair, which fell to her shoulders in soft waves and
shone like pure silk. Her wide, guileless eyes were the
blue of a summer's sky, belying the sharp wits of their
owner and a tongue that was at times apt to cut and
thrust with the deadly speed of a rapier.

'Yes, I know,' Caroline Manners replied. 'I would
not go, except that Lucy begged me to – and I rather
like her. She can't help her dreadful mother after all.'

'No, indeed.' Sally pulled a face. 'Such a foolish
little woman.'

'I must admit I find her company tedious, but for
Lucy's sake I suppose it must be endured.'

The dressing table was cluttered with all kinds
of expensive trinkets. Sally picked up a narrow blue
glass scent bottle; it had embossed silver stoppers at
both ends and could contain two different perfumes.
She dabbed a little of one behind her ears.

'This is a lovely fragrance, Caroline,' she said. 'I
must buy some. Why the Thorntons could not have
held the wedding in town I do not know.'

'Too expensive perhaps?' Caroline reached into her dressing-table drawer and took out a bottle of French perfume. 'Have this, Sally. I don't care for it as much as I thought I would.' She pressed it into the older woman's hands and turned back to her mirror before Sally could protest. 'I doubt the Thorntons are all that well breeched, and Sir Malcolm is a little too fond of the card tables.' Caroline laughed suddenly, her eyes alight with mischief. 'Look at it this way, Sally – if we are out of town we shall miss the crush at Carlton House.'

'Caroline!' Sally was amused. 'Don't you know there are those who would willingly die for an invitation from the Regent?'

'Social climbers!' The younger woman grimaced. 'They may have mine and welcome. Next time he lays his podgy hand on my thigh under the table at dinner I swear I shall scream!'

'You are supposed to consider his attentions an honour.'

'An honour to be pinched by that – that grossly oversized son of a lunatic!'

'Caroline, stop,' Sally commanded. 'Such comments are tantamount to treason. We all know that the King has these unfortunate attacks but we do not speak of it. Besides, the Regent is a fine figure of a man.'

Caroline made a face at her in the mirror and began to quote:

> 'By his bulk and by his size,
> By his oily qualities,
> This [or else my eyesight fails]
> This should be the Prince of Wales.'

8

'Caroline! I'm shocked.'

'They are Mr Charles Lamb's words, not mine.'

'I am still shocked,' Sally said with an expression of reproof. These are not the words I expect to hear from you. I know you do not mean to be unkind, but . . .'

'You are right, of course,' Caroline agreed. 'I am ill-tempered today, and you are an angel to put up with me.'

Sally smiled and picked up a heavy silver brush. She was not a maid but she knew that Caroline was often soothed by having her hair brushed, something her mother had often done when she was a small child.

'What ails you, my love?' she asked as she began to stroke the long tresses. A widow with scarcely a penny to her name, Sally was grateful to the young woman who had taken her in as a companion. Caroline was generous to those she cared for. 'Something is on your mind – did you have one of your restless nights?' She gave her a sympathetic look. 'Would you like a tisane?'

'I'm not ill,' Caroline said. 'Just a little bored.'

She got up and paced about the room, then turned to her companion with a rueful twist of her lips.

'What's wrong with me, Sally? Why can't I be content? I seem to have everything that any young woman could reasonably want. Money, position, friends – and you, my dearest friend of all. Yet sometimes . . .' She sighed and shook her hair back so that it fell almost to her waist. 'Yes, I think we shall accept Lady Thornton's invitation. It will be a change of scenery if nothing else.'

Caroline's eyes moved round the crowded room without interest. She had met everyone here before and there was no one whose company amused her. In fact she wondered now why she had bothered to come to a country wedding at all. Perhaps the Regent's ball would have been more interesting . . . Her gaze was drawn across the room towards two men who had just entered. Both were tall, dark and attractive, though one had a slight limp.

'He has come!' Caroline's hostess gasped with pleasure and laid a hand on her arm. 'I never dreamt he would accept, though naturally I invited him.'

Lady Thornton's remarks surprised Caroline, and she politely restrained her hostess from charging across the room to greet her unexpected guests immediately.

'Who are they?' she asked. 'The man with the limp . . .'

'Why, Lord Carlton,' Lady Thornton replied, amazed. 'And his cousin Will, of course. Excuse me, my dear Miss Manners. I must go to them.'

The two men were much alike, though his lordship had more presence. Caroline watched them for a while, noting the way Will Carlton greeted his hostess with a warm handshake compared with the arrogant lift of his lordship's brows. The man looked as if he regretted coming at all, thought Caroline, then, as he turned towards her, she felt his sadness pierce her like a lance.

What suffering had he endured to make him look like that?

The next moment he was frowning, averting his gaze, which piqued her. Almost every other man she had ever summoned with a look had been only too eager to hurry to her side. What made Carlton so special as to be indifferent to her charms?

She moved away, losing herself in the crush. If his

lordship was indifferent, there were many who were not. She was stopped at every turn by admiring gentlemen – not to mention ladies who wished to cultivate her acquaintance. For if Lady Thornton considered herself to have captured Lord Carlton, there were others who thought *Caroline's* presence here a greater triumph.

Caroline was the latest rage to have taken London by storm. She was considered beautiful, amusing – and she was extremely wealthy. There was no house that closed its doors to her, no hostess who did not write her name near the top of her list, and at least a dozen eager gentlemen had expressed a wish to make her their wife. So far she had shown no preference for anyone, thus earning the name of a heart-breaker.

She decided to seek the cooler air on the terraces, and made her way towards the French windows. She turned as someone touched her arm, feeling surprised when she saw it was Lord Carlton's cousin. She gazed into his rather appraising eyes, which were more blue than grey.

'Miss Manners?' he inquired. 'Forgive me. I meant to ask our hostess to introduce us but she fluttered away like a butterfly and I was left with no alternative but to approach you personally.'

His description of their hostess was very apt and amused her.

'I know who you are,' she said. 'Lady Thornton mentioned your name to me earlier.'

'I believe you mean she mentioned my cousin's name,' he corrected, a faint smile in his eyes. 'It is on behalf of Lord Carlton that I have approached you. If you would be so kind as to consent, he would like to meet you.'

Caroline looked for his lordship, frowning when

11

she did not see him. Mr Carlton's request was a little unusual. Gentlemen did not usually request a lady to come to them – unless they happened to be the Prince Regent, of course. On the last occasion Caroline had acceded to such a request the outcome had been a hasty retreat from the Prince's private apartments.

'Fitz has taken sanctuary in a quieter place,' Will explained. 'But if you would follow me . . .'

'I'm not sure. I must speak to Lucy or she will think I am neglecting her.'

'I believe the new Lady Bramley will excuse you for a moment,' he murmured, his hand on her arm. 'Please, Miss Manners, I beg your indulgence.'

Curiosity overcame Caroline; she allowed herself to be drawn across the room and into the library, where Carlton was sitting in a high-backed wing chair, his face turned away.

'Fitz,' his cousin said. 'Permit me to present Miss Caroline Manners. Miss Manners – my cousin Lord Fitzroy John Carlton.'

Lord Carlton turned his head at once, acknowledging her with what she fancied a curt nod. Accustomed to homage, her hackles went up as she saw the cool disinterest of his stare.

'Your cousin insisted on presenting me, sir, but I believe you might prefer to be alone?'

'Forgive me if I don't get up,' Fitz drawled and half rose from his seat before sinking back. 'This damned leg of mine is the very devil.'

'Fitz has recently risen from his sick bed,' Will seemed to apologise. 'I begged him to take my arm but he would not and now he suffers. We should not have come were it not that Lucy Thornton was always a particular friend.'

'I was not aware that you had been ill.' Caroline felt

disadvantaged. Why had his cousin not told her. 'I am sorry if your leg troubles you. Did you fall from your horse?'

'Fitz was with Wellington,' Will explained. 'He was wounded at Salamanca and more recently at Waterloo?'

So he was a hero of the French wars! Terrible, wearisome wars that had dragged on for far too long, causing soaring prices and high taxes.

'Forgive me. I did not realise.'

'Why should you? So tiresome, but I must sit often to ease the pain.'

Caroline noticed the scar at Lord Carlton's temple. Because his hair was longer than was now fashionable it hid all but a tiny fraction of what was probably a sabre cut.

'Perhaps you would have done better to keep to your bed, sir?'

A smile flickered about his mouth, revealing a different man – a man she thought she might like to know.

'Perhaps I should,' he agreed. 'It was good of you to give me a few minutes of your company, Miss Manners, but I must not keep you. Your friends will be missing you.'

'It was a pleasure to have met you, sir.' She bobbed a curtsey. Insufferable man! He was just beginning to win her good opinion, but his cavalier dismissal annoyed her, though she was too well schooled to show it.

Well, what was all that about? Why had he asked to see her? It did not matter. She was sure she did not mind if she never saw either him or his cousin again!

*   *   *

The next morning dawned bright and clear. Caroline rose early, washing in cold water left in a jug from the previous night and donning her riding habit without the help of her maid. She ran down the back stairs she had carefully noted on her arrival, escaping before she could be pounced on by her vigilant hostess.

Now that the wedding was over she was wishing herself miles away, but there were another two days to get through before she could decently make her excuses and leave. What she needed was a good gallop.

If the grooms were surprised to see her so early they made no comment, but saddled up a spirited mare and led it out into the yard. Caroline used a mounting block and rode off. She needed no grooms to accompany her, though she knew her behaviour might shock her hostess. What did it matter? She would probably never visit the Thorntons again.

She galloped through the park and across an open stretch of meadow, up a slight rise and then slowed her horse to an easy canter through the wooded area the other side. It was such a glorious day and she was beginning to feel much better. The wooded area had given way to meadows now, and she rode on, enjoying the sunshine and forgetting all sense of time or place. At last, seeing a stream, she dismounted and tethered her horse loosely to the overhanging branch of a tree. She wandered by the bank of the stream for a while until she came to a small wooden bridge.

The sun was high in the sky now and she took off her hat, sitting down beneath the spreading branches of an ancient oak and closing her eyes. It was so peaceful, so pleasantly warm . . .

When she awoke – suddenly – it was to find a man standing over her. For a moment she was blinded by the sun and she shaded her eyes to look up at his face. His expression was one of such anger that she was shocked, and it was a moment or two before she could find her voice.

'Mr Carlton?' she said uncertainly.

'Miss Manners.' His tone and expression were cold as he offered his hand to pull her to her feet. 'Your horse was found riderless and I thought you must have had an accident.'

His eyes swept her from head to foot, showing his disdain for her dishevelled appearance. Caroline was suddenly very conscious of her crumpled gown and the dampness beneath her armpits.

'I meant only to sit for a moment . . .' She reached for her hat and set it anyhow on her head. 'I – I must have fallen asleep in the sun.'

'Not a wise thing to do,' Will Carlton said, then stretched out his hands, adjusting her hat. 'It wasn't straight . . .'

There was an odd expression in his eyes that disturbed her. Caroline jabbed her long hatpin through the velvet, wishing it had been his hand. How dare he criticise her? How dare he regard her as if she were some kind of a hoyden?

'My horse?' She tossed her head imperiously, looking for it in vain.

'Found it's way to our stables,' he replied, his tone becoming colder still. 'I had seen you ride by earlier and I thought it must be yours. I've had a dozen men out looking for you.'

His manner told her that he considered it a waste of labour. He was reprimanding her as if she were a fool not even capable of caring for her own horse!

'I tied its reins to a branch,' she said. 'Wretched thing! It must have pulled free and wandered off.

I'm sorry you've been put to so much trouble, sir.'

He looked contrite, as if belatedly remembering his manners. 'Forgive me,' he murmured. 'I was anxious for your safety. Please – will you let me take you up to the house and offer you some refreshment? It is not far.'

'Am I on your land then?' She had not realised she had come so far. Remembering her wild gallop she accepted that it would be a long walk back to the Thorntons' house.

'Thank you,' she said. 'If your housekeeper could give me some tea I should be grateful. And I apologise again for wasting your time.'

'No, no,' he said, anxious to make up for his rudeness. 'Mrs Brandon will give you nuncheon and the carriage shall be brought round to carry you back to the Thorntons. A groom can be sent to return your horse and allay any anxiety they may feel.'

Caroline was humiliated. She would have liked to refuse and ride off without further ado, but having placed herself in an uncomfortable position was obliged to accompany him.

They crossed the bridge and walked over a grass hump, which had blocked the house from her view, towards the stables and kitchen gardens. Carlton led her round by a narrow gravel path which came eventually to the door of the west wing.

Situated on the site of a much older manor, the house was large, built of pale buttery stone at the beginning of the century and having particularly gracious lines. In other circumstances Caroline would have made her admiration known, but feared her sentiments might be misunderstood. It might even be thought she had engineered this visit to Pendlesham, one of the richest estates in the country.

Fortunately for her peace of mind, her guide handed her over to the housekeeper once they were inside the house, excusing himself on the pretext of business.

'I fear I have caused some trouble,' Caroline said as she was shown into a pleasantly sunny parlour. 'Mr Carlton has much to do, I suppose?'

The housekeeper inclined her head. 'His lordship leaves everything to Mr Carlton.'

'Because of his wound?'

'Yes, Miss Manners. I expect so.'

As the housekeeper departed to arrange for her meal, Caroline was left to admire some fine paintings by Van Dyck, her curiosity unsatisfied. Clearly Mrs Brandon was very discreet.

She glanced out of the window, frowning as she saw his lordship and Mr Carlton standing by an ornamental pond not far from the house. They appeared to be arguing; Lord Carlton was shaking his head and seemed agitated. For one moment he glanced towards the house, causing Caroline to draw back hastily in case it was thought she was spying on him.

She felt her cheeks become warm. Had they been discussing her? Perhaps Mr Carlton had told his cousin of her presence in the house, suggesting he might like to speak to her – in which case it might mean that he had been refusing?

She turned, trying to hide her deep embarrassment as the housekeeper brought in a tray.

'Would you kindly ask the coachman to be ready in ten minutes, please?'

'But your nuncheon, Miss Manners . . .'

'All I require is some tea, thank you.'

She had an urgent desire to escape. If her presence

17

here was unwelcome to its owner she would not stay another moment!

'Shall we go up to town?' Caroline asked of her companion. 'I am wearied of the country, Sally. I shall die of boredom if the rain continues.'

They were sitting in the rather dreary front parlour of her Norfolk house, and it had been raining intermittently for almost a month, ever since her return from the Thorntons.

'What has upset you?' Sally asked. 'It isn't just the weather, is it? You've been out of sorts since we came here.'

'How well you know me, Sally.' Caroline laughed reluctantly. 'Hand me those cards if you please. I shall tell your fortune.'

Sally shook her head. 'I know my fortune well enough, Caroline. Why don't you do it for yourself?'

It had not been lost on Sally that Caroline's restlessness had started after the wedding breakfast at which Lord Carlton had been an unexpected guest.

'It's bad luck to tell your own fortune,' Caroline replied, her eyes staring into the distance. 'Come on, Sally, there might be a tall, dark and handsome stranger in your future.'

Sally gave in. Caroline always won in the end.

'In truth I would rather be your companion than wife for a second time,' she said.' But if it will please you . . .'

She shuffled the cards and cut them as Caroline directed, watching as the girl began to turn them up and forecast the future. Caroline often told fortunes for her friends, and because she was intelligent and a keen observer of life, she was able to tell them things about themselves they imagined no one else knew.

More than one happy event had come to pass that she predicted, and she was gaining a reputation for her skill.

'You will definitely meet someone,' Caroline said. 'Wealth is coming your way, Sally, but not marriage. First you will pass through an emotional experience and you may lose a friendship you value.'

'Indeed, I hope I shall not,' Sally cried, looking less than pleased. 'For I value your friendship more than any other.'

'Oh, you won't lose that,' Caroline said, laughing at her expression. 'Besides, it's all nonsense. Surely you know that I make it all up?'

'Well, yes, I suppose I do,' Sally said doubtfully. 'But you often get things right.'

'If some foolish girl has been making eyes for weeks at a man her mother is encouraging, then it's safe to wager that she will announce her engagement in the near future. It's a matter of being observant, nothing more.' Caroline's eyes clouded 'Of course I can't really tell the future – I don't believe anyone can.'

'Why don't we play picquet?' Sally asked. 'Or would you prefer to embroider while I read to you?'

Caroline got up and went over to look out of the window at the gardens, dripping with moisture. If only it would stop raining! Perhaps then she could go for a walk or a ride. She was so tired of being cooped up inside.

Although she would never have admitted it, Caroline was a little disturbed by an attempt she had made at reading her own fortune a day or so earlier. She had turned up the tall dark stranger again and again, but always in a position of adversity to her own card. The stranger meant danger for her!

'It's all nonsense,' she murmured to herself without

conviction. Once or twice when reading the cards she had seen something tragic or evil. Not that she would have dreamt of frightening her friends by such tales. Fortune telling was merely a diversion for wet afternoons. Except that she had seen death three times in Amelia Cartwright's cards and Amelia had died suddenly in her own bed that very night. Curiously the doctors could find no cause for it. She had been a young woman in perfect health, but her heart had simply ceased beating.

Afterwards, Caroline had stopped telling fortunes for a month. She was racked with guilt. Why had she done nothing to stop it? Had she brought about Amelia's death by tempting fate?

After a while she recovered from the shock and realised she was being silly. It was just the way the cards fell, and could mean nothing. Nevertheless, she was now troubled by the stranger in her own cards.

'Yes, why don't you read one of Lord Byron's poems?' she said, without turning round.

She was certain the stranger she had seen in the cards was Lord Carlton. He reminded her vividly of the poet who had been lionised by society but had lately fallen from grace somewhat, on account of scandalous rumours that were circulating about his relationship with his half-sister Augusta Leigh. Lord Byron had certainly brought danger and pain to Lady Caroline Lamb, who had risked everything for his sake and been finally rejected. Would the hauntingly-sad eyes of Fitz Carlton be the downfall of Caroline Manners?

She had left Pendlesham vowing never to speak to its owner or his cousin again, but she had not been able to put the incident out of her mind. Why had Mr

Carlton been so angry to find her asleep in the sun, and why had his lordship snubbed her?

Her cheeks stung with embarrassment as she realised it could only be that they believed she had contrived the whole incident. Perhaps Lord Carlton assumed she was interested in his fortune – which was of course nonsense! Caroline had inherited more money than she would ever need from her own parents, who died together in a coaching accident when she was fourteen. She had been left to the care of an elderly maiden aunt, a governess, and her guardian Silas Tavener.

Silas had been her father's business partner and was a wealthy man in his own right. He had watched over her from afar during her formative years, taking good care of her fortune but leaving her wellbeing in the hands of the women. For the past several years he had been abroad, but she had received a letter telling her that he was returning to England soon and would call on her.

Caroline did not imagine that his return would much influence her life. She had an adequate allowance but knew that the bulk of her fortune was in trust until she married – and as yet she has met no one that she would care to make her husband.

She would naturally require a title if she were to bestow her person and her fortune on a man, but being a fastidious creature she wanted more. The man she married must have good manners – that excluded the Carlton cousins for a start! – be intelligent, witty, interesting, handsome . . . Caroline allowed herself a smile. Where would she ever find such a paragon? Every man she had been introduced to during her first season was lacking in some respect: the handsome ones were either dull or foolish; the intelligent ones were too old or had run to fat.

She had heard that Carlton had a brilliant mind . . . perhaps she might be persuaded to accept his lack of social graces if he satisfied her other criteria. Besides, he represented a challenge, and Caroline relished a challenge above all else. It would be amusing to have him begging her forgiveness after his rudeness at Pendlesham.

Suddenly, her mood lightened. She was smiling as she turned to her companion.

'You read so well, Sally. You have quite cheered me up.' She sat down at her writing table and rang a small silver bell. 'I shall change for dinner now, and so should you.'

Sally paused at the door of her boudoir as Caroline's maid appeared. 'Has something upset you, my love? You have seemed in low spirits of late.'

'No, nothing,' Caroline lied. 'I have made up my mind, Sally. You may instruct the maids to pack. We shall go to town on Friday.'

It was not night, it was not day. The light was unreal as the mist swirled around her – a strange, choking mist that clogged mouth and nose, making it difficult to breathe.

She was a small child again, at the top of the stairs looking down at a man and a woman struggling; the woman was screaming, weeping and begging for forgiveness. She clawed at the man with her hands, falling to her knees in supplication.

'Forgive me . . . I beg you, Henry. Forgive me.'

The man struck her about the face several times and she fell across the bottom stair, weeping bitterly.

'Lala . . . Lala . . .' Caroline cried in her dream, and

the woman looked up, her face ravaged with tears and grief.

'Caroline . . . my baby . . .'

The woman got to her feet and reached out towards Caroline, but the man caught her arm and dragged her away. She fought him desperately, but he drew her screaming and weeping from the house, away into that swirling fog.

'Lala . . . Lala . . . come back.'

Caroline awoke with tears on her cheeks. She'd had the nightmare again, the one that had haunted her throughout her childhood.

Who was Lala? Who was the woman who called out to her? Not her mother, that much was certain.

She remembered perfectly well the way her parents had died. Her mother had been dressed in a beautiful ballgown, her father resplendent in velvet coat and knee-breeches. Her mother had kissed her before they left that last evening. Caroline remembered too, her elderly aunt and her governess coming with the news of their death the next day. Why should she be haunted by that dream?

Yet the man hitting the woman was her father, though she could never recall Lala's face when she woke from her dream.

Henry Manners had been a cold, hard-faced man, who had never shown any true affection either to Caroline or her mother. She remembered her mother so well – a soft-voiced, gentle woman. Caroline could still smell her perfume sometimes, and there were moments when she ached for the touch of her hand, the love that had been so cruelly snatched from her.

Getting out of bed, Caroline went over to the window and looked out. It was a clear, moonlit night, the rain clouds finally gone. Her lovely face was wistful as she gazed at the gardens. How beautiful they looked, turned to silver by the moon. She was aware of loneliness, her sense of need . . . for what she knew not.

In that moment when Lord Carlton had let slip his guard she had seen something that touched her heart – the heart she usually protected so well. It was not a man's love she wanted, for instinct told her that men were cruel, unforgiving creatures. And yet she had felt something when she gazed into his eyes, though it might have been more a meeting of kindred spirits than pangs of love.

Her irritation returned as she recalled her last meeting with Will Carlton. Neither he nor his aristocratic cousin were of the least interest to her! She would in any case be unlikely to meet either of them in future since Lady Thornton had told her they never went up to town and she had no intention of visiting Pendlesham ever again.

Chapter Two

'Damn it, Fitz, not another shilling shall you have from me this evening,' cried Will Carlton and tossed his cards onto the table in mock disgust. 'I'll swear you have the devil's own luck!'

Since he had spent the past three hours trying to lose all the golden guineas he had previously won from his cousin at the tables, Will was hard put not to grin. His lordship pushed back his elegant gilt chair and limped over to the fireplace that had been designed by Robert Adam and was a handsome thing, fitting indeed for the room of one of the country's wealthiest men.

Lord Fitzroy John Carlton stood with his back towards the younger man, holding his hands out to the dying embers of the fire. Will's pensive grey eyes rested on his cousin's broad shoulders – shoulders that filled so well the exquisite cut of his blue superfine wool coat. He needed no one to tell him that Fitz was feeling the pain in his leg, or that one of his black moods was on him. If the truth were spoken, his lordship was hellbent on losing his fortune to his cousin and drinking himself into an early grave. Will was equally determined to coax his kinsman back to health. It was a battle of wills between two stubborn men and one that neither was likely to win.

'Old Hookey did me no service in banishing me to

Pendlesham,' Fitz complained. 'My damned leg hurts like hell in this accursed weather. I had far rather be with the army. Death on the battlefield is preferable to an empty life, Will.'

'Self-pity does not become Carlton of Pendlesham!' Will's tone was harsher than he had intended, and it brought his cousin round to face him in a hurry.

'Damn you, Will!' Fitz snapped. 'Are you the keeper of my conscience now?'

Will got to his feet and took two steps towards him. They were very alike, both tall, handsome men with aristocratic features, jutting, square chins, dark, almost black hair and grey eyes, though Will's appeared more blue in a certain light. His lordship looked older than his seven and twenty years, however, the lines of pain etched about his mouth and his eyes dark-shadowed by sleepless nights. Will on the other hand had health and strength, and his mouth was a little less hard than his cousin's.

The difference between them was explained by their lifestyles these past few years. His lordship had been away fighting with Arthur Wellesley – now the Duke of Wellington – in Spain and France, leading many a reckless charge to glory and a score of wounds, the most recent against Napoleon Bonaparte on the field of Waterloo. His shattered leg had been nearly a year in the mending and was still far from healed. Will had spent those same years caring for the family fortunes and keeping Pendlesham in good heart for his cousin's return.

'If you resent my remarks, I apologise,' Will said stiffly. 'But I refuse to stand by and see you throw your life away. You are the head of the family, Fitz, and you owe it to yourself and your name to put the past behind you.'

His lordship held up his hand for peace. 'We shall not speak of *her* if you please,' he said, and there was a deep sadness in his face. 'Do not think I resent your remarks, Will. I know well you speak for love of me, and I have not forgotten my duty. Would that I could, or that *she* would let me.'

'I fear you have lost me, Fitz?' Will was puzzled by the oblique reference to Julia – the woman Fitz had loved and lost – but his cousin shook his head.

'It is nothing,' he muttered, a faint smile flickering across his mouth. 'I doubt you would believe me if I told you.'

When his lordship smiled he looked young again. Will turned away, not wanting to show he was moved. He was very fond of his cousin and would have been determined to see him happy even had he not been the head of the family. To Will, that in itself was very important.

Will had loved Pendlesham and all that it stood for from the moment he was brought here as a young lad by his widowed mother. His uncle – Lord Gerald Fitzroy Carlton – had taken in his brother James's wife and her only child, treating the boy as another son and teaching him to care for the rich Suffolk land that had always been the source of their wealth.

Fitz had never shown any inclination for running the estate, preferring to idle his time away at Oxford writing poetry and reading the classics. At least his father had called it idleness, though Fitz's tutors said that he had one of the finest minds ever to pass through their hallowed halls.

It was at about the time that he was due to leave Oxford that he met Julia and his fate was sealed.

Will had only met the beautiful but fragile Julia

27

Winterton once, just a few weeks before she died of an inflammation of the lungs, but he had cursed her name a thousand times since. If it were not for her, Fitz would never have gone off to the Peninsula to fight with Wellesley in a mood that could only be called suicidal. If he had remained at home he might still be the strong, healthy man he once was, with a good wife and a nursery already filled with sons to ensure the succession.

'A penny for them, Will?'

Will met his cousin's questing eyes for a moment, realising that he would never dare reveal what was in his mind. Women were the devil in disguise! Julia had died in Fitz's arms while he vowed to love her for the rest of his life – a promise he unfortunately showed every sign of keeping.

No woman would ever do that to Will! He had never met one worth a night's sleep, let alone a lifetime's devotion.

'I was thinking that perhaps you should spend a few days in town now that you're on the mend,' Will said. 'Attend some parties, get out in company, take your mind off things.'

'Perhaps.' Fitz stared moodily at the polished toes of his expensive boots. They had been burnished to a high gloss with a secret mixture prepared by his valet, which no doubt contained some of his second-finest champagne. It was no secret that any leftover champagne inevitably disappeared down his servant's throat, but since the man had accompanied Fitz at Salamanca and various other battles, his position was secure.

Fitz brought his gaze up to meet Will's. 'Why don't we go together? Open the town house up for a month or so.'

'I'm needed here,' Will protested. 'You're the one who craves diversion.'

Again that smile flickered on his lordship's mouth. 'It won't wash, sir,' he mocked. 'You had far better give up your plan to marry me off to the beauty and save yourself the trip. Marry her yourself and get an heir for Pendlesham. I doubt I'll keep you waiting long for the title.'

'Damn you, Fitz!' Will glared at him. 'I'll have no more of this morbid talk. You've spent long enough sulking here. If you wish it, I shall of course accompany you to London. As for your marriage, that is your own affair.'

'Thank you, Cousin.'

His lordships's meekness did not deceive Will, but at least he had emerged from his black mood.

'Laugh at me if you please,' Will said, his anger gone as swiftly as it had flared. 'If I pointed out Miss Caroline Manners as a suitable candidate for your attention, it was merely because you seemed to like her when we met at the Thornton's wedding breakfast last month.'

'She amused me,' Fitz said. 'A shrewish temper, Will, but by heaven, what a beauty! Those eyes – I've seen none bluer, I'll swear – and that hair. It's the colour of sunlight on ripe corn.'

Will smiled inwardly at his cousin's poetic waxing. Fitz was not the only man to have been impressed by Caroline Manners. Half the gallants in London were dying of love for her and must needs continue if the stories were true. The lady was proud but cold in her ways. For himself, he thought her too much of a spoilt brat and in need of a good spanking. She had a reputation for breaking hearts, but Will had noticed her eyes appraising Fitz and he believed her interest was caught. Which might explain why she had let her horse wander off that morning he'd found her sleeping in the sun, while half his servants were out searching for her. Something he had found unaccountably irritating. She had surely done it on purpose: she wouldn't be the first young woman to try and get herself invited to Pendlesham. It was odd how often the carriages of eligible young ladies seemed to come to grief at the gates of the estate.

Nor was she alone in admiring his lordship for himself. Fitz had a haunted, brooding look that attracted women like bees to a honeypot, and the scars of battle only added to his lustre. His ability to quote poetry at any given moment added to his allure, and caused many a female heart to flutter.

Will hid his amusement. Fitz was completely unaware of the sensation he caused whenever he deigned to attend any of his neighbours' gatherings. It was so seldom that he accepted invitations, that any hostess lucky enough to capture him was assured of success. Indeed, Fitz would have been surprised to learn that he had unwittingly broken a few hearts.

He was, in any case, immune to beauty. His heart lay forever in the grave with Julia. Caroline Manners could have his body and his title, but her claws and sharp white teeth would not hurt him. If he had not been sure of that, Will would never have selected her as the most likely bride for his wayward cousin.

Will, of course, was not in the petticoat line. His duty was to the estate and Carlton. Once Fitz was safely married he might think of taking a wife. But he would choose sensibly. A woman of good birth and modest fortune, not a wealthy beauty who might enslave him in her toils. He had seen enough of love secondhand to know of its destructive effects.

'I think I shall go to London,' Fitz said, a gleam in his eyes. 'And you, my dear Will, shall come with me.'

The candles were flickering low in their sconces and it had turned colder as the fire died. Will inclined his head, admitting defeat.

Will rose at a quarter to seven the next morning, as was his habit. Before breakfast he wanted to ride out to inspect some fields that had lain fallow the previous year and were about to be ploughed. After that he wanted to meet with one of the gamekeepers, who had reported an outbreak of serious poaching in the home woods. A few birds taken here and there for the pot was one thing, but Briggs seemed to think it was more serious this time; he had complained of a tribe of gypsies in the area. And then there was the problem of the labourers' cottages, some of which needed repair.

Glancing through his window, Will noticed that the yew hedge was looking a bit straggly in places, as though it needed replanting. Shrugging on a coat, which was as well cut as any his lordship owned but of a servicable broadcloth in a sober grey hue, Will left his rooms and went downstairs. In the hall he was stopped by Mrs Brandon.

'Could I have a word with you, sir?' the housekeeper asked respectfully.

'Yes, of course.' Will gave her the warm smile he seemed to reserve for the servants.

'It's about the linen, Mr Carlton. If his lordship is thinking of having guests, it's time some of the sheets were replaced.'

Pendlesham had been without a mistress for many years. Lady Carlton had died in childbirth when he and Fitz were still lads, and Fitz's father had never remarried. By tradition the Carlton men generally remained faithful to their women, seldom marrying more than once – which did not always hold true of the women. Will's own mother had remarried six months after his father died, to an Italian count who had carried her off to live in his villa in the hills of Tuscany. She wrote occasionally to invite Will to stay, though he'd never had the time nor the inclination to visit her. Contact between them was confined to the occasional letter.

'Send for what you need, Mrs Brandon,' Will said now. 'You may apply to me for the necessary funds in the usual way.'

'Yes, sir.'

Will picked up his hat, gloves and riding crop. He imagined that other linen and soft furnishings might also need replenishing. There was no shortage of money for such things, but they were rightly a woman's business. He knew nothing about style or colour, though he could appreciate a well-appointed room as readily as the next man.

Pendlesham needed a mistress to bring it back to life again. Until Fitz's return from the army, Will had lived here alone with only the servants for company and he had noticed a certain shabbiness creeping in. Nothing that a woman's touch could not cure, but below the standards expected at Pendlesham.

It hadn't mattered when there were no guests, other than for the occasional shoot Will organised for his neighbours. That was conducted outdoors, and gentlemen took no account of such things. However, something must be done now that Fitz was thinking of entertaining once more.

Walking across immaculate lawns towards an orna-mental temple, which had over the years been much favoured by the Pendlesham ladies, Will was startled to see his cousin taking the air. Fitz was unshaven, his hair escaping from its ribbon to fall about his face in lank whisps, and there were dark shadows beneath his eyes.

'You're about early?'

'I could not sleep,' Fitz acknowledged. 'I have been sitting out here since before the birds were awake and calling.'

'You'll catch your death!' Will was anxious; his cousin had had several bouts of a virulent fever and they had at one time feared he might die of a congestion of the lungs.

A wry smile touched his lordship's lips. 'No, Will, don't accuse me so. I am stronger than you might imagine. Besides, *she* will not let me take the easy way.'

Seeing the sadness in Fitz's eyes, Will experienced a spurt of anger towards the woman who still haunted his cousin after so many years. What kind of person had she been, to reach out and hold him in thrall from beyond the grave?

'What do you mean?' he asked. 'Did you make her more promises?'

'I promised Julia I would love her forever,' Fitz said, a nostalgic smile transforming his harsh features. 'No, I've made her no other vows, but she will not let me throw my life away for her sake.'

'I don't understand.'

For a moment Fitz was silent, his eyes staring into the distance. 'You will not believe me. You will say it was but a fevered dream.'

'Tell me, Fitz,' Will said, suddenly alert. This could be important; it might be the key to his cousin's moods.

'It was after Salamanca,' Fitz said, a soft, dreaming note in his voice. 'I was wounded in the shoulder and in my fever I knew no one. Then out of the pain a voice spoke to me – it was her voice. I opened my eyes and I saw her . . .'

'Go on,' Will prompted as he stopped. 'What did Julia say to you?'

'She was not a figure of mist floating in the air,' Fitz said, his brow wrinkled in remembrance. 'She was as solid and real as you. She touched my forehead and her hands were cool; they made the pain seem easier. Then she told me I must live. "If you die without fulfilling your mission in life we shall never be to-gether," that's what she said.' Fitz met his cousin's eyes. 'You think it merely a dream of course.'

'You are convinced she came to you, aren't you?'

'Yes.' Fitz looked rueful. 'I don't know how such a thing is possible, but I do know that after she kissed me both the pain and the fever were suddenly gone.' Fitz gave a harsh laugh. 'Am I mad, Will?'

For a moment Will was silent. He was firmly convinced that it had been a part of his cousin's illness. Such things were not possible, but if it gave Fitz some comfort, it was not to be dismissed as a triviality.

'There are many things in Heaven and Earth . . .' Will smiled at him. 'No, you're not mad, cousin, far from it.'

He had cursed Julia a thousand times, but now he blessed her as a saint. If Fitz believed Julia wanted him to live he would not take his own life – something Will had feared.

'What did she mean by your mission in life?'

'I wish I knew!'

'Perhaps she wants you to be happy – with a wife and family?'

'Do my duty and produce an heir?' Fitz's smile was sardonic.

'You don't have to break your promise to Julia. It isn't necessary to love your wife, merely to get her with child.'

'Poor wife,' Fitz said. 'A cold and cruel fate awaits the woman who takes me for her husband. I cannot give her love even if I would.'

'Then choose a woman who wants a title and position and will not be hurt by your indifferences. A woman who prefers to live in town.' Will saw that he'd given his cousin pause for thought. He let his words sink in, then, 'Once you have your heirs you may both go your own way and live amicably apart.'

'Do you really see life as that simple?' Fitz asked after a moment or two, and there was an odd expression that might have been pity in his eyes. 'Have you never loved, Will?'

'I was – am – fond of my mother, but I have never loved a woman deeply. Not in the way you mean.'

'You have missed so much, my friend. Better to love deeply and die than never love.'

'Perhaps.' For a moment Will thought of a woman asleep in the shade of an ancient oak, then blocked the vision swiftly from his mind. 'If I ever fall in love I dare say it will make a fool of me. But we were talking of a marriage of convenience. How many men do you know who love their wives? They may be infatuated for a few months, but the gilt soon wears away after marriage. Or women who love their husbands for that matter? How many are faithful to their vows?'

'Julia would have been faithful, as should I to her.' Fitz's voice carried the ring of conviction.

Will digested this in silence but made no comment. He did not believe in eternal love, or romantic love at all for that matter. However, it was not for him to destroy Fitz's illusions.

'Then marry a woman who loves no one but herself,' he suggested. 'You will not hurt her or yourself. Do it for the sake of the estate.'

'Caroline Manners?' Fitz nodded, looking thoughtful. 'You think she has no heart?'

'She is cold and they whisper she dislikes men. She will marry for position and a title, believe me.'

'Poor Caroline,' Fitz said. 'If what you say is true, she must be very unhappy. Do you suppose she has been hurt by a man?'

'Who knows?' Will shrugged. 'No doubt there are others as willing, if she is not to your taste.'

'If I could be sure she would not suffer from my indifference. I would not deliberately hurt her or any other woman, Will.' Fitz looked troubled, but Will could see he was swayed by his arguments. He decided not to push the subject further for the moment. Though Fitz could be stubborn, left to himself he would see where his duty lay.

'But you will think about marriage?'

Fitz was silent for a long time, then he inclined his head. 'I suppose it is my duty,' he said. 'Yes, I shall think about it.'

Chapter Three

London was thin of company; the season was over and many of Caroline's friends had departed for Bath or their country estates. There were of course those who, like her, found the country tedious and preferred to live permanently in town. It meant smaller, more select gatherings, which were on the whole more pleasant than the fashionable crush earlier in the year.

This summer there had been no shocking news from France to enliven the fashionable drawing rooms with stories, such as that of Bonaparte's triumphant return at the head of an army. Wellington had the previous year taught that scallywag a lesson and sent him off to exile on Saint Helena, there to dream of his hundred days of glory and reflect on his sins, and in exile he remained. So the gossip was all of the Regent's latest unkindness to his unfortunate wife, poor Caroline of Brunswick – a lady not known for her prudent behaviour, who had nevertheless aroused the sympathy of many.

This particular evening Caroline Manners and her companion, Sally, were attending a small supper dance given by Lady Blackstone at her house in the Strand, for her eldest daughter. Rachel Blackstone had gone through the season without attracting an offer of marriage, perhaps because she was a tall, thin, plain girl whose conversation consisted entirely of horses and hunting. Her mother, however, was a pleasant, woman, who had confided to Caroline in a moment of despair, that she doubted she would ever get the girl off her hands.

'You are giving up too easily,' Caroline cried with a laugh, for she liked Rachel despite their opposing interests. 'I'm sure there must be a gentleman somewhere who loves horses and hunting as much as Rachel does.'

'Then I pray he will appear before my impatient daughter drags me back to the country and her beloved horses! She vows this dance is the last she will attend this year.'

Most of the Blackstones' guests had already arrived when Caroline and Sally entered the elegant reception room, which was massed with banks of hothouse flowers and was already rather warm. Caroline's eyes swept over the assembled company, coming to rest at last on a vivacious group, laughing and chattering excitedly in a corner by the velvet-draped window. Her heart missed a beat as she saw the two men at the centre of all this attention. What an outstanding pair they were, she thought, and how surprising to find them both at what she had expected to be an unremarkable party.

Her hostess came bustling up, silk gown rustling importantly; she was obviously dazed and excited by her triumph. 'It is the most thrilling thing, dearest Caroline,' she carolled. 'Sir Charles happened to bump into his lordship in the street, and, learning he had that day arrived in town, he straightway invited both Lord Carlton and his cousin for this evening.'

'A fortunate meeting indeed,' Caroline murmured,

her eyes bright with amusement. 'You must be the first to welcome his lordship to town.'

'Yes, indeed.' Lady Blackstone fanned herself vigorously, her cheeks almost as red as her elegant gown. 'I am overcome with the honour. I never dreamt they would actually come.'

Had she known it, Lady Blackstone owed her triumph to her husband's having mentioned the name of one particular guest – that of Miss Caroline Manners, herself a cool vision of loveliness in lemon yellow silk. Happily for both ladies, neither of them had the least idea that this news had swayed his lordship in favour of attending an insignificent dance.

'If he should offer for Rachel . . .' the ecstatic mother sighed. 'It would be the answer to all my prayers.'

'Lord Carlton?' Caroline asked, surprised at the woman's ambition.

'No, I am not a dreamer, Caroline.' Lady Blackstone gave a rueful laugh. 'I was thinking of Mr Carlton. Such a pleasant gentleman. We met once at the Thorntons' two years ago, and he was kind to Rachel when her horse went lame. He lent her another from his own stables.'

'His lordship's stables?' Caroline questioned.

'Mr Carlton keeps a string of good horses himself,' Lady Blackstone informed her. 'He breeds and sells hunters to his neighbours. And I declare a better judge of horseflesh could not be found.'

'Then Mr Carlton should have something in common with Rachel.'

'Exactly.' Lady Blackstone looked blissful. 'She would make him an excellent wife.'

'Yes, I suppose she would.' Caroline glanced across the room once more, but the Carlton cousins had their backs towards her.

The champagne was flowing freely as people moved about the spacious rooms, loosening tongues and adding to the atmosphere of this cordial occasion. In the light of magnificent crystal chandeliers, jewels flashed from throats and fingers, eyes sparkled and laughter tinkled. The evening would undoubtedly be declared a success.

Her hostess turned inquisitive eyes on Caroline. 'Have you met Lord Carlton? I believe you would like him.'

'What makes you think that?'

'He has such a quick, clever mind – just like you, my dear. And the poor man has been so ill. You would be good for him, bring him back into society where he belongs.'

'He may not wish to be in company too much just yet,' Caroline replied, but there was a pensive look in her eyes. 'When last we met he was in a great deal of pain with his leg.'

'It was not his leg I was thinking of,' Lady Blackstone said with an arch smile. 'But I shall tell you another time, when we are alone and can enjoy a good gossip. Excuse me now, I must greet Mrs Harris and her son.'

Caroline smothered her irritation, unaware that she was frowning and that Will Carlton was watching her from across the room. How very annoying it was when people hinted at a secret then refused to reveal it!

She noticed that Sally had settled herself amongst the matrons and was about to join her when someone tapped her arm. Her mood was not improved when she saw who it was.

'Captain Royston,' she said. 'Are you still in town? I quite thought you would have left for Hertfordshire by now.'

Now this man might be Rachel's perfect partner, Caroline couldn't help thinking. The last time they had met he had bored her for quite half an hour with talk of his hunting exploits.

'Do you dance this evening, Miss Manners?'

'Why yes, sir, I certainly mean to,' she replied. At least if they were dancing he couldn't talk the whole time!

The carpets had been rolled back in the spacious drawing-room and a small group of musicians were already playing a waltz. At a select private gathering such as this Caroline had no hesitation in dancing without the express permission of her hostess. Such strict rules were for the haughty patronesses of Almack's or the Assembly Rooms.

Captain Royston was a more accomplished dancer than conversationalist, and Caroline gave him a warmer smile when he relinquished her as the music died. She was immediately besieged by half a dozen eager gentlemen and her card was soon filled. She kept the supper dance free, though had little hope of being approached by the partner she hoped for. Lord Carlton's leg was surely not healed enough for dancing.

During the evening she twice observed Will Carlton twirling Rachel Blackstone about the floor and was piqued that he had not chosen to add his name to her card. Not that she especially wished to dance with him, but it did not sit well with her pride to be ignored. Was it that the Carlton cousins found her unattractive?

Her pride was eventually placated when at last Mr Carlton approached her, just before the supper dance. She noticed how well he held himself, and the exquisite cut of his coat. He dressed plainly but with a certain elegance and stood out from the company, needing no padding for shoulders that were if anything broader than his cousin's.

'Miss Manners,' he said. 'It is a pleasure to see you again. I trust you are well?'

'Very well, thank you, sir – and you?' She extended her hand as he murmured something, and he touched it with his fingertips. 'I am surprised to see you here this evening. I imagined you settled in the country for the hunting and shooting.'

'Fitz had an urge for company and he cannot ride at the moment,' Will replied. 'Now that he is feeling better in himself he needs diversion. For myself I should prefer to be at home – there is much to be done – but he would have me come, and here I am.'

'Everyone should forget their duty sometimes.'

'Do you think so, Miss Manners?' His eyes seemed to search her face intently, as if trying to penetrate her thoughts.

'All work and no play . . .' she challenged, tipping her chin at him.

'Do I seem dull to you?'

'I did not say that!' she denied. 'You wrong me, sir.'

'You implied it.' A wry smile curved his mouth. 'Perhaps I deserved it. However, duty has always been important to me.'

'You are devoted to Pendlesham, I think?'

'Indeed. It is my life.'

'You do not care much for London?'

'He shrugged. 'I can enjoy it on occasion.'

'Then you do not agree with Doctor Johnson?'

'That when a man is tired of London, he is tired of life?' Will raised his brows. 'I think there may be more to life than that implies, don't you?'

'But then you are a countryman. You live for horses and hunting, I presume?'

'I think I would rather agree with Wellington: "Being born in a stable does not make a man a horse." I find many things agreeable, Miss Manners, don't you?'

'I have never cared for the country, though it can be pleasant at times.'

'You prefer to be constantly in company perhaps?'

'Yes . . .' Caroline sighed. It was not always true. She enjoyed interesting company, but until recently she had been as happy at home with a good book or her embroidery. 'In good company. I need stimulation. I cannot bear to be bored.'

'Do I bore you?'

'No, of course not,' she cried and realised it was true. He might not be the most polished of men, but his company made her feel brighter, more alive. Seeing Captain Royston bearing down on them, she lowered her voice. 'But the captain does. I am not committed to him but cannot refuse. Rescue me, I beg you!'

Will glanced over his shoulder, smothering a laugh. He had endured several of Captain Royston's tales himself. He held out his hand. 'Will you dance, Miss Manners?'

'Gladly, sir.'

Caroline pretended not to see the captain's disappointed look as she was whisked from under his nose.

'Will you have supper with Fitz?' Will asked. 'He sent me to beg for the favour of your company.'

She wondered at Will's readiness to act as his cousin's messenger.

'Is his leg paining him again?'

'He is seldom without pain but does not complain.'

'That must be hard for him.' Her sympathy was aroused. 'He is young to have suffered so much.'

'Fitz has suffered too long and too often.'

Caroline looked up. In the candlelight, his eyes seemed to have lost their former harshness. 'You are fond of your cousin, I think?'

'He is Carlton,' Will replied, as if that were sufficient answer. 'I would do anything for him. Yes, I am fond of him. We were raised as brothers after my own father died. My uncle made no difference between us. We shared favours and beatings equally.'

'Were you often beaten?' She was diverted by his direct way of speaking, which she found refreshing.

'Only when we deserved it.' Will grinned, and she drew breath as she glimpsed the man beneath the unemotional mask. 'That was often enough. We were always up to some mischief, each as bad as the other.'

'You were lucky to have each other,' Caroline said, a wistful note in her voice. She gazed up at him, unaware of the revealing expression in her clear eyes.

'You were an only child?'

'Yes. My parents died when I was fourteen. I was brought up by an elderly aunt and a governess – and my guardian, though I seldom saw him.'

'I see. That was unfortunate.'

'Perhaps. I still miss my mother.'

'But not your father?'

'He showed neither my mother nor I much affection.' Why was she telling him all this? It was something she never spoke of, except to Sally.

'Ah.' Will nodded and looked thoughtful. 'Do you see men as harsh, uncaring creatures, Miss Manners?'

'Many of them are,' she replied. 'But tell me more

about your cousin, sir. He has been wounded several times, I imagine. He has such sad eyes . . .'

'Yes. It makes him a romantic figure, does it not?'

'You mock me, sir!'

'Indeed I do not. Other women might sigh for his looks. You, Miss Manners, are more level-headed, I think? I believe you know exactly what you want from life, as my cousin does. You would suit each other well.'

Caroline missed a step and almost trod on his foot. 'If you are suggesting . . . ' Really, this was too much!

'I suggest nothing,' Will said. 'I would not presume to be so forward. My cousin's wits are not impaired, though his health is not yet as good as it once was and will be again given the right circumstances. If he has anything to say he will speak for himself. And I hope you will accept his invitation?'

'Very well,' she said, and laid her hand on his arm. 'You may as well take me to him, since you will give me no peace otherwise.' She realised her reply must have sounded ungracious. 'Forgive me, that was rude.'

'I deserved worse,' he murmured and there was a hint of laughter in his eyes. 'I provoked you deliberately for the sheer joy of it. You look very beautiful when you are angry, Miss Manners.'

'Flattery will not wash with me, Mr Carlton! It is the refuge of the insincere and the social climber.' She gave him a stern look, but in reality was mollified.

'You are a sensible woman, Miss Manners. I remarked it at our first meeting.'

'You did not think me sensible when my horse found its way to your stables,' she reminded him.

'Wanderer by name, wanderer by nature. She merely came home, that's all.'

45

'Ah yes, you breed horses, I believe? You did not tell me you had owned the horse, or that you were an expert on bloodlines.'

'I would not dream of boring you with such topics, Miss Manners,' Will murmured. 'Perhaps you may find Fitz's conversation more to your taste.'

'But . . .' She stared at him in surprise as they paused outside a door. She knew the house well and he had not brought her to the dining-room, where a sumptuous cold buffet was laid out for the guests. 'This is the library . . .'

'Nevertheless, your supper awaits you.' Will gave her a gentle push towards the door. 'Excuse me please, I am promised to Miss Blackstone for supper.'

Caroline hesitated for a moment as he turned away, then opened the door and went in. The library was a large, pleasant room, its walls lined with mahogany shelves filled with leather-bound books that looked as if they had never been opened. In the middle of the room was a large drum table with a green leather top; several smaller tables were dotted about in convenient corners, one of which had been set for two persons. Only a handful of candles were burning, giving the room an intimate atmosphere, and champagne was already poured into crystal glasses. Lord Carlton had been so certain she would come then.

As she hesitated on the threshold, he rose from the high-backed wing chair that had hidden him from her view and stood before the fireplace, smiling at her.

'You are welcome, Miss Manners. Please be seated. I daresay you are hungry.'

'Why have you done this, sir?'

'Once before you were offered hospitality but left before it could be rendered. My fault, I believe? You

46

were offended because you were my guest, and I did not come to greet you. This is my way of apologising, Miss Manners. It was unforgivable of me, but I pray that you will relent.' He waved his hand towards the table. 'Our good hostess has thought of everything, I believe. May I serve you a little cold chicken, or some of this fine ham?'

She took a step towards the table, fascinated by him despite herself. 'Why did you not want to meet me that day? I saw you arguing with your cousin from the window.'

'Ah!' His eyes were understanding. 'I see why you left. Such rudeness deserved no less. I was still feeling rather sorry for myself because of . . .' He shrugged his shoulders. 'A poor excuse but my only one I fear. Now what may I serve you?'

'I will have some of that ham and a spoonful of green peas,' Caroline said. She sat down and took a sip of the champagne. 'You intrigue me, sir. I had thought you did not care for my company – and now all this.'

'But I have an ulterior motive of course.' Fitz's eyes were quietly amused. 'I have come to town to entertain, yet I have no hostess. As a bachelor I cannot entertain ladies, unless I can persuade someone to take pity on me.'

'You are asking *me* to be your hostess?' An unmarried woman: it was an impossible idea!

'You and Mrs Croxley jointly, of course,' he corrected himself at once and smiled. 'Come, Miss Manners – what do you say? Will you take pity on me?'

There were a dozen ladies of mature years and superior reputations he might have asked. This was merely an excuse to widen the scope of their

47

acquaintance, and after his cousin's heavy hints she could not mistake his intentions. Caroline toyed with a sliver of the delicious ham he had placed on a plate for her. If she accepted, she would be opening the way for an offer of marriage in the near future. By taking this unusual and bold step he was rushing his fences, which could mean only one thing. He was thinking of making a marriage of convenience. If it was not her, it would be someone else – someone prepared to marry for the sake of a title and position.

Caroline was not to be rushed. She ate her ham then reached for a peach. Lord Carlton took it from her, peeling it with his own knife and cutting it into thin slices. She thanked him, revising her opinion of his decorum. Perhaps it was his temper that was uncertain? Well, she would discover that on closer acquaintance. She had almost made up her mind to accept his offer to act as a hostess, though she would not tell him so just yet.

'You must allow me a little time for reflection, sir.'

'Of course.' He sipped his champagne, then refilled her glass. She noticed that his movements were still rather stiff, but if he was in pain he did not show it. 'How soon would it be convenient for you to give me an answer?'

'I shall write to you tomorrow,' she said. 'If my answer is no, you will need to approach someone else.'

'I would be grateful if you could find it in your heart to accept,' he said. 'I believe you have special qualities that would ensure the success of my modest entertainments, Miss Manners.'

How appealing he was when he spoke in that soft voice, that was almost a caress. For a moment she wondered what it would be like to be kissed by that generous mouth. Not unpleasant, she surmised. In fact she felt she might come to like him rather well. His reserved manner pleased her, and he had a sense of humour to boot. She did not think he would demand too much of her.

'Can I tempt you to some grapes?' he asked, picking up a pair of silver scissors and snipping off a tiny branch.

'Thank you no, I think I have eaten enough,' Caroline said. She pushed back her chair and stood up. 'You were kind to think of this, sir – and I have forgiven you. I shall give my answer to your flattering offer tomorrow.'

'Not flattering or kind,' Fitz said, a brooding expression on his face. 'You would probably be wiser to refuse me.'

Caroline saw the sadness in his eyes and was once again struck by it. 'Perhaps,' she acknowledged. 'But I shall think about it and give you my answer when I am a little more certain.'

He bowed his head and let her go. Caroline was thoughtful as she made her way upstairs towards the bedroom set aside for the ladies to tidy themselves. She was much in need of a few moments alone. However, at the top of the stairs she met her hostess, who gave her a knowing look.

'Did you enjoy your supper, my dear?' she asked. 'Lord Carlton was feeling poorly and he asked me to arrange it so that he might have the pleasure of your company privately for a few moments. I think he is very taken with you.'

Caroline shook her head, slightly irritated with her friend. 'We hardly know one another.'

'But love is a bolt from the blue.' Her ladyship

sighed. 'It would be so wonderful if poor dear Lord Carlton were to fall in love with you.'

'What do you mean?' Caroline furrowed her smooth brow.

'Do you not know his story?' Lady Blackstone was surprised. 'He was engaged to be married to a very beautiful girl when he was nineteen. She died – in his arms so they say. Since then his name has never been linked with another woman . . .' She gave Caroline a mischievous smile. 'Until now.'

'Engaged to be married?'

That would explain everything, of course. Mr Carlton had prepared the way for his cousin by telling her that he needed to be coaxed back to health, and what better way than by taking a wife? Lord Carlton had asked her to be his hostess because he wanted a shortcut to finding a new mistress for Pendlesham. Obviously, he did not feel up to a long drawn out courtship. She had been selected as suitable – and available, seemingly.

Caroline was not sure whether to be furious or flattered. But Lord Carlton had denied that his offer was flattering. Indeed, he had almost recommended she decline it.

'Excuse me,' she said. 'I must tidy myself a little before I go down. I have a partner waiting.'

As Lady Blackstone sailed away in full bloom, Caroline went into the bedroom. She was relieved to find it empty. She paured some cold water into a bowl and splashed her face, patting it dry with a soft towel. Then she stared at herself in the mirror.

What was she to make out of all this? It would need some careful thought. For the moment she must make an effort to put it out of her mind.

* * *

It was easier thought than done, however, and Caroline was glad when she and Sally were finally allowed to leave. She had seen nothing more of either Lord Carlton or his cousin and she presumed that they had left after supper. She was so quiet on the way home, that Sally looked at her anxiously as they went upstairs.

'Has something upset you, Caroline?'

'Not upset me, no.' She explained that Lord Carlton had asked them to be his hostesses. 'Of course it will really be you, Sally,' she said. 'I could not do it on my own.'

As an unmarried lady it would be unheard of for her to be a gentleman's hostess, but with her companion it would be tolerable. In this way Sally would be the official hostess, and she, Caroline, would merely help greet the guests.

'I expect he will make you a handsome present.' Caroline laughed as she remembered telling her companion's fortune. 'There – I told you wealth was coming your way.'

'Yes, you did.' Sally looked struck, then shook her head and laughed. 'I hardly think it will make me wealthy, my love. I shall do it if you wish, of course.'

She looked at Caroline curiously, for the reasons behind such a request were not lost on her. Caroline smiled and kissed her cheek.

'I shall tell you what I think tomorrow,' she said. 'Goodnight, dear Sally. Sleep well.'

Having dismissed a sleepy maid, Caroline undressed alone in her room, scattering her clothes and jewels carelessly about the furniture. She sat down before the mirror and brushed her hair. She did not feel in the least tired. Besides, she knew sleep would elude her. Going to the little velvet cushioned seat under the window she gazed out at the silent streets. Nothing was stirring.

To acceept Lord Carlton's offer did not mean that she was forced to accept an offer of marriage if she found she disliked him, but unless she was prepared to go along with his suggestion she would never know her true feelings. Then he would approach someone else. Caroline knew a dozen eligible ladies who would jump at the chance she had been offered. Fitz Carlton would have no trouble in making his marriage of convenience.

Caroline dwelled on her prospects. Marriage might not suit her. Sometimes she thought she might prefer to become an old maid, and yet that threatened to be a lonely state. Her aunt had never married and she certainly did not wish to live like that – year after year of becoming a dowd, slowly slipping into shabby gentility with nothing to look forward to, no family and only a few crabby old ladies for company. No, a marriage between two civilised people who knew what to expect of each other might be just what she needed. It would certainly be better than being a hostage to her emotions.

Chapter Four

Caroline slept very little that night. She had always meant to accept Lord Carlton's offer, of course, but it had caused her to look deeply into her own emotions. A single lady had little influence in society; even if she had sufficient means to live comfortably she would be looked upon as an oddity or an object of pity. Marriage was a woman's duty, as was the begetting of heirs, but it also opened up life in a way that was not possible for a spinster.

A married woman could take a lover if she was discreet. She could enjoy pleasant intrigues or simply amuse herself with entertaining and gossip; she could choose her own guests and live much as she pleased, providing she had a compliant husband. A marriage of convenience could have much to offer.

For a moment a picture of her mother's face flashed into Caroline's mind: Helena Manners coming from her husband's study, a red mark on her cheek. Her eyelashes wet as though she had been crying.

'Are you unhappy, Mama?' Caroline asked.

'No, my dearest child,' her mother whispered. 'Not when I am with you.'

Caroline had sensed a deep sadness that she did not then understand, but now suspected was due to cruelty on her father's part. It had sometimes made her wonder if marriage was a desirable institution.

Sally too had made it clear that she did not care to be married again. 'Marriage can be heaven or hell,' she had told her once. 'Take care to choose wisely, Caroline.'

Would it be wise or even sensible to marry a man she hardly knew? She had met no one else she would even consider marrying. Lord Carlton certainly attracted her, and though she had at first thought him rude, she knew better now. His moods and dark glances were caused by pain, not ill-temper. When someone had suffered as much as he, allowances must be made. Her womanly instincts had been aroused – he so obviously needed a wife to take care of him.

Caroline suddenly laughed out loud. All he had done was to ask her to host a few dinners; he might discover he detested her and they would part with mutual relief. She was making too much of it all.

She drew her special lilac writing paper towards her and began to compose a suitable letter of acceptance.

'I do so admire Mr Constable's work, don't you?'

It was a little later that same morning when Sally gazed up at various paintings adorning the walls of the Royal Academy, lodged in Somerset House since before the new building was commissioned. A house had stood on this site in the Strand from 1550, when it was built for Lord Protector Somerset, who had given it his name.

Caroline murmured assent to Sally's question, though she was not really paying attention, for a gentleman had just entered the hall with a young lady on his arm.

'Isn't that Rachel – and Mr Carlton?' Sally remarked. 'Shall we speak to them?'

'Let them come to us if they wish. We should not intrude.'

She turned her attention back to the paintings, studying them in silence for several minutes.

'How tastes do change,' she remarked at last. 'The vogue is all for romanticism. I am not entirely sure that I approve. I think that perhaps the old masters had more power.'

'Are you an expert, Miss Manners?'

The man's deep voice startled her. She swung round to find herself being appraised by a pair of amused blue-grey eyes.

'Forgive me,' she said and blushed. 'I imagined myself to be addressing Sally.'

Her eyes flicked beyond Will Carlton to where Sally and Rachel were deep in conversation.

'I had not thought you interested in art, sir?'

'Had you not? I was brought up to appreciate its worth,' Will replied. 'At Pendlesham I believe you would discover many paintings you might prefer – if you have a taste for the old masters, of course.'

Caroline gave him an icy stare. 'Of course I admire Mr Constable's work. Mr Gainsborough's, too. I am not such a fool that I cannot appreciate the modern as well as the old.'

'How fortunate then that Fitz has just purchased a new landscape from Mr Constable.' Will tipped his hat. 'Excuse me, please. I believe Miss Blackstone is ready to move on.'

Caroline stared after him in irritation. She believed she might come to like his lordship very well albeit that his cousin really was quite the rudest man!

*　　*　　*

It was almost two weeks later and the day of Lord Carlton's dance. Caroline had been busy for days making sure that everyone who should be invited had been included on the guest list, checking that flowers had been arranged and that his lordship's staff had ordered enough food and champagne, but now she was resting in her boudoir with an afternoon caller to keep her company.

'Would you tell my fortune, Caroline?' Rachel Blackstone asked. 'It might help me to make up my mind.'

'Do you have a problem? Would it help to talk?'

Rachel sighed and shook her head. 'Read my cards – please?'

'Very well, but you know it's only a game, don't you?'

'Yes, of course.'

Rachel shuffled the cards and handed them to Caroline. She placed four cards face up from one pack, then dealt four more in a circle.

'The queen of hearts is you, Rachel' she said. 'The ace of hearts is your lucky card and the king is the man you will marry. The knave of clubs is the dark stranger. His place in the circle tells you your fortune as regards love and romance.'

She turned up the card at the top of the circle; it was the knave of clubs. She smiled at Rachel.

'You have met someone you like very much – is that true?'

Rachel's cheeks turned pink and she nodded. Caroline flipped up the next card, which was the knave of hearts. She frowned as she tried to imagine what might be behind her friend's request for her fortune to be told. Suddenly it was obvious.

'There is another man in the picture – someone you don't like as much?'

Rachel nodded again, and her cheeks grew even pinker.

The king of hearts followed. Caroline shook her head and turned up the next card which was the ace of hearts.

'What does it mean?' Rachel said, frowning.

Caroline hesitated, then, 'It means that you will marry the man your mother approves of, but not necessarily the one you prefer.'

Rachel nodded gloomily. 'I knew that's how it would be.'

'The cards aren't always right,' Caroline said. 'You mustn't take any notice of them. I only do it for fun.'

'But it's all so true,' Rachel cried. 'I've had an offer at last, you see.'

'Oh . . .' Caroline stared at her thoughtfully, then nodded. 'Yes, I see.' She played with the cards in front of her. 'Your mother thinks you should accept of course.'

'Yes.' Rachel bit her lip. 'Only I'm not sure. I like him but I don't know if I want to marry him. You won't say anything to Mama, will you?'

'I wouldn't dream of it,' Caroline assured her. 'But the cards are just for fun, Rachel. You must make up your own mind.'

'I've asked him to give me a little time,' Rachel said. 'but this evening I shall see him again and perhaps I shall know what I want then.'

'He is to be at Lord Carlton's dance?'

'Yes.' Rachel looked shy. 'Oh yes, he will definitely be there.'

Could she have received an offer from Will Carlton? Caroline mused. It was certainly what Lady

57

Blackstone had been hoping for – and they *had* been together at the Royal Academy.

Caroline wondered why it seemed so implausible a match to her. In the eyes of the world it would be eminently suitable. Rachel had breeding and a handsome dowry: Mr Carlton was well born but of moderate means, with no real expectation of a title – and they both had an interest in horses.

A sensible match then, but all wrong for both of them, Caroline thought. Rachel was a sensitive girl, easily crushed by a harsh word or a sharp look – and Carlton would surely be bored with her meekness inside a month!

It was not for her to voice an opinion. She had nothing to say about an affair that did not concern her.

Caroline determinedly changed the subjet, and after a few minutes Rachel called for her carriage and departed, obviously still feeling low – though why she should feel that way when she had at last achieved her ambition was hard to say. And who was the dark stranger? Surely not Lord Carlton himself!

Until recently Rachel had shown no real interest in any of the gentlemen to whom her mother had introduced her, so if Will Carlton had proposed . . . well, poor Rachel. Caroline's heart went out to her friend. Even if she withdrew, she did not believe there was the slightest chance of his lordship offering for Rachel.

What a desperate business this marrying was! It would all be so much more comfortable if women could have children and lives of their own without men.

Yes, there were times when Caroline longed to experience a warm, loving relationship that would bring her happiness. Was it possible to love in such a way that nothing else mattered, to be ready to give up everything – even your life – for the one you loved?

'Nonsense,' Caroline reprimanded herself, as she went to change for the evening. 'Marriage is a contract like any other. Love is a myth . . .'

As she stood with Sally and Lord Carlton to receive their guests that evening Caroline was convinced that this was an important event in her life: to have position, respect and influence, that was what she craved. As Lord Carlton's hostess she had achieved a tiny but subtle improvement in her social standing.

She saw knowledge and acceptance in the eyes of the ladies she greeted that evening. Sally was the official hostess, but the significance of her presence was not lost on matrons well versed in the rules of society: they would expect an announcement very soon.

The evening progressed smoothly. There was dancing in Lord Carlton's magnificent ballroom, and cards for the gentlemen and another table for ladies who liked to wager their pin money at Loo. And, naturally, fountains of the very best champagne. Although late in the year for a dance the rooms were satisfyingly full. It would have been surprising if it had been otherwise, for the combination of Lord Carlton and Miss Caroline Manners was a powerful draw.

'I always expected dear Caroline to snatch the most glittering prize of the year,' said Lady Blackstone to her daughter. 'It will be an ideal match for her.'

'Yes, Mama.' Rachel's eyes moved across the room, brightening as she saw someone. 'May I go to Caroline please?'

'Of course.'

Caroline turned as her friend approached. She gave her her warmest smile and turned to the gentleman at her side.

'Pray excuse me, Captain Royston, I must circulate. Why don't you ask Miss Blackstone to favour you with this dance?'

He obeyed instantly, and Rachel accepted. She seemed unusually animated as she was led away, and Caroline smiled.

'A penny for them?'

Caroline started at the voice of Will Carlton and swung round to face him, a faint guilty colour in her cheeks.

'My thoughts are my own and not for sale, sir.'

Little did he know that she had just done her best to promote a match between his intended and another man!

'The evening goes well, I think?' There was satisfaction in Will's eyes as they moved over the elegant gathering.

'Did you doubt it, Mr Carlton? This is the first mixed affair your cousin has given; there could be no possibility of failure.'

'Not with you as his hostess, Miss Manners.'

'How gallant. Yet many ladies would have served his purpose as well. On the whole though, it does have a certain piquancy, don't you think? A delicious hint of something suggested but not yet declared? Pure nectar for the gossips.'

'I believe I have made no secret of my opinions. You are all that I could wish to see in Carlton's hostess.'

Caroline accepted the further compliment with a cool smile.

'Excuse me,' she said. 'I must circulate.'

He laid a restraining hand on her arm. 'Do you not dance this evening?'

'Perhaps later,' she replied. 'For the moment I have duties?' Her smile flashed out, cold and cutting. 'Isn't that what you most admire, sir – a devotion to one's duty?'

'A hit,' he murmured, a flicker of something like admiration in his eyes. 'Let me not stand in the way of duty, Miss Manners. I shall delay you no more.'

Caroline moved away from him, her feathers more ruffled than his. He was the most irritating man she knew. Compared to him, his cousin was sweetness and light. Indeed, she had begun to discover a softer side of Lord Carlton that she found pleasing. When not in one of his black moods, he could be a charming and considerate companion.

Glancing round the card tables she was surprised to see that Lord Carlton was not seated there. Surely he could not be dancing? A brief foray into the ballroom confirmed that he had not taken to the floor either, though Mr Carlton was there dancing with Rachel. Well, if he was determined to have her it was his affair.

Caroline frowned and went away to search for his lordship. She came upon him at last in his library, a glass of brandy at his side and a book of poems in his hand.

'Come, sir,' she cried in a rallying tone. 'This will not do. Your guests will think you have deserted them.'

'Why should they want me when they have you?' His smile was a challenge. 'You look very beautiful this evening, Miss Manners.'

'Thank you, my lord,' she replied. 'But you will not win me over with pretty compliments.' She hesitated, then, 'Is your leg paining you dreadfully?'

'No,' Fitz said. 'Forgive me, Miss Manners. You are right – it was rude of me to hide myself away in here, and after you have done to much to make the evening a success.'

'I have done very little.'

'To that I shall not agree.' He stood up, gazing down at her with serious grey eyes. 'Tell me not, Sweet, I am unkind . . .' he quoted.

Caroline laughed. 'I know well you would prefer to fly to battle, sir. But you must make up your mind to a peaceful life from now on.'

'You know the verse then?'

'Tell me not, Sweet, I am unkind, That from the nunnery, Of thy chaste breast and quiet mind, To war and arms I fly.' Caroline saw the look of appreciation in his eyes. 'Colonel Lovelace, and one of my favourites.'

'Ah, I see I shall have my work cut out to confound you, Miss Manners.'

'I have always read a great deal, sir.'

'This little book has travelled many a mile with me.' He showed her the worn cover. 'It has oft been my solace in times of despair.'

'I believe you write poetry yourself?'

'I am an indifferent poet, Miss Manners.'

'Perhaps you will show me some of your work one day?'

'Perhaps.' He studied her face for a moment. 'Everyone is leaving town. Would you and Mrs Croxley consider coming to stay at Pendlesham? It is time I entertained my neighbours. The house needs opening up. I believe it has become a little shabby. I need a woman of taste and style to advise me what is to be done.'

'I should consider it an honour,' Caroline replied with a smile. She had no more need to delay her decision. Lord Carlton would suit her very well. 'When did you intend to go down to the country?'

'I have a dinner this coming Friday, as you know, I thought on Sunday.'

'Then Sally and I will join you the following Tuesday – if that will suit you, sir?'

'Admirably, Miss Manners.'

'Good.' She gave him a scolding look. 'Can I not persuade you to rejoin your guests, sir?'

'On one condition, Caroline.' He raised his brows. 'I think we could become a little less formal in private now, don't you?'

'Certainly, Fitz – in private' she said. 'Is that your condition?'

'No. It is that you should dance with me.'

'Dance?' She was surprised at the invitation. 'But your leg?'

'Is much recovered,' he told her with a sheepish look. 'I fear I have been using it to get me out of such affairs, but you and Will are perfectly right to scold me. It is time I came out of the sullens. So if you will bear with my clumsiness . . .'

'I should be delighted,' Caroline said. 'I am sure you are an excellent dancer.'

'I was once,' he agreed. 'We shall see if I have forgotten all I knew.'

'If you have, I shall teach you how to become an excellent dancer once more.'

A gentle smile touched his mouth. 'Shall you teach me how to live again, Caroline?'

'I shall certainly do my best,' she replied. 'But in

the end I think you will do as you please.'

Fitz laughed softly. 'You know I like you, Caroline. At first I was not sure, but I now think we shall get along famously.'

She smiled and waited, surely he meant to speak now? He did not, merely offering her his arm to escort her back to the ballroom. Caroline laid her hand lightly on it. She knew that a clever reply from her could have brought him to the point, but she preferred to let things go on as they were for now. He had asked her down to Pendlesham and now that she had accepted the outcome was not in doubt.

Lord Carlton would ask her to marry him and she would accept.

Caroline sat propped up on a pile of satin pillows, reading her letters. By her side was a tray with a pot of hot chocolate, some tiny almond comfits and sweetmeats. She smiled and nodded to herself as she read the letter of thanks from his lordship for the way the party had gone, then frowned over a similar note from his cousin. How could two men say the same thing in such different ways?

'*My dear Caroline,*' Lord Carlton had written. '*Please accept my sincere gratitude for the other evening, especially the dance. I do hope that my clumsiness has not made you wish yourself a thousand miles from my company. My cousin and I look forward to receiving you at Pendlesham very soon. Yours with deepest respect, Fitz Carlton.*'

His cousin had written thus: '*Dear Miss Manners, Carlton has told me you have accepted an offer to stay at Pendlesham. I leave town at once to prepare for your visit. Please accept my thanks for the other evening. You will of course be very welcome at Pendlesham. Yours, Will Carlton.*'

Caroline was tempted to crush the offending note into a ball, but as her fingers curled about it there was a tap at her door and Sally wafted in, dressed in a wrapping gown of pink satin.

'How are you, my love?' she asked with a cheerful smile. 'I have received the kindest letter from Lord Carlton – and a very handsome present.'

Caroline did not ask her what Lord Carlton had sent. He had inquired what she thought would be proper. She had told him that Sally had very little money of her own, and would probably prefer something practical.

'He has told me I may buy myself some new clothes and have the bills sent to him,' Sally babbled excitedly. 'I am to purchase whatever I need for my stay at Pendlesham and think nothing of the cost. Now what do you say to that?'

'It is no more than you deserve,' Caroline said. 'Without you to act as his hostess, Carlton could not entertain in the way he wishes.'

'You know very well it is you he wants to welcome his guests,' Sally contradicted with a laugh. 'But you could not do it alone, so perhaps I am useful in my own little way.'

'You are much more than that,' Caroline said. 'You are my closest friend, Sally. I am very fond of you, as you must know.'

Sally nodded and fiddled with the sash of her pale lilac morning gown. 'I shall miss you when you marry, Caroline.'

'I have no intention of leaving you in the lurch,' Caroline said. 'We shall come to some amicable arrangement – unless you meet that tall dark stranger we spoke of.'

Sally laughed and shook her head. 'Well, there is no

need to be thinking of these things yet. Unless Carlton has already made you an offer?'

'No, not yet,' Caroline replied. 'We scarcely know one another, Sally. No doubt we shall both be surer of our own minds in a few weeks from now.'

'I thought you were sure?'

'Yes . . .' Caroline stared into the distance. 'I suppose I am.' She would surely not otherwise have accepted his invitation, but caution kept her thoughts from leaping too far ahead.

'I like Lord Carlton,' Sally said. 'He sometimes has odd moods, but he is generally considerate. A good trait in a husband, my love.'

'Yes,' Caroline agreed with her. 'Tell me, Sally — what do you think of his cousin?'

'Mr Carlton?' Sally looked at her in surprise. 'He seems pleasant enough. He is, I believe, devoted to Pendlesham and the family. I hadn't really thought about it much. You are not considering . . .'

'No! God forbid,' Caroline cried in horror. 'I do not think Mr Carlton likes me very much. It might be a little awkward in the future, don't you think?'

'He is merely his lordship's agent,' Sally said. 'As the mistress of Pendlesham you will not need to fear Will Carlton's displeasure.'

'He has a great deal of influence with Fitz. They are more like brothers than cousins. He told me they were brought up together.'

'Even so it can make little difference to your position, Caroline.'

'No.' Caroline reached for an almond cake and bit into it. She chewed in silence, then, 'No, I don't suppose it matters what he thinks of me.' She laughed all at once and threw off her mood. 'I shall get up, Sally, and we will go shopping together. We must see what we can find that suits you – make the most of Lord Carlton's generosity.'

'Oh, I must not abuse his kindness,' Sally said. 'Perhaps a new bonnet or a shawl . . .'

'Nonsense!' Caroline declared. 'Fitz would be insulted. He will expect you to buy at least two or three gowns, with all the bonnets and shawls you fancy.'

Sally's cheeks tinged with pink. 'Well, if you think so, Caroline.'

'I am sure of it,' she said. 'Go and dress, Sally, and I shall be ready in half an hour.'

As Sally went off, Caroline noticed a letter she had not yet read. Slitting it open, she saw with some surprise that it came from Silas Tavener.

'My dear Miss Manners,' her guardian had written. 'I sail for Portsmouth next week and expect to be in England within the next ten days. I shall call on you as soon as it is convenient at your London house, since that is where your solicitors informed me you expect to be for the forseeable future.'

It was dated twelve days earlier, which must mean that he was already in England. Caroline stared at the letter, feeling a mild flutter of irritation. If he did not call in the next day or so he would find her gone down to Pendlesham. She would leave him a letter telling him of her whereabouts, and he could follow her down to the country if he wished.

For the first time it occurred to her that she would need her guardian's permission to marry. Her aunt had never imposed much restraint on her wishes and for the past several months she had done just as she pleased, with none to gainsay her. But until she was twenty-one her guardian did have the power to refuse her permission to marry if he so chose.

Of course he would not do so. Once she was

married he would be saved all further responsibility for her, which would no doubt be a relief to him. Besides, he had never bothered with her much in the past and she doubted he would do so now. There was nothing he could possibly object to in a marriage between her and one of the wealthiest men in England.

Chapter Five

Silas Tavener was not a man to be crossed. Forty-three years of age, he looked older; his thin face was deeply lined, giving him a hangdog expression even when his mood was cheerful, and his complexion was still sallow from a bout of fever he had suffered before he left India. There had been days when he hovered between life and death, and only the devotion of his dusky-skinned servant woman had saved him.

For a moment as he stood on the bustling dockside, pausing to watch the unloading of a ship, he thought with regret of Anais. On her knees, clinging to his legs as she begged him to take her to England with him. Silas had been resolute as he thrust her away, ignoring her as she lay on the floor at his feet, shedding bitter tears.

'You know it's impossible,' he said harshly. 'You will not starve, Anais. I've given you money to last for a month or two. And Sahib Jarvis will take you for his woman after I am gone, if you are cooperative.'

She rose to her feet, her eyes looking straight into his. 'Am I a dog to be passed from one master to another?'

For a moment the burning anger in her eyes had shocked him. Silas had been used to her unquestioning devotion; she had been a passionate lover and he would miss her. The exotic smell of the perfumed oils she used on her long black hair clung to some of his belongings still, even after his sojourn in Portugal, reminding him sharply of her sensuous, pliant body moulding itself to his with a passion he had matched. Of all the women he had known, she had been the one who suited him best. And he knew he was being unfair to her.

'Sentimental fool!' he muttered, and turned away from his contemplation of the busy docks: men shouting to one another; the rattle of a hoist and the rumble of waggon wheels, a heady mix that made Silas restless. He had always been a traveller, a dealer, buying and selling, making money and spending it as easily on women, gambling and wine. He was a connoisseur of all three. Land and the sedentary life of a gentleman held no appeal for him, though he had been born a gentleman's son and might have lived all his life in England had it not been for her, the woman he had lost. But she had been a pale beauty, a goddess to be worshipped from afar. Though once, just for a while, he had hoped for more. It was his bitter disappointment that had shaped his nature, making him the man he now was.

Dismissing old memories, Silas thought again of his dusky servant's beautiful face and voluptuous body. The memory stirred his blood, making him feel slightly sick with desire. He had not been in love with Anais, but she had adored him and in her arms he had found a kind of fulfilment. He looked around him at the wet pavements and the dull greyness of dilapidated buildings. What was he doing here in this cold, miserable country? He should have stayed in India and taken Anais as his wife.

His mouth twisted with anger as he recalled his last meeting with Harry Jarvis.

'Get out of India before I have your throat cut,' Jarvis had threatened. 'You're finished here, Silas.'

Finished and ruined, Silas reflected morosely. The larger part of his fortune had been tied up in the trading company he and Jarvis had started together. Like a fool he'd thrown it all away. He'd been drunk that night and jealous . . .

Silas brought the curtain down on his bitter thoughts abruptly. He'd never been one to let the past prevent him from making a future, though he'd had enough cause. He wasn't finished, not yet. He would never be able to go back to India, not after what he'd done, but there was a way out of this mess. All he had to do was keep his head and stay away from the cardtables for a while.

His business in Portsmouth had delayed him. Now that it was finished, he was free to set out on his journey to London – and his ward. Silas was thoughtful as he turned away from the docks and hailed a passing hackney cab.

If his courage had not failed him he would have slit Harry Jarvis's throat that night, and it would all still have been his. No one need ever have known that he had tossed his share of the company away on the turn of a card. It was useless to look back. He had stopped short of murder, and so he must pay the price.

Next time he was required to be ruthless he would show no mercy.

Chapter Six

Caroline had heard nothing more from her guardian. She had written a letter, which she intended to leave with her housekeeper, informing him that she would be away for some weeks.

'You may reach me at Lord Carlton's estate in Suffolk,' she had written. 'I am sorry to have missed you and trust we shall meet soon. Respectfully yours, Caroline Manners.'

'It is so long since I saw Mr Taverner that I doubt I should know him,' she confided to Sally as they sat together in the parlour, the afternoon before they were due to leave town. 'To tell the truth, I wish he had stayed in India a few more months.'

'Has he come straight from India?' Sally asked.

'No, he broke his journey,' Caroline replied, looking thoughtful. 'When he first wrote to say he was coming back to England he was in Portugal. On business, I expect.'

'His business was in India, I thought – spices and silks, was it not?'

'Yes, that's so,' Caroline agreed. 'But he seems to have sold his interests there. I think he means to import wines from Portugal into this country now.' She shrugged carelessly. 'Not that it concerns me. I doubt I shall see him often. I did not much care for him as a child. He was a strange silent man. Still, he saw to it that my fortune was in good hands before he went off to India, so I suppose I have much to thank him for.'

She remembered her guardian, who was then her father's business partner, visiting with her mother a day or so before the accident. They had been talking earnestly but stopped when she entered the parlour. Her mother had looked guilty and sent her away to fetch a handkerchief.

'Yes, I imagine you have. I wonder why he has decided to come back . . .' Sally broke off as the maid came in to announce a visitor.

'Miss Blackstone has called, Miss Manners.'

'Show her in, Mary.' Caroline rose and went to greet her visitor with a kiss on the cheek. 'How lovely to see you, Rachel. We leave for town in the morning, so you have just caught us.'

'Yes, I know,' Rachel said, her voice animated. 'I wanted to tell you, Caroline – I've said yes. I'm going to be married.'

To Will Carlton, for sure!

Caroline felt as if her heart had ceased pumping. 'So you are engaged . . .'

'Mama is delighted,' Rachel said. 'At first she was cross with me because I turned Mr Bertram down, but . . .'

'Mr Bertram?' Caroline blinked, bewildered. It took her a moment or two to realise who Rachel was talking about. 'Would that be Sir Malcom's nephew?'

She had never even considered the gentleman in question, had hardly noticed him, and had certainly not realised he was paying court to Rachel. So much for her powers of observation!

'Yes,' Rachel said, and sighed with satisfaction. 'But after Lord Carlton's dance he – the dark stranger – called on Mama and . . .'

'Please explain,' Caroline begged. 'I don't know what you mean – who called on your Mama?'

'Captain Royston, of course!' Rachel cried. 'The dark stranger in my cards. It was he I hoped would offer for me, and now he has. He said that he never realised before you mentioned it how well suited we were, and once he started thinking about it, he discovered he was in love with me.' Rachel threw her arms about Caroline and hugged her. 'You guessed that I was in love with him, of course. How can I ever thank you?'

Caroline felt light-headed. She laughed at her friend's excitement and hugged her back. 'I'm so glad for you, Rachel, so very glad. I always thought you and Captain Royston would suit.'

'I'm so happy,' Rachel said. 'And it's all due to you. If you hadn't helped me, I should have been forced to accept Mr Bertram. When you told me it was my decision, I knew I could never marry just to oblige Mama.'

'You really love Captain Royston, don't you?' Caroline studied Rachel's glowing face. When happy, like now, she was actually quite a pretty girl.

'Yes, I do.' Rachel said, glowing. 'Forgive me, I cannot stay. But I could not let you leave town without telling you the wonderful news. And you will come to my wedding, won't you?'

'I wouldn't miss it for the world.'

Rachel kissed Caroline and Sally, then left them in a rush. After she had gone there was silence in the parlour.

'Did you know she was in love with him?' Sally asked at last.

'I had no idea,' Caroline confessed. 'I thought they were ideal partners, but . . .' She shrugged and turned away. 'For some reason I was quite mistaken about Rachel's sentiments. I imagined her to be in love with Lord Carlton.'

'And that his cousin had proposed to her?' Sally's troubled eyes followed her about the room as she paced restlessly. 'Is that why you spoke to Captain Royston?'

'Rachel was unhappy . . .' Caroline picked up a small Derby figure and pretended to examine the detail of the delicate painting. 'I would have hated to see her marry the wrong man.'

'What about you, Caroline? Are you about to make the same mistake yourself?'

'Sally!' Caroline cried and swung round to face her. 'What is this?'

'Is it Lord Carlton you truly want – or his cousin?'

'I have never considered marrying Mr Carlton,' Caroline answered honestly. 'He is an impossible man. I could never live with him. Why on earth should you think that?'

'Forgive me, my love,' Sally said. 'It was just a feeling I had. Obviously I am mistaken.'

'Very much mistaken,' Caroline said. 'Lord Carlton is a gentleman – his cousin has no graces, absolutely none!'

'Do you not think you are a little harsh?' Sally asked. 'I have always found Mr Carlton a perfect gentlemen.'

'Indeed?' Caroline's eyes sparked dangerously. 'Then perhaps it is only when he is with me that he forgets to behave like a gentleman.'

'I see that he had seriously displeased you,' Sally murmured, hiding a smile. 'Whatever has he done to upset you so?'

'He . . . he is always trying to promote a match

between his cousin and I,' Caroline fumed, her finger-nails drumming angrily on the immaculate surface of a polished table. 'He deliberately provokes me because it amuses him and, oh, I don't know! It is just the man himself. He annoys me. We cannot be together five minutes without disagreement.'

'Dear me,' Sally tutted. 'How distressing all that must be for you.'

Caroline stared at her in sudden suspicion. 'Are you laughing at me, Sally?'

'Only a little, my love. Surely you can see the amusing side to all this?' Her tone became soothing. 'After all, you do want to marry Lord Carlton, don't you? So why be angry because Mr Carlton has helped to arrange it? It seems to me that far from disliking you, he has paid you a great compliment.'

'What do you mean?' Caroline stopped her pacing and stared at her.

'If Mr Carlton approves of you as his cousin's wife, he must think highly of you.'

Caroline turned to glance out of the window. There had been an unexpected shower of rain and the pavements were wet. She suddenly felt her spirits plunge. How depressing London could be in the rain; she would be glad to leave for Lord Carlton's country estate.

'Then why do we always quarrel?'

'As to that, I cannot say. My advice would be to give him a chance to know the real you, Caroline. Sometimes . . . just now and then . . . you can seem cold and haughty, my love. Oh, not to me! Never to me, but to others who do not know you.'

'I suppose I may have been at fault. We started out on the wrong foot.' Caroline's mood lightened and her mouth curved. 'To be honest, Sally, I quite enjoy sparring with Mr Carlton. I find it exhilarating for some reason?'

'Do you, my love?' Sally hid her smile. 'Now I wonder why that should be?'

'Perhaps I should be kinder to him.'

'Perhaps you should.' Sally picked up her needle-work. She was working on an exquisite tapestry panel which she intended to have set into a wooden pole screen as a gift for Caroline. 'I think I shall change for dinner now.'

'Yes, do,' Caroline said absently. 'I shall come up in a moment or two.'

Pendlesham was a treasure house; it contained so many beautiful paintings, it would take weeks to view them all, and a lifetime to appreciate them fully. Every room was furnished in a particular style, ranging from dark oak and the rich mahogany so popular in the previous century to the lighter, daintier pieces of the day. There were many fine show cabinets and each one was stuffed with delicate porcelain, silver and *objets d'art*. Many of the carpets were silk; there were Gobelin tapestries from France, ivories chased with gold and silver, fine clocks, elegant furniture made by the best craftsmen, Italian marbles and Venetian glass chandeliers. Clearly more than one member of the Carlton family had been on the grand tour and brought back his finds from Europe, but of late it seemed that things had been neglected and some of the curtains were threadbare in places. Nothing very terrible was needed but improvements could certainly be made, Caroline thought.

Will showed her the royal apartments, which were very grand and furnished with gilded furniture, dark blue drapes and gold damask.

'We have had Queen Anne staying here, the Duke of Marlborough too. At different times, of course.' Will smiled. 'It was after they had fallen out and soon after the house was rebuilt.'

'Which was at the very beginning of the last century, I think?'

'It was begun in 1694,' Will said. 'But not completed until 1705. We have all the records, including the bills down to the last detail. Perhaps you would like to see them one day? They make fascinating reading.'

'You are very proud of Pendlesham, aren't you?'

Will nodded and led the way to the music salon. It was a long, airy room and there many beautiful instruments, some of them from an age long gone, including a set of virginals, a viol and a harp. There was also a fine spinet that Caroline immediately wished to play. She contented herself by running a finger over the delicate ivory keys, before following Will into yet another elegant reception room.

'Carlton wanted to show you the house,' Will said to her as they paused in the portrait gallery to admire his ancestors. 'But since he is unable to greet you himself at the moment, he asked me to stand in for him. The fever came on him suddenly when we returned and he has been ill for two days.'

'How distressing for him,' Caroline replied. 'I'm so sorry. It is the wrong time to visit. We shall leave in the morning.'

'I wish you would not,' Will said. 'The illness is recurring but usually brief. Fitz should be himself again in a matter of days.'

'But you cannot want guests in the house at such a time?'

'You are more than a guest, Miss Manners. Surely you know that?'

'Yes.' Caroline flushed as she met his eyes. 'Then we shall stay if you think it best.'

'Please do,' he said. 'If you could bear to visit Fitz occasionally while he is recovering, I am sure it would help him to get back on his feet. He needs something – someone – to live for.'

'And you believe I am that someone?'

'Yes.' Will's voice throbbed with conviction. 'Perhaps I should tell you his story, Caroline – may I please call you that?'

'I see no reason why not,' she replied. For the first time she found she was not angry over his assertion that she was the right wife for his cousin. 'I have been told that Fitz was once engaged to someone.'

Will nodded, his expression one of grave concern.

'Her name was Julia Winterton. She was a pretty girl, though unfortunately fragile. She died of what seemed just a little chill, but turned to an inflammation of the lungs. My cousin was overcome with grief. He went off to join the army and I believe for a time he hoped never to return.' Will paused, then, 'Fitz has remained faithful to her memory, but it has been killing him little by little. Until recently he was drinking too much and had terrible moods, but with the pain, who could blame him? He has ceased to drink so much since he met you. In fact he has even begun to smile again.' Will's eyes seemed to burn into her. 'Can you understand why I am so anxious to see him married?'

'Yes, of course. He needs a wife to take care of him. But why me particularly? You encouraged Fitz to look in my direction, did you not?' She gazed up at him. 'Why – when you hardly knew me?'

'Because – because you will not ask for more than Fitz can give you.'

'What . . .' Caroline's gaze narrowed. She felt a coldness spread through her. 'You believe I mean to marry for a title and position, don't you?' She had begun to think that Sally was right, that he did have a high opinion of her. But this was a slap in the face.

'Is that not the reason you are here?'

Caroline controlled the overwhelming urge to hit him. 'I could have married a duke within days of my coming out party had I cared only for that,' she said in a low, furious voice. 'I will not deny that I require both a title and position from marriage. Nevertheless, I would not dream of accepting a man I could not like or admire. Your cousin has many qualities I find pleasing.'

'You do not say love, Miss Manners?' He had gone back to a cool formality that belied the wintry glint in his eyes.

'Love is a myth,' Caroline snapped, her temper betraying her. 'I prefer a comfortable arrangement that suits both parties.'

'I agree with you entirely. Why should we quarrel over this? If I offended you by my clumsy words, I apologise. It was not intended. You too have admirable qualities. I hope very much that you will be my cousin's wife.'

'Do you indeed?' Caroline asked, icy cold now. 'Let me tell you, sir, that it will be despite your efforts if – and I say if – I accept any offer your cousin may make me.'

She turned on her heel and walked off, leaving him to stare after her.

'I do not believe in love, Sally,' Caroline said to her companion a little later. 'Not romantic love, anyway. I imagine it is possible to care deeply for someone – to be kind and considerate in one's daily life, but that's all.'

'What about a wild passion that sets your blood throbbing in your veins? A madness that makes you want to scream for pure joy – that makes you long to lie in a man's arms?'

'Sally!' Caroline chided. 'Have you ever felt like that? I thought you did not particularly care for being married?'

'I didn't – but I was in love once. If he had been free it might have been different. I married Mr Croxley because my parents were dead and I had no money. I have only ever loved one man.'

'And he was married to someone else? Poor Sally, how unhappy you must have been. I had no idea.'

'There was no reason to speak of it. John died before my husband. My marriage was not happy, and I prefer to live my own life now rather than remarry.'

'But if you found a man you could love?'

'I would have walked through fire for my John.' She blushed. 'How foolish you must think me?'

'No, not foolish, but I am surprised. I had not thought love could endure so long. Would I have to live with Julia's ghost do you suppose?'

'Lord Carlton would not ask you to be his wife if he could not forget her.'

'No – perhaps not,' Caroline agreed, but was not convinced. If Fitz were still in love with Julia, it explained many things.

Caroline visited Fitz in his apartments that evening. He was sitting up against a pile of fat pillows with a book lying open on the embroidered satin coverlet beside him. The bed had four posts and was hung with heavy damask curtains, and the furnishings were all in the same dark shades of mulberry and grey. Caroline thought it a depressing room and made a mental note that the curtains needed replacing.

Fitz had been shaved and made presentable by his devoted valet. The yellowness brought on by the fever was beginning to fade, but there were dark shadows beneath his eyes and his face looked drawn.

'This is a sorry welcome to Pendlesham,' he said and held out his hand to her. 'Forgive me, Caroline.'

'You are not at fault,' she replied, taking his hand loosely in her own. It felt quite cool, so the fever had obviously gone. 'I understand it is a recurring illness?'

'Unfortunately so,' Fitz said. 'Sometimes I feel as if I bring it on myself. Will scolds me for not taking more care, but I fear I am a lost cause.'

'Surely not!' Caroline rallied him. 'In a day or so you will be feeling more yourself, and then we shall begin to make our plans. I have not been idle since I arrived. Your cousin has shown me over the house and I have some ideas to discuss with you when you feel up to it.'

'No need to tell me,' he said. 'You have excellent taste, Caroline. I have remarked it in your own apparel. I shall give you carte-blanche in the matter of furnishings.

'Shall you indeed?' Caroline murmured, a husky, teasing note in her voice. 'I may spend a great deal of your money, my lord.'

'Fitz,' he reminded her, an answering smile on his lips. 'You are very good for me, Caroline. I am so glad you came to Pendlesham.'

'Thank you.' Caroline felt her cheeks grow warm.

He did need her, whether he realised it or not. She would stay for his sake – at least until he was completely recovered.

It was the first time Fitz had left his room in a week. Caroline smiled as she watched him walk downstairs unaided. His limp was less pronounced now, and some of the shadows had left his face.

'You look much better this morning,' she said. 'I am happy to see you down again.'

'With two such excellent nurses how could I fail to recover?' he asked. 'My valet is quite put out because Mrs Croxley's tisanes have done me more good than his.'

'Oh dear, that will never do,' Caroline laughed. 'But I shall ask her for the recipe and give it to Mr Brown for safe keeping. Should you need it in future, he will have it to hand.'

'You will make him a friend for life,' Fitz said. 'Will tells me that you already have my entire staff eating out of your hands.'

Caroline went to take his arm and they walked into the drawing-room together. 'I merely asked Mrs Brandon for her advice,' she said. 'We have discovered there are some drapes packed away in trunks that I have ordered brought out for some of the smaller rooms. I have listed those rooms I think need new furnishings and made suggestions as to colour and style. New drapes will be needed for all the main reception rooms, of course. Perhaps you would care to cast an eye over the list?'

Fitz shook his head. 'I trust your judgement, Caroline. Such things are rightly a woman's province. Now, I have been thinking that we should give a dinner party this weekend.'

'Are you sure you feel well enough?'

'Quite sure, thank you. It was for that I asked you to stay, not to play nurse to an invalid. I fear I may have given you a dislike of Pendlesham?'

'No, indeed you have not,' she replied. 'I have seldom enjoyed myself more. You have a wonderful house, Fitz, full of beautiful treasures. I think all your books and pictures should be catalogued and recorded. Some of them are important works. If you could bear it, you should open your house to the world once a year and let people see them.'

'You are an unusual and intelligent woman,' Fitz said. 'I'm glad you have not been bored during your stay here.'

'I could never be bored here,' Caroline cried, breaking off as Will Carlton came into the room.

'Fitz, can you spare a moment?' he asked, then frowned as he saw Caroline. 'Forgive me. I did not mean to intrude.'

'You are not intruding, Fitz said. 'What is it, Will? You look worried.'

'It's about that damned poaching,' he replied. 'Briggs is sure it is those gypsies in the wood.'

'Gypsies usually take only what they need for food,' Fitz said. 'I would tend to doubt Briggs' judgement on this: he was always disliked the travelling folk.'

'Yes, I know,' Will said. 'And I agree with you. I know these gypsies; they are not thieves, though they may take some game for the pot occasionally. But this is not a light matter, Fitz. So many of your birds have been taken, it will not be worth holding a shoot this year.'

Fitz shrugged his shoulders. 'A pity but not the end of the world.'

'Poaching on this scale is a hanging matter,' Will replied. 'It has to be stopped, Fitz. But if I'm right . . .'

'You think you know the culprit?'

'Yes, I'm almost sure of it. He's an unpredictable character, but I hesitate to set a trap. Even a rogue like Tom Hay doesn't deserve to hang.'

Fitz nodded, and glanced at Caroline. 'We'll talk of this another time, Will. We were just discussing a dinner party this weekend.'

'Yes, of course.' Will looked awkward. 'Forgive me if I have upset you with talk of such matters, Miss Manners, but . . .'

'Come, come,' Fitz said. 'We cannot have this, Will. You do not need to be so formal with Caroline.'

'I am not upset,' Caroline said. 'Poaching is a serious matter. I think you should apprehend your thief, Mr Carlton. You could warn him in such a way that he understands he will be handed over to the magistrates if he offends again, could you not?'

'There, Will,' Fitz said and laughed. 'See how easy she makes everything? She will put us all to rights in no time at all. Set your trap for Tom Hay and if he falls into it, get Briggs to deal with him. He must bear his punishment like a man. Next time it will not be just a beating?'

'If that's what you want?' Will gave Caroline a cold look. 'Excuse me, I shall see to it at once.'

Caroline watched him walk from the room. She turned to her companion with a little frown. 'Have I upset your cousin by speaking out of turn, Fitz? I did not mean to imply that he was not doing his duty by you. Only that if he did not care to see the man hanged, he could warn him off.'

'It was what I should have suggested myself,' Fitz said. 'Tom Hay has a widowed mother and a large family to feed. They rely on what he earns, but he was a weaver and you know they cannot find much work these days, not since the new power looms were brought in. Will has offered him, employment as a labourer on the estate, but he is too proud to accept. If he were hanged as a poacher his family would be flung on the parish, or more likely they would run off somewhere and starve rather than go into the work-house. Poor devils! You cannot blame Tom for taking the birds, but of course it has to be stopped.'

'I did not know,' Caroline said.'

Fitz patted her arm and smiled reassuringly. 'How could you? Leave it to Will. He will see to everything. No one knows Pendlesham and its people better. If the truth were spoken, he would make a far better lord of the manor than I could ever be. Will is a good master, Caroline. He cares for our tenants and labour-ers as if they were all a part of his family. No doubt he was hesitant to punish Tom because we played to-gether as lads, but it has to be done.'

Chapter Seven

Caroline went riding the next morning. She refused the offer of a groom to escort her, feeling the need for a little time alone. A good gallop would clear the cobwebs from her mind and ease the slight tension she was experiencing.

The estate was large and kept in good heart, as was the village which lay just beyond the woods, and consisted of one long street with cottages on either side, all with flourishing gardens, flowers growing beside the vegetables and chicken runs. Some of them had a sty with a breeding sow, and from beyond one cottage came the plaintive lowing of a cow.

The street had been cobbled to make it passable even during the winter, and there was a blacksmith, an inn, and of course the church. The cottages were of the usual design with one large room at the front that served both as a kitchen and living room, a lean-to and store at the back with two tiny bedrooms, but they were not the tumbledown hovels that so many labourers were condemned to occupy. The women who chatted over their scrubbed doorsteps looked healthy and happy.

They watched Caroline curiously as she walked her horse through the street to the church. God's house was a small stone-clad building with a single tower and a few tiny stained-glass windows. It must have been built by one of the early Carltons as a place of worship for his family and his dependants, and the architecture was more functional than impressive.

Just beyond the church was a rather pleasant house with a thatched roof, black timbers and white-washed walls. The garden was filled with flowers, some fading and straggling after the summer but many still blooming in a riot of colour, much appreciated by the bees probing their centres. Clematis climbed the walls and the scent of musk roses mingled with lavender and the last of the sweet peas.

As Caroline approached, a woman came out to the gate to meet her, smiling in welcome.

'Good-morning. We're having another warm spell – have you come to see the Vicar?'

'No. I was just out for a ride and I stopped to admire the church.'

'My husband is proud of it,' the woman said. 'Though it's not in any way remakable from the outside. Would you care to see inside? You will find the Vicar pottering about somewhere.'

Caroline nodded. She tied her horse to a tethering post and went into the church. It was not large but there were several good wooden pews, many supplied with tapestry cushions. Some of the stonework was exceptionally well carved and the altar was covered in a magnificent cloth of blue and gold.

'You must be the guest staying up at Pendlesham?'

Caroline turned at the sound of the Vicar's voice. He was of medium height, stout, with thinning hair and a benevolent smile. He walked towards her with his hand outstretched.

'I'm Thomas Makepeace,' he said, clasping her hand firmly. 'And you must be Miss Manners.'

'You know my name?'

'Mr Carlton mentioned it,' the Vicar replied. 'He called to see me a few days ago and said there were guests at Pendlesham. A Mrs Croxley – and a very beautiful young lady.'

Caroline blushed and shook her head at the compliment. 'Does Mr Carlton often visit?'

'Most weeks, just to see how things are, you know. Between us we manage to keep our little flock from straying too far.' He beamed at her. 'And what do you think of my church?'

'I like it,' she assured him. 'It has an air of . . . of comfort. That may sound odd, but one does not always feel that in a church. I mean physical comfort, of course.'

'Ah yes, the cushions. The late Lady Carlton was a great believer in comfort. She maintained it was better to entice folk rather than coerce them.' His eyes twinkled. 'But I hope we offer a measure of spiritual comfort as well.'

'I'm sure you do,' Caroline said. 'If one needs it.'

'You have no need of my services?'

'No. I came only out of curiosity, I'm afraid.'

'You are welcome, whatever your reasons.' He closed the bible on his lectern. 'Would you care to come into the Vicarage for a glass of Mrs Makepeace's excellent elderberry wine?'

'Yes, I think I would, thank you,' Caroline said. 'If it is no trouble?'

'No trouble at all. Mrs Makepeace loves to entertain.' He gestured to her to follow him. 'This way, Miss Manners. Perhaps you would care to see my gardens as we go? My marrows are doing very well this year.'

*   *   *

It was almost an hour before Caroline was allowed to leave, having heard much that interested her about his lordship, Mr Carlton, and the more notable among the Carltons' neighbours. The Vicar and his wife enjoyed a good chat, and she had liked them. She felt mellowed as much by the company as the two glasses of Mrs Makepeace's rather strong wine she had been pressed to taste.

As she passed the rustic bridge and the oak tree where she had once fallen asleep, she was tempted to get down and sit for a while, but resisted. She had been absent long enough and she was not anxious for Mr Carlton to send the servants out to look for her again.

She doubted that he had yet forgiven her for her interference the previous day, nor could she blame him. Her visit to the village had taught her that, whatever his feelings about her personally, Will Carlton was an excellent steward of his cousin's estate. He certainly did not need her advice.

Caroline became aware that she was being watched. A man had walked onto the bridge as she passed and was staring after her. For a moment she thought it was Will Carlton, but then she saw that he wore a red scarf around his neck and had a gold ring in his ear. She guessed he was one of the gypsies said to be camping in the woods.

The wind had got up and it was getting cooler. Some of the trees had begun to shed their leaves; it was autumn already. In the past she had hated the onset of winter in the country, but now she thought it might be pleasant at Pendlesham with the huge open fireplaces and the smell of fragrant logs; a long table set for dinner guests and good company to while away the dark evenings. And yet she wondered whether it would be right to take advantage of Fitz's vulnerability. She knew that he was coming to rely on her, to listen for her step in the hall, and he seemed to lose his expression of sadness when she sat with him in the parlour, talking of poetry and the future. Supposing Sally was right; supposing she were to fall in love with someone else one day. No, no, it was out of the question. Love was not for her.

Leaving her horse at the stables, she walked towards the house, catching sight suddenly of a girl creeping out from the shrubbery, dressed in what could only be called rags. Her manner was furtive and she kept glancing over her shoulder, as if afraid of being seen. She was surely not one of the servants.

Caroline called out to ber. 'Who are you? What do you want?'

The girl froze. Caroline approached her, smiling reassuringly. The girl was quite a pretty thing beneath the dirt, albeit thin and undernourished. Her eyes were unusual, with a luminous quality. Caroline felt pity for her, and reached into her pocket for one of the coins she kept to reward the stablelads for helping her.

'Don't look so frightened,' she said. 'What is your name, girl – and what are you doing here?'

The girl hesitated, as if she were trying to decide whether or not to trust this grand lady. 'I'm Katya, yer 'onour – I mean yer ladyship,' she said, and made an awkward curtsey.

'I am merely Miss Manners,' Caroline said, amused. The girl was only a little younger than herself and very nervous. 'You're one of the gypsies, aren't you?' Her smile faded as she recalled the man on the bridge and the outbreak of poaching. Perhaps it was the gypsies after all. 'What are you doing here – have you come to steal from Lord Carlton?'

'No, miss. I swear I've stolen nothing,' Katya cried, her eyes dark with fear. 'I wanted to see 'im – the one who looks after everythink. We knows they're all sayin' as 'tis us what takes them birds of 'is lordship's, but 'taint. Jake wouldn't have none of that – skin any of 'is people alive he would, what touched anythin' on his lordship's land.'

'If you are telling the truth, none of you have anything to fear. Besides, Mr Carlton believes he knows the real culprit.'

Katya's face brightened. 'We know who 'tis,' she said, 'but we thought no one would believe us. I came because we've been threatened with the law if we don't move on.'

'The poacher is a villager . . .'

'No, 'taint,' Katya contradicted. ' 'Tis Briggs 'isself . . .'

Caroline stared at her in astonishment. 'You mean his lordship's gamekeeper is stealing the birds himself? That surely cannot be true!'

'Jake said as no one would believe 'im. I thought that one what rides about the place might listen. 'ee were kind to me once – but 'tis always the same. We're called as liars and thieves.'

'Who is Jake?'

'He's our leader.' The girl turned as if to leave.

'No, don't go. I think I do believe you, Katya. Have you seen Mr Briggs taking the birds?'

'Yes, Miss, Jake has. He sells 'em to someone from away, local being too dangerous, so Jake says. He could tell 'im more if he was to come to us afore we go. You tell him that, miss, you tell him.'

'Yes, I will.'

'I gotta go afore anyone sees me.'

'Here,' Caroline reached into her pocket and took out a half sovereign. 'Please take this for your trouble, Katya.'

The gypsy girl stared at the coin in surprise, then bit it. 'I can't take this, 'tis too much. Jake'll skin me.'

'Tell him you earned it telling my fortune,' Caroline suggested and the girl smiled, showing teeth that were surprisingly white and even.

'You have this then,' she said, giving Caroline a small silver object. ''Tis a good luck charm. Jake makes them himself. 'Tis to hang on a chain about your neck, see.' She showed Caroline a little loop.

Caroline looked at the workmanship of the charm; it was beautifully done, though she was not sure what it represented.

''Tis a pixie,' Katya told her. 'Keep it close to you and 'twill protect you.'

'Thank you.' Caroline slipped the charm into her pocket. 'I think it a fair exchange, Katya – and I shall tell Mr Carlton what you've told me.'

She watched as the girl ran off into the shrubberies, then frowned. If Katya was telling the truth she had better speak to Will before he arranged his trap for the poacher. He would no doubt inform the gamekeeper of his intentions, and it would all be in vain.

'Will!' Caroline called breathlessly as she saw him coming from the direction of the bailiff's room at the west end of the building. 'Mrs Brandon told me I might find you here. Please, I must speak to you before it is too late!'

He stopped and stared at her in surprise. 'Caroline – is something wrong? It's not Fitz . . .'

'No,' she said and gasped for breath. 'You mustn't

set that trap for Tom Hay. It isn't him – he isn't the thief.'

Will's brow furrowed as he looked down at her. 'What are you talking about, Caroline? I've already spoken to Briggs about him.'

'But you mustn't,' she said, her breast heaving as she tried to recover her breath. 'It's him, Briggs: he's the one who has been stealing the birds all along.'

'Briggs? Are you mad? He's the best gamekeeper we've ever had. Why should he steal the birds?'

'He's selling them to an outsider. That's why he keeps blaming the gypsies. But Katya swears it isn't them.'

'What on earth are you talking about?'

Caroline explained about her meeting with the gypsy girl. He listened, his expression one of disbelief, then made a gesture of dismissal.

'Do you expect me to believe such a ridiculous tale?' he asked harshly. 'I've known Briggs for years. I trust him implicitly.'

'At least question him,' Caroline said. 'Why should the gypsy girl lie to me? Why would she dare to come looking for you?'

Will slapped his thigh with his riding crop. He was obviously beginning to wonder if she might be on to something. 'You think she was telling the truth, don't you?'

'Yes, I'm sure of it.'

'I was sure it was Tom Hay. I saw some pheasant feathers near his kitchen door last week when I called unexpectedly, and I thought he looked guilty.' Will was thoughtful. 'I suppose I could be wrong.'

'Perhaps Tom took a bird for his dinner,' Caroline said. 'You would not see him beaten or hung for that, would you?'

An odd expression came into his eyes. 'Why are you pleading for a man you have never met?' he asked. 'You said you thought he should be punished.'

'And why do you think so poorly of me?' Caroline cried, a flash of temper in her eyes. 'Do you think I have no heart, no compassion? When I spoke so thoughtlessly I did not know that he had a widowed mother and a large family to support. I did not know that he was once your friend and that it would hurt you to see him punished.' Tears hovered as she looked up at him. 'Please stop it happening, Will,' she begged, 'for my sake and your own. You will never be able to forgive yourself if he is innocent.'

'You care so much . . . ?' Will said softly, looking at her in bewilderment. He reached out to touch her face with his fingertips. 'I thought . . . Caroline, forgive me.'

'Will . . .' she whispered. 'Oh, Will.'

He made a sound of anguish deep in his throat, then, still looking dazed, he reached out and drew her close against his chest. Caroline lifted her face to his, her mouth opening softly beneath his as he kissed her. At first he seemed hesitant, then his mouth became more urgent, intensifying the kiss to one of hungry passion.

Caroline felt as if she would swoon. Her head was spinning and she melted against him, knowing only that she wanted this wonderful feeling to go on and on forever. It was like nothing she had ever experienced, nothing she had dreamed of; a heady, delicious sensation that made her press herself to him, her body pliant, willing to surrender itself to anything he asked of it.

'Will . . .' she breathed, as his lips drew away from her. 'What does this mean?'

For a moment he stared down at her in silence, then his expression hardened to one of anger. 'It means nothing,' he said harshly. 'Nothing more than a moment's folly.'

'How can you say that?' she protested, feeling as if he had struck her. 'Did it mean nothing to you?'

'Nothing at all,' he said, and gave her a cruel smile. 'Men are often tempted by a pretty face, Caroline. I am not a saint, nor am I immune to your charms. When you look at a man so invitingly you risk being taken at your word. But if you wish to marry Carlton, you should take care not to let him see you making eyes at other men, at least until he has his heirs. He may seem easy going, but I assure you he has a temper when roused.'

Caroline stared at him for a moment, then she lashed out, striking him hard across the face. 'You are insulting, sir,' she said. 'If I marry your cousin, I shall not invite attention from other men. I do not know why you hate me so much.'

'I do not hate you . . .'

'Perhaps it is all women you dislike,' Caroline said, her tone icy now. 'You are right, it was a moment's folly, nothing more.' She turned with a flounce of her skirt and began to walk away from him.

As she did so something fell from her pocket and Will stooped to pick it up. He saw it was a tiny silver charm such as one sometimes found at a fair. It lay in the palm of his hand, tempting him to call her back, then he shrugged and slipped it into his waistcoat pocket.

Caroline ran into the house. She was angry and close to tears. How dare Will Carlton treat her so? He had

96

implied that she had invited him to kiss her, that she was some kind of a flirt, a *wanton*!

'Caroline,' Fitz's voice called to her from the parlour. 'Stay a moment if you please. I want to talk to you.'

Caroline hesitated. She longed to run up to her room and weep. But why should she shed tears for a man she had always known disliked her. She brushed a hand across her face, lifted her head and turned with a dazzling smile on her lips to meet Carlton.

'Fitz,' she said. 'I was just going to change my gown.'

'Have you been riding?' His eyes searched her flushed face. 'Are you upset about something?'

'No, no, of course not,' she lied, and went to take his arm. 'I've had such an adventure, Fitz. I was on my way from the stables when I met this poor creature. She was a gypsy girl, a pretty little thing but half starved.'

'She hasn't been eating my pheasants then.' Fitz raised his eyebrows. 'What did you say to her?'

'It was what she had to say to me that mattered.'

Caroline went on to explain, leaving nothing out but the kiss and her quarrel with his cousin.

'No wonder you seemed upset,' Fitz said. 'It would have been a grave mistake if Tom had been beaten for another's crime. He's been taking the odd rabbit and wood pigeon for years, but we've always turned a blind eye for old times' sake.'

'You don't doubt the gypsy girl then?'

'No – not if you believed her.'

'Will was less inclined to believe me,' she said ruefully.

'Will is often too stubborn for his own good.' Fitz gazed down at her, tipping her chin towards him

97

with one finger. 'You must not let Will's brusque manner upset you, Caroline. He does not trust women, perhaps because of his mother.'

'His mother?' Caroline's eyes widened.

'She married again six months after his father died. I don't think he has ever quite forgiven her. He adored his father, and he felt that she had betrayed his memory. Then, of course, she went off to Italy and left him here.'

'I see . . . Poor Will indeed!' Caroline turned away to hide her emotion. 'So he believes all women to be faithless.'

'Something like that,' Fitz agreed. 'One day he will fall in love and I dare say it will come as a great shock to him, but until then . . .' he paused, then, 'Do you think you could bear to live here, Caroline. With an invalid and a man who thinks so little of your sex as companions? Of course, you could have as many guests as you chose to enliven the tedium, but I should not want my wife to be always in town.'

'Fitz . . .' She stared up at him. 'I – I don't understand you.'

'Surely you do?' he said with that gentle smile she had come to find so appealing. 'I am asking you to be my wife, Caroline. We should go up to town for the season, of course, but your life would be here with me – and our children if we were fortunate enough to have them. I like you very much, far more than I had expected. It would suit me to be married, and it would make me a very happy man if you would be my wife.'

So it had come at last, as she knew it must.

He had not mentioned love, but she had never expected that. She looked up into his face, searching for something, though she knew not what.

'Are you sure you wish to be married, Fitz? I know you think it your duty, but . . .'

He reached out to take her hand, carrying it to his lips to kiss it gently. 'I have thought about this a great deal, Caroline,' he said. 'I shall not insult you by pretending to a grand passion – I believe such is beyond me – but I think we could find happiness together.'

'You really want me?' she asked a little tremulously.

'I believe it must be you or no one,' he replied. 'I thought I had no wish to live, yet you have made me realise that there is still goodness and hope in a cruel world, Caroline. In time . . . no, I shall make no promises. Only that I shall make you as happy as I know how.'

Caroline's throat tightened with emotion. How could she refuse such a noble offer? He needed her. His memories still held him to the past, but he cared for her as much as he was able to care for anyone. His gentle appeal had touched her heart, and she knew that she had come to care for him. Not with the wild passion that Sally had spoken of, but with a quiet concern, much as she had for her closest friends.

She reached up and kissed him on the cheek. 'If you want me I shall marry you, Fitz,' she whispered. 'I am honoured by your offer and I shall always do my best to make life pleasant for you.'

'Then I am content,' he said. 'We shall make life pleasant for each other.' He tipped her chin towards him again.

His kiss was soft and tender. Caroline accepted it but made no attempt to respond. She felt none of the joyous singing in her blood that Will's passionate embrace had aroused, and her eyes stung with tears.

'Will you excuse me for a moment? I should like to change my gown.'

'Of course.' Fitz turned away, then looked back. 'Perhaps we could ride together from now on? I believe my leg is strong enough at last.'

'I should like that,' Caroline said, 'I shall see you at nuncheon.'

She walked quickly away before the tears could fall. Fitz stared after her with a puzzled expression in his eyes, then he crossed the room to stand looking out towards the park and the woods beyond.

'Have I done right, Julia?' he whispered. 'Why don't you come to me, my love? Come to me, tell me what you want from me.'

Chapter Eight

Will was thoughtful as he strode towards the game-keeper's cottage, which was situated at the edge of the woods. He could hardly believe that Briggs could be stealing the birds himself, but Caroline had seemed so certain that it had given him pause for thought.

Caroline. For a moment a picture of her face hovered before his eyes blotting everything else from his mind. He had long considered her the most beautiful woman he had ever met, but had believed her to be cold and heartless, loving only herself and ambition. It seemed he was wrong – very wrong. A woman without pity would not have looked at him in such a way, nor begged for mercy for a man she did not know. She had looked so vulnerable, so soft and inviting that he had lost his head. He had used her shamefully and then slandered her for not rejecting him.

Such hypocrisy!

It was not her fault that he had behaved improperly. For an instant he had desperately wanted to make love to her, forgetting she was here because his cousin needed a wife.

Cursing himself, Will banished the memory of how sweet and welcoming her lips had been. She was not for him, even if he wished to marry – which he most certainly did not. Fitz was on the point of speaking out; if there had ever been a chance for him it was gone. He had no right to entertain such thoughts of her, and he would never do so again. He would not allow himself to look back with regret.

Will was suddenly alerted by nearby shouting. He was in sight of the keeper's cottage now, and he observed a fight in progress between two men by the gate. One of them was the leader of the gypsies whom he knew well enough from the past; the other, the head gamekeeper. Will broke into a run, but already the fight was over and Briggs lay on the ground, wiping a hand across his bloodied nose. He looked up as Will approached, an uneasy expression in his eyes.

'I was trying to throw this gypsy off his lordship's land, sir.'

'He has my permission to be in the woods,' Will said, 'just as he and his people had my uncle's. I've told you before, Briggs, it isn't the gypsies who are taking the birds. At least no more than the odd wood pigeon now and then.'

''Tis he that's the thief,' Jake the gypsy growled. His dark eyes met Will's angrily. The two men were of similar height and build but very different in their features. Will knew Jake to be much the same age as his lordship. He hesitated, not sure whose word to trust – that of a gypsy or a man whose loyalty was now suspect.

'Look in his kitchen, if you don't believe me,' Jake said.

Briggs had struggled to his feet, a flicker of fear passing across his surly face. 'He lies, sir. You wouldn't take the word of a dirty gypsy against mine. I took the birds off him after he snared them and was about to bring them to you when he set on me.'

'I believe I might take the word of this gypsy,' Will replied. 'If the birds are there you leave Pendlesham today, Briggs.'

Will strode towards the back door of the cottage. The gamekeeper came running after him, grabbing at his arm in an effort to disuade him.

'He's a liar, sir. I took them from him. I was bringing them to you . . . I swear it.' Sweat stood out on the keeper's brow. To Will, he had the look of a guilty man.

'Take your hand from my arm.' Will gave the keeper a haughty, stare and his hand fell away.

Will entered the kitchen. It was cluttered and untidy, the floor unswept. On the table lay four dead pheasants. They had been shot cleanly by someone who was used to handling a gun, not snared as was the gypsy way. Will picked them up and took them outside, dangling them before the gamekeeper. Briggs had gone grey, his eyes rolling in terror.

'You deserve to hang,' Will said in a quiet, dangerous tone. 'Get out of the cottage and be gone by tonight, Briggs. If I see you on Carlton land tomorrow, I'll shoot you myself.'

'I needed the money for my sick sister, sir.' Briggs was blabbing now, blood mingling with saliva on his chin. 'Please give me another chance. Her husband died and she has six children to feed . . .'

'No more of your lies and excuses!' Will said, his face hard. 'If you had come to me, I would have helped you. But you blamed others – you would have seen another man beaten or hanged in your place. You disgust me. I have no pity for you. Get out of my sight before I change my mind and hand you over to the magistrates; they'd show no mercy, I'll be bound.

It would be a hanging or transportation at the least for you.'

For a moment the gamekeeper glared at him, then he hung his head and slouched past him into the cottage. Will turned to the gypsy, who had watched in silence. They measured each other, look for look, then Jake nodded.

'You know, don't you?' he said.

'I know that my uncle said you were to come and go as you please. Nothing more.' If Will suspected the reason for that freedom, he would not say.

'A still tongue is a rare blessing,' Jake said. 'We are going tomorrow. We shall not return now that the old lord is dead.'

'That is your choice.'

'There's a new master here now. He might resent our presence on his land.'

'I can speak for his lordship.'

'Mebbe, but 'tis best if we go.'

The gypsy turned and strode into the woods, head high. For a moment longer Will stood staring after him, his brow creased in thought. It was best this way. He had kept his silence while his uncle lived, he would keep it now that he was dead.

Chapter Nine

Silas was angry as he turned away from the house in Bedford Square. He had made a long and tedious journey for the sole purpose of calling on his ward only to find that she had gone off to stay with friends in the country. It was too bad of her, after he had written to say he would be calling. Well, he was damned if he was going to go chasing after her at once. Their meeting could wait until he had completed his own business.

'Forgive me,' Silas apologised as he bumped into a passer by. 'My mind was elsewhere.' He broke off to stare at the other man. 'Aren't you Edward Brockleton?'

There was a slight momentary awkwardness, then the second man nodded. 'Couldn't place you for a moment – Silas Taverner, ain't it? You were a friend and business partner of Henry Manners. I heard you were in some outlandish place or other.'

'India,' Silas replied and turned up his coat collar. The wind was bitter and he was feeling the cold. 'This is a fortuitous meeting – I was hoping to find you in town. I've a bit of business I wanted to discuss.'

'The past is gone, Taverner. Why not let it lie?'

'This has nothing to do with Helena. I gave you my word on that years ago.'

'Yes.' Edward Brockleton looked at him with

thinly-disguised dislike. This was the man he secretly blamed for his sister's tragic death. 'Very well then. I'm going to my club. You may as well accompany me. Would you care to join me for dinner?'

'That's very civil of you,' Silas replied. 'I'll be glad to get indoors out of this wind.'

'I suppose you feel it after India.' The other man nodded. 'I'm surprised you've come back. I thought you would settle there after . . . well, no need to mention any of that, is there?'

'None at all,' Silas said. 'I've never spoken of your little secret to anyone and I never shall.'

Brockleton nodded. 'She's at rest now. No sense in stirring up old wounds.'

'My opinion entirely,' Silas agreed. 'The truth could only be harmful, don't you think?'

'I've always thought so, that's why I never did anything about it at the time.'

Now in perfect harmony the two men walked on through the gathering dusk.

Chapter Ten

Caroline awoke with a start and lay shivering in her bed. She'd had the dream again, and this time it lingered even after she was awake. She seemed to see the face of the woman her father was dragging from the house – and it was her.

'It's just a dream,' Caroline muttered. She lit the candle on the table beside her bed, then threw back the covers and got out, pulling on a warm, quilted dressing wrap before going over to the window. 'Just a silly dream.'

She had woken early and dawn was just breaking. The birds had begun to trill, first a blackbird piping from a rowan bush outside her window, then the melodious song of a thrush and many others she could not identify as the chorus swelled to a joyful welcome of the new day.

Caroline shrugged off the lingering memory of the dream. Her father was dead; besides, he had never harmed her. She believed he had hurt her mother more than once, however. Though Helena Manners had never complained of her husband's cruelty, Caroline had noticed bruises on her arms and shoulders from time to time.

'Have you hurt yourself, Mama?' she would ask. But her mother would not look her in the eye.

'I banged myself on a door – wasn't that careless of me?'

She had lied to protect Caroline, of course. Sitting, staring out into the gardens as the light strengthened, Caroline wondered what made some men take pleasure in hurting their women. Her flesh suddenly went goose pimply, and she shivered as though an icy wind had blown through the room.

Lord Carlton was not that kind of man. She was quite sure it would be beneath him to strike a woman, whatever the provocation – so what had brought on her nightmare? She had the oddest feeling, as though some evil force were casting a shadow over her life.

What nonsense! She was safe at Pendlesham. Fitz would not allow anyone or anything to harm her. She had everything in the world to look forward to and nothing whatsoever to fear.

From her vantage point she could see a man walking across the lawns. Obviously, he had not been able to sleep either. He paused for a moment to glance back at the house. She thought at first he was looking directly up at her window, then she dismissed it as mere imagination. Why should Will Carlton look for her? He despised her.

Her thoughts turned to Will Carlton. She remembered the wild, wonderful sensations that had set her body trembling with delight as he kissed her. She had wondered, in those first heady seconds, if this was love. Then he looked at her in that cruel way, and pricked the bubble of her dream.

'A moment's madness, nothing more.' His words wre imprinted into her mind in letters of fire.

She had fled from the humiliation of his rejection to the undemanding kindness of Fitz Carlton's arms, and now she had promised to be his wife, a promise she could never break. Before dinner he had presented her with a beautiful sapphire and diamond ring.

'It belonged to my mother,' he said as he slipped it on her finger. She was surprised to discover it fitted perfectly. 'I shall buy you a ring of your own choosing, of course – but wear this just for now. I thought we would announce our engagement at our dinner party next week – if you agree?'

'An excellent idea.' Caroline admired the ring on her finger. 'This is lovely, Fitz. I need no other.'

'But you shall have one nevertheless. You must allow me to spoil you a little, Caroline. It will give me pleasure.'

His cousin had walked in at that moment and Fitz swung round with a smile of welcome. 'Congratulate me, Will – Caroline has consented to be my wife, isn't that splendid news?'

'The best,' Will replied. 'I congratulate you both and wish you every happiness for the future.'

His tone was warm and even. Was it her imagination or had there been a flicker of pain in his eyes? If it was ever there it was banished in seconds.

'Caroline – please, may I have a moment of your time?'

Caroline paused in the hall as she heard Will's voice. She had succeeded in avoiding him for almost a week, but knew she must face him eventually. Reluctantly, she went to join him in the small front parlour that looked out towards the rose gadens.

'Yes,' she said in a cool voice. 'You had something to say to me?'

He threw her a frustrated look.' This can't go on,' he said. 'We have to live in the same house. If you persist in this – this coldness – Fitz is bound to notice.'

'I believed you warned me of his temper if I should smile at you too often?'

'I said far too much that morning,' Will replied ruefully. 'I behaved badly altogether, and I beg you to forgive me.' He gave her an odd, almost shy smile. 'I'm asking if we could begin again, Caroline? If you could possibly give me a chance to be your friend?'

His smile was so genuine and wistful that her heart seemed to stop beating and she felt light-headed. At this moment he was so like Fitz – and yet they were so very different. Will was vital, full of strength and energy and so very alive. Beside him, Fitz, for all his presence, was almost a shadow caught in a twilight world of his own.

How strange that she should only see that now. At first Fitz's haunted eyes and pale face had captured her imagination, but now Will had become the stronger influence. But to think like that was treachery.

Her eyes moved round the room, taking in the pretty pastel shades of greens and blues in the curtains and rugs, the delicate gilt chairs and comfortable sofas. It was a favourite room of hers, but from now on – since *he* seemed to use it too – she would avoid it.

'Do you think it possible for us to be friends, Will?' she murmured at last.

His eyes seemed to burn into her. 'What else can we be?'

'I don't know,' she whispered, taking a step towards him despite herself.

'You are right,' he said and retreated towards the elegant marble fireplace, where he stood, facing the fire. 'I hoped – but no, it would not work. You were right to avoid me, Caroline.'

'Perhaps, once I am married . . .'

'No!' He spun round, anguish in his face. 'We can only be enemies – or lovers.'

'Then it is hopeless.'

'Yes,' he said in a low voice. 'I must leave here.'

'Where would you go?'

'To my own estate in Hampshire. It was my father's and is but a small house and park – but it would be best. Just until you are married and I am more settled in my mind.'

'Please don't,' Caroline said. 'I am leaving in two days time – after the party – to prepare for the wedding. Stay here where you belong, and when I come back we shall begin anew. We shall try to be friends, Will.'

'Yes, perhaps you are right. We are both civilised people are we not?' He was back in control of his emotions. 'I wanted to tell you – you were right about Briggs too. He has been dismissed.'

'I know. Fitz told me.' She smiled as the tension eased between them. 'The gypsies have gone, too. I wanted to find Katya, but it was too late.'

'Perhaps it was for the best. Gypsies are proud people; they do not take kindly to charity.'

'I just wanted to help her.'

He nodded and sighed. 'You have a generous nature, Caroline.'

'You did not always think so.'

'I am a fool.' His smile flashed out, catching at her heart. Then he took something from his waistcoat pocket and held it out to her. 'I believe this is yours. You dropped it the other day.'

The silver pixie lay on his palm. Caroline reached out to take it, then shook her head. 'It is supposed to bring luck,' she said. 'You keep it for me, Will.'

Then she turned and walked away, leaving him staring after her.

It was the evening of the dinner party. Caroline sat at the head of the long table, looking down its impressive, shining length to Fitz at the other end. The array of silver and crystal was breathtaking; in the middle a magnificent three-tier epergne was dressed with flowers and fruits from the hothouses; smaller epergnes were set at intervals down the table, the perfume of exotic blooms subtly pervading the room, mixing with the pungent heat of burning candlewax. Along each side of the table were seated ten guests – mostly neighbours and friends of Carlton, who had accepted his invitation to dine with curiosity – and of course her faithful, loyal Sally.

Caroline smiled as she heard the laughter and chatter around her. This was what a house like this should be like, full of laughter and people and light. It gave her a warm feeling to know that she had been responsible for bringing it back to life. Her heart skipped a beat as Fitz stood up and raised his wine glass to her.

'Ladies and gentlemen, friends. I believe you have all guessed the reson for this celebration. I wish to announce my engagement to Miss Caroline Manners, and to ask you all to drink the health of this beautiful and gracious lady who has made me the happiest of men . . . To Caroline . . .'

'To Caroline . . .' they all chorused, lifting their glasses to her and drinking. She blushed, then bit her lip as Will got to his feet, his eyes meeting hers across the table. 'Happiness to Caroline and Fitz,' he said. 'May theirs be a long and fruitful marriage.'

Caroline looked down, her cheeks fiery. She sipped her wine but it almost choked her. Will was staring at her so oddly. As if the last thing he wished her was happiness?

The announcement made and toasted, it was time for her and Sally to lead the ladies into the drawing room, leaving the gentlemen to their port.

Lady Thornton came bustling up importantly, tapping Caroline's arm with her fan, and smiling archly. 'To think that it was at my house you met,' she said. 'I am *so* glad we shall be neighbours, my dear Miss Manners. You must not be a stranger. It will be as it was in the old days. Oh, the parties and balls Carlton's mother gave! You must reinstate all the old traditions.'

'Yes, I intend to – after we are married,' Caroline said. 'Will you take some tea, Lady Thornton?'

One by one the ladies came to congratulate her. These were the closest and oldest friends of the Carlton family, who had watched the decline of a great house with sorrow, and were pleased to see its old grace and charm being restored.

Caroline made the acquaintance of two ladies she especially liked, making a mental note to call on them once she was living at Pendlesham. Lady Ross in particular could tell her many of the things she wished to know about the duties of Pendlesham's chatelaine. Once she was Lady Carlton she meant to take an interest in the village and its people, and she fancied that Lady Ross was like-minded.

'I am so glad that Fitz has found you,' Lady Ross confided to her. 'You will be so very good for him, my dear.'

It was not long before the gentlemen joined the ladies for cards and music. Lady Ross was persuaded to sing, and Caroline played for her. Afterwards, Caroline moved about the room conversing with some of the gentlemen, who were as curious as their wives about the woman who had persuaded Fitz Carlton to marry at last.

'A damned fine gel if you ask me,' Lord Ross said to his wife as they were leaving. 'He'll get an heir by her, I shouldn't wonder.'

His wife laughed and pursed her lips. 'You men!' she said with a shake of her head. 'The succession is everything with you. I only hope she will be happy with her bargain.'

'What do you mean?' He glanced at her frowningly. 'Now what bee is in your bonnet, Maudey? It's a splendid match for the gel.'

'Yes, I suppose it is,' his wife replied. 'You know I liked her, Ronald. I liked her very much.'

Since everyone was of the same opinion as Lady Ross, the evening was declared a resounding success.

'You have them all eating out of your hand already,' Fitz declared as he said goodnight to her. 'I am very fortunate, Caroline.'

He kissed her hand. Over his shoulder, Caroline saw Will watching them.

'You have been very quiet these past two days,' Sally said as she pulled on her gloves. 'Are you sad to be leaving Pendlesham sooner than you planned?'

'No, for I shall return as its mistress,' Caroline replied, and studied her reflection. 'Is my hat on straight?'

'Not quite – stand still, my love. There, that is better, is it not?'

'Much,' Caroline agreed and picked up her own gloves. 'Of course I need Mr Taverner's permission, but I hardly think he will refuse it. In six months I shall be twenty-one and able to please myself. Under the terms of my father's will I can take control of my fortune, marry whom I please and generally go to hell at my own speed.'

'Caroline!' Sally looked shocked. 'What a thing to say.' Her expression became troubled. 'You have not begun to regret your promise to marry Lord Carlton – have you?'

'Not in the least,' Caroline said. 'There, I think I have everything – shall we go?'

They were due to leave for her property in Norfolk. Caroline had decided to have it put up for sale now that she was to settle at Pendlesham she would not need it. It was a cold, bleak house, too large and ugly for her ever to wish to visit there, but there were certain things – china and personal items that had belonged to her mother – that she wished to keep. She intended to have them packed into trunks and delivered to Pendlesham before her marriage.

'Are you sure?' Sally laid a hand on her arm. 'It is not too late to change your mind, my love. I know your engagement has been announced locally, but it is not to be inserted in the *Times* until you have spoken to Mr Taverner.'

'I have given my word to Fitz,' Caroline said, thinking of the consternation it would cause amongst his neighbours if she were to break it off. 'I could not break my promise even if I wanted to, Sally – which I don't. Fitz needs me and I am comfortable with him.'

'I thought you might be in love with someone else?'

Caroline's laugh was a little too harsh. 'How you do go on,' she cried. 'Love is a myth as I have always told you. Oh yes, I know about your wild passion, but I believe that is something quite different – something perhaps akin to lust.'

'No, no,' Sally denied, upset. 'You are quite wrong.

Lust can, indeed does, play a part in love, but they are not the same. 'Oh, I wish I could make you see.'

'You worry too much,' Caroline scolded. 'I know you are fond of me, Sally dearest, but I have made up my mind.'

'And nothing will change it.' Sally shook her head. 'You are so stubborn.'

'Then pray do not waste your breath.' Caroline took her arm. 'Let us go down now.'

Fitz was waiting in the hall to say goodbye. He kissed her cheek, then pressed something in her hand. She saw it was a leather-bound book of poems, a new edition of the one he treasured.

'I thought it would keep you company on the journey,' he said, looking into her face earnestly. 'Please take care of yourself, Caroline, and come back to us soon.' He touched her cheek. 'You are a little pale. You are not ill I trust?'

'I am perfectly well,' she reassured him. She glanced over his shoulder, half hoping to see his cousin. 'You will say goodbye to Mr Carlton for me?'

'You must begin to call him Will once we are married,' Fitz scolded gently. 'Will is like a brother to me, my love. He is off on some business for the estate, or he would have been here to say goodbye himself.'

Fitz turned from her to say his farewells to Sally and press a purse of guineas on her. She blushed and refused but was eventually prevailed upon to accept.

Caroline stood waiting, her back towards them. Why was she so disappointed that *he* was not here to see her off? She had not really expected it.

'The carriage is waiting.'

Caroline turned at the sound of the familiar voice, her heart thumping. So he had come after all!

'You got back then,' Fitz said to Will. 'Caroline asked where you were.'

'I just wanted to wish you a safe journey,' Will said. 'And you, Sally. You must not be a stranger here, must she, Fitz?'

Will's smile was for Sally, but his eyes never left Caroline's face.

'Just what I was telling her,' Fitz said. 'She says she is to visit her sister-in-law after the wedding, but she will always be welcome here.'

They moved outside to the waiting carriage as a group. Will opened the door and helped Sally in. He whispered something to her, slipping a small package into her hand. She nodded and smiled at him.

Caroline saw it all but took scant notice. She had been aware of a growing friendship between her companion and Will Carlton, no doubt it was a small keepsake.

Fitz took Caroline's hand and kissed it. 'I shall miss you,' he said. 'The house will not be the same without you – what do you say, Will?'

'No – it will seem empty indeed.' He sounded as though he were forcing out the words.

Caroline could not look at him. She reached up to kiss Fitz's cheek.

'Thank you,' she whispered huskily. 'You must promise to take care of yourself. I do not want to hear that you have been ill again.'

'I shall try not to be,' he promised. 'I am much stronger now.'

'I'll take care of him for you, don't worry,' Will said.

Caroline glanced at Will, then away. 'Thank you,' she said, accepting the hand he offered to help her into the carriage. 'Goodbye.'

For a moment their eyes met and held. Then Will was closing the door after her. She waved from behind the window as they rumbled off, sitting forward to see the last of the two cousins before the carriage swept down the drive and away.

Caroline closed her eyes. It was several minutes before she opened them again to become aware that Sally was proffering a small package.

'Will asked me to give this to you,' she said.

'Surely it was meant for you?'

'He gave me something yesterday in private. Go on – take it.'

Caroline opened the box reluctantly. Inside was a heavy gold chain and an oval locket. A large double C was engraved on the front and chased with vine leaves and flowers.

'Caroline Carlton,' she whispered. 'Lady Carlton . . .'

'May I see?' Sally held out her hand, and Caroline passed it to her. Sally opened it. 'Oh, it has an inscription.' She immediately handed it back with a guilty flush.

'For Caroline of the tender heart, with love,' Caroline whispered, then snapped it shut. 'Don't look like that, Sally – he meant it only to mock me.' She replaced the gift in its box and slipped it into her muff. 'It isn't a message of love.'

'Are you quite sure?'

'Quite.' Caroline glared at her. 'He may not be immune to my charms, but he doesn't love me. Mr Carlton does not like or trust women in general, and me in particular.'

'He has always been very kind to me.'

'He likes you.'

'He likes you more,' Sally countered.

'Not another word, Sally. Not another word!'

Seeing the set of Caroline's jaw, Sally gave up with a sigh. The wedding could not take place for at least another month. Perhaps by then Caroline would have come to her senses.

Chapter Eleven

Silas Taverner felt sick as he looked at the deeds lying on the table in front of him in the club's private room. The property they represented did not belong to him, though he had power of attorney over them. Once he signed, the transaction would be legal, and the house in Norfolk, together with its pasture and woodland, would no longer belong to Caroline Manners.

Silently, he cursed himself for a fool. He should never have let Edward Brockleton put him up for membership of the club, knowing that gambling took place on the premises. He had never had much luck at the card tables – and he had vowed he would never play piquet again. Not after that last time in India, when he'd lost everything to Harry Jarvis. But the curse was in his blood like a fever, and he had been helpless in its grip.

And this time, it wasn't even his own money he'd thrown away. How was he to explain it to his ward? But he could not explain; he would have to buy it back.

'Is something wrong?'

Silas glowered at the young aristocrat who was looking down his long nose at him. From his expression it was clear that he thought Silas was beneath his class – good enough to play cards with, but not to meet on his home ground. He would never be invited to dine at this young man's home. Silas knew the type and despised them. It made him all the more angry because he had to ask a favour.

'I shall sign of course,' he said, picking up a pen and dipping it in the ink. 'But I beg you not to sell for at least a month – by then I shall be in a position to buy it back.'

'I can give you three weeks,' the bored voice drawled. 'I have debts of my own to meet, sir. Settle by the seventeenth of November, or I shall sell to the first bidder.'

'Very well.' Silas signed, tight-lipped. 'I shall meet you here on the sixteenth at noon – my word as a gentleman.'

'Certainly. Good-day, sir.'

Silas watched him place the deeds in his inner pocket, then pushed back his chair. He was scowling as he left the club and made his way back to his lodgings. Now he had no choice. He would have to visit this place of Lord Carlton's . . . Pendlesham or whatever it was. He needed Caroline's signature on some papers. He had power of attourney over her property, because her father had given it to him years before, but he needed to liquidate other assets in order to buy the damned house back again.

He paused outside his lodging house, looking around him with distaste. Not the best neighbourhood, but all he could afford in his present predicament. He went inside, nose wrinkling at the stink of stale cabbage and ale. He would be glad to leave the wretched place.

There was a letter lying on the hall table. Silas recognised the handwriting as Caroline's; it must have been sent on by her solicitor. He picked it up with a prickle of unease. Not once until now had he abused the trust her father had placed in him.

He waited to read the letter until he was back in his own room. A good fire was burning – he had left instructions that it was never to go out, because he was still susceptible to the cold – and there was brandy waiting. The fire warmed him and the brandy gave him courage. He opened the letter, reading it swiftly and then more slowly.

Lady Luck must be on his side! Caroline was getting married and wanted to sell the Norfolk property. That would make things considerably easier. He could convince her that her investments needed adjusting, and with a little jiggling of the figures she would never know that she hadn't received payment for the house.

It was strictly temporary, Silas promised himself. He hadn't set out to cheat her. Once he'd sold that consignment of Portugese wine . . . but he would need a sizeable sum for reinvestment. Damn it! She was rich enough thanks to him. He'd more than doubled the fortune her father had left her by his shrewd investments on her behalf. She wouldn't miss a few thousand pounds. Besides, he had no alternative.

Silas finished his brandy and refilled the glass. He sat back in his chair, closing his eyes and relaxing as the warmth flowed into his bones. He could almost imagine himself back in India, smell the perfume of Anais' hair, feel the smooth silk of her skin as he thrust deep into her. How he longed for her, for the warmth and colour of India, the spiced food – everything was so bland and tasteless here – the flowers and the brightness, but above all Anais.

It was no use, he could never return. He had

stopped short of murder but he had mutilated and disfigured Jarvis in that drunken brawl. If ever he entered India again Jarvis would keep his promise to have him killed.

He could go somewhere warmer, of course. Spend a part of the year in Spain or Portugal, selecting his wines. A smile touched his mouth as he dwelled upon it. Spanish women could be beautiful too.

Damn it, but he needed a woman!

But first and foremost he needed money, far more than he could raise from his own sources. Finishing his brandy, Silas stood up and yawned. Best get some sleep if he were to travel to Norfolk first thing in the morning.

Chapter Twelve

Will stood gazing out over land that had been autumn ploughed; there was a white frost on the soil and it was still freezing. This was good, rich land, high yielding and profitable. At Pendlesham they clung mostly to the old ways: wheat, rye, oats and barley with one year fallow, but there were new methods of farming, new ideas, and it was true that the root crops cleaned the soil, giving better yields for the traditional harvest the next year. Still, he and Fitz preferred the old way, and there was no lack of land.

The Carltons were good stewards; they had never believed in the enclosures that led to terrible deprivation and starving amongst the common folk, thus robbed of their ancient rights and their living. There were few fences on the estate, except for the perimeter wall on the high road and hedges to keep the sheep from straying. Villagers were free to graze their cows and pigs on the common; the far wood provided fuel and rabbits for any who chose to snare them, and the river was teaming with fish for those with the skill to catch them. Years of prudence and careful management had made the Carltons too wealthy to be concerned if some of the game that was rightly theirs found its way to a poor man's table.

It was a nuisance about the pheasants though, Will reflected. It hadn't been worth holding a shoot this year, which had disappointed their neighbours, but it couldn't he helped. Briggs had been replaced, though his successor was less adept with the birds. How many years had Briggs been cheating them and getting away with it, he wondered. He might still have managed to shift the blame on to someone else, but for Caroline's intervention.

Will turned away from his contemplation of the land. What was he going to do? Pendlesham had been his life; it would devastate him to leave it. But how could he bear to stay?

The past two weeks had seen some easing of his tension. With Caroline gone, he managed to empty his mind of her for hours at a time, though she often returned to haunt his dreams. Of late he rose earlier than in the past, unrefreshed and heavy-eyed. Only when he was out walking the estate, consulting the bailiff, or his grooms, could he put her face out of his mind.

What torture it would be when she became his cousin's wife.

Hearing the thud of a horse's hooves, he turned to see Fitz cantering towards him. As he reined in, Will could not help but notice his cousin's general air of well-being. It would not be long before he was back to being his old self. All thanks to Caroline.

'There you are, Will,' Fitz hailed. 'I thought I might find you here. I was thinking of taking a ride over to the Thorntons'. Would you care to join me?'

'Not this morning,' Will replied. 'I heard that Lucy was visiting. Give her my regards.'

Fitz gazed down at him. 'You were always more her friend than I. I even thought once that you might marry her: you should find yourself a wife, cousin.'

'I'm not the marrying kind.' Will avoided his eyes. 'Perhaps one day . . .'

'Yet you were set on it for me,' Fitz reminded him with a smile. 'And you were right. I received a letter from Caroline this morning. She's expecting to see her guardian any day now. As soon as he gives his consent I shall put up the banns. No sense in delaying it.'

'No,' Will agreed. 'None at all.'

'I'll be off then.'

Will watched his cousin ride away, going from a canter to a gallop across the meadow, and frowned at his rashness. It was but a few days since he'd got back on a horse after a long abstinence caused by his leg wound. If he were to fall and break his neck . . . If Fitz were killed it would all be his: Pendlesham, the land . . . Caroline.

He groaned aloud. What was Caroline doing to him that he could entertain such thoughts. Perhaps he was bewitched.

Even as he berated himself, he saw a man emerge from the woods directly in Fitz's path, and raise his arm. The horse reared up on its hind legs, throwing its rider to the ground.

Then Will was running and praying as he ran, and begging silent forgiveness for his wicked thoughts. Fitz was still, face down in the grass. Will knelt beside the comatose form, throwing a hateful glance at the man whose thoughtless act had caused the accident – Fitz's former head gamekeeper. He stood meekly a few paces away, clearly in dread of retribution.

'Is he alive, sir?'

'If he is, it's no thanks to you, you dunderhead!' Will snapped. He grasped Fitz's shoulders, turned him onto his back. 'Damn you, Fitz, don't you die on me.'

Fitz's eyes fluttered open and he smiled faintly. 'It

would take more than a tumble from a nag to see me off, old fellow.'

'Thank God for that.' In his relief Will grinned back foolishly. 'Where are you hurt?'

Fitz moved his arms then his legs, and a sharp cry of pain escaped him.

'It's my leg again, blast it. Must have twisted it in the fall.' He cast around. 'Is my horse all right?'

'Yes – yes, he has bolted, that's all. We'll see to him later.' Will ran his hands over Fitz's leg. 'It does not seem to be broken.'

'Is there anything I can do, sir?' Briggs asked timidly.

'Haven't you done enough?' Will snarled at him. 'I'll have you locked up for this . . .'

'No, Will, no,' Fitz said soothingly. 'Give me a hand up, will you?'

Supported by his cousin, Fitz strugged to his feet. He turned a mildly curious gaze on the shamefaced keeper.

'Perhaps you would care to explain your actions, Briggs.'

'Yes sir.' The keeper shuffled his feet abjectly, his eyes downcast. 'I just wanted to speak to your lordship, sir. I can't get work . . . I . . . I was hoping you would take pity on me, sir.'

'Pah!' Will would have liked to wring the man's neck. 'Behind bars is where you belong, my man.'

Fitz patted Will's arm. 'No, no, that won't do. The man's a fool, but that's no reason to take his freedom away.' He squared up to the keeper, who dropped onto one knee. 'You will leave Pendlesham at once, Briggs. If you set foot on Carlton land again I will have you flogged. Is that understood?'

'Yes, my lord.' Briggs was close to grovelling. 'I

wouldn't have harmed you for the world, sir. You was always good to me.'

'Right, now be off with you.'

'And look sharp about it,' Will added.

The keeper backed off in a flurry of bows, then turned to run. Will flung a curse after him to speed him on his way.

'I'm sorry to go over your head, Will,' Fitz said. 'But I am not one for revenge.'

'Then maybe you should be.' Will's expression was stony. 'You showed him charity once, and how does he repay it?'

'Will was more shocked by events than he cared to admit – the more so because of his own wicked thoughts immediately before the accident occurred.

Fitz tried to take a step forward and winced.

'Sit down, cousin. I'll fetch my horse and we'll ride home together, the way we used to when we were boys.'

Chapter Thirteen

Caroline took the gold locket out of its box for the umpteenth time and examined it, fingering its smoothness in her restless hands. It was such a lovely trinket – could Will really have meant the inscription to mock her? Sally was certain not, but then he had been unfailingly kind to her and she was unaware of his cruel words to Caroline. Besides, whatever the inscription was intended to mean, it could make no difference to her intentions.

Sighing, Caroline put the locket back in its box and glanced at the sapphire and diamond ring on her finger. That too was beautiful, and she had accepted it in good faith. It would be unthinkable to break her promise to Fitz. In any case, she wasn't even sure that Will liked her. He might well *desire* her, but that was not the same. Men did not always like and respect the women they lusted after.

She was brought out of her reverie by a tap at the door of her boudoir.

'Come in,' she called, as Sally put her head round the door. 'I'm ready. I was just about to come down.'

'You look very elegant, my love,' Sally said, entering on a cloud of flowery perfume.

Caroline had on a dark blue morning gown with puffed sleeves and a narrow, figure-hugging skirt caught up in high waist with a pale blue sash. She had worn it only twice previously. Sally was also dressed in one of her best gowns: a pale lilac with flounces at the hem. They were dressed to receive an important caller – Silas Taverner.

'Thank you, Sally,' Caroline said, then seeing that she was clutching a piece of notepaper, 'Was your letter exciting?'

'It is from Miss Bridget Croxley,' Sally replied, wrinkling her brow in an uncertain frown. 'You know I planned to visit her after your wedding . . .'

'Yes . . .' Caroline sensed her hesitation. 'Is something wrong?'

'Bridget has not been well,' Sally said. 'She has asked if I will go down to her next week. Of course I shall tell her it isn't possible.'

Sally was quite fond of her sister-in-law, more so than she had been of her husband, and obviously torn two ways.

'But why?' Caroline asked, understanding her dilemma at once. 'If you are afraid of putting me out you need not be. I shall be here in Norfolk only another week or so, then I shall go up to London for long enough to buy my bride clothes, before returning to Pendlesham for the wedding.'

'It would be so awkward for you,' Sally said and shook her head. 'No, no, it is impossible – and with Mr Taverner arriving this morning . . .'

'He will stay no more than a day or so,' Caroline assured her. 'Besides, I have a houseful of female servants to preserve my propriety, and I am engaged to Carlton now, so there can be no difficulty there. I have my maids. Rosa and Mary are to go with me to Pendlesham when I leave this house. And don't forget, Mrs Lambert will be here until the end of the month, so I am well protected.'

Sally nodded. 'Yes, I suppose it will be all right – if Mrs Lambert is here.'

Caroline's housekeeper was past sixty, a dour-faced woman of strict morals. She had been both care-taker and housekeeper over the years of Caroline's minority, and had decided to retire to her married daughter's home only now that the house was to be sold.

'I wouldn't have deserted my post if you needed me, Miss Manners,' she had told Caroline. 'But my daughter could do with a hand now that she's expect-ing her sixth child. It will give her a chance to put her feet up occasionally.'

'Yes, of course,' Caroline said. 'I'm glad you have somewhere to go; though I'm sure the new owners would have been delighted to keep you on.'

'No, no, Miss Manners,' Mrs Lambert insisted. 'It's time I looked after my own.'

She had asked to leave at the end of the month, which meant that the house would be closed until a buyer could be found. She had promised to arrange for someone to come in from the village now and then to keep an eye on the place.

'I shall miss you, of course,' Caroline said to Sally, as she touched a little cologne behind her ears. 'But I shall send both you and Bridget an invitation to my wedding. You can both come and stay at Pendlesham – if your sister-in-law is well enough, of course.' She got up as she heard carriage wheels outside. 'That must be Mr Taverner arriving. We should to down now.' Taking Sally's arm, she smiled at her. 'Write and tell Miss Croxley that you will come at the end of next week. Then I shall be only three or four days alone before I leave for London.'

'Very well, if you wish it,' Sally sighed, still uneasy

about leaving Caroline without her companionship, but relieved to have it settled.

'It is not that I want to part with you,' Caroline assured her, giving her arm a little squeeze. 'But we shall see each other soon and you must always write to me, of course. If you are ever unhappy you can come to me for a visit and stay as long as you like. There are so many rooms at Pendlesham that I'm sure it would not matter even if you took up permanent residence.'

'You and Lord Carlton are both so generous,' Sally said and tears sparkled in her eyes. 'I hope to visit as often as I can, but Bridget has asked me to make my home with her and I believe she needs me. She has the rheumatics, you know, and is beginning to find it hard to get about. She talks of spending the winter abroad somewhere.'

'That would be nice for you,' Caroline said.

'But of course I shall come for your wedding whatever happens!'

Caroline nodded and said no more. Sally would make up her own mind as circumstances allowed.

They came to the top of the stairs. In the hall below, Mrs Lambert was helping a gentleman off with his heavy cloak and several mufflers. Caroline was able to observe him for a moment or two before he became aware of them.

He was of average height – or perhaps she thought that because the Carlton cousins were taller – and much thinner than she had remembered, with a sallow complexion, and dark wiry hair that had begun to turn grey. Despite his complexion, however, he had strong features and a certain physical attractiveness that she thought might appeal to older women. For a moment she wondered if she should persuade Sally to stay on longer after all. Then he glanced up at her and she changed her mind, instinctively hostile. There was something about him that she instantly disliked – something she had been unaware of as a child; the look in his eyes made her flesh creep. He was staring at her intently, as if he were stripping the clothes from her body, and she dropped her own gaze.

'Mr Taverner,' she said, summoning a smile of welcome as she went down the stairs to greet him. 'How good of you to come all this way yourself. A letter of consent would have been sufficient.'

He moved to meet her, continuing his almost insolent appraisal. 'I should have been failing in my duty towards you had I not come in person,' he said. 'Marriage is a serious business, Miss Manners. There are contracts to be arranged, investments to be discussed . . .'

'Surely Lord Carlton's lawyers and mine can sort that out,' Caroline said with a lift of her chin. He seemed to be censuring her and she did not care for it. 'I am sure his lordship intends to make a generous settlement. He is after all one of the wealthiest men in England; my fortune can mean very little to him.'

'Your fortune is not insignificant,' Silas demured. 'Your investments have prospered under my care.'

'Yes, of course. I did not mean that.' Caroline reminded herself that, no matter what she felt about him personally, he was her guardian. Moreover, she owed him a great deal for his careful stewardship in her years of minority. 'You have had a long journey, sir. Please come into the parlour and take some refreshment with us.' She turned to Sally. 'I do not believe you have met Mr Taverner? Sir – this lady is my companion, Mrs Sally Croxley.'

'Ma'am.' Silas bowed over her hand. 'I have heard excellent things of you from Miss Manners, of course, and it is an honour and a pleasure to meet you.'

His smile was warm and sincere. Sally dimpled with gratification and Caroline wondered if she had misjudged him. The expression on his face when he first saw her could have been a trick of the light. She had been a rather thin, un-prepossessing child when they had last met, and he may have just been surprised, probably thinking of her still as a child. It would not do to jump to conclusions about what manner of man he might be. Besides, she need only be polite to him for a few days, and then he would be gone. Once she was married their paths need never cross again.

'I'll ask Mrs Lambert to bring tea to the parlour, shall I?' Sally suggested.

Caroline nodded and she rustled away, leaving Sally to lead their visitor into the parlour. It was a dark, depressing room, furnished in heavy oak and dull colours, as was most of the house, and did not present much of a welcome even though a fire was crackling merrily in the large fireplace.

'This place doesn't change,' Silas said, going to rub his hands before the fire. 'I'm not surprised you want to be rid of it. I could never understand why Henry bought the place – I suppose he just wanted somewhere in a hurry after . . .' Silas stopped abruptly and shuddered slightly. 'I cannot seem to get warm since I've been back in England.'

'I thought my father had always lived here,' Caroline said, frowning. 'Did we live once somewhere else?'

'He brought you here when you were about two years old, as I remember.' He seemed reluctant to speak of it.

Caroline had no memory of having lived elsewhere. 'Why did we come here?'

'I've no idea,' Silas said, then as Sally returned, 'Could I trouble you for something a little stronger than tea, Mrs Croxley? A drop of brandy for medicinal purposes perhaps? This cold weather affects my chest.'

'It has been rather cold,' Sally agreed, 'and of course you would feel it after India.'

As she went off again, Caroline fixed him with a determined stare. 'Please – you do know something. I sensed it just now.'

'If you insist,' Silas said grudgingly. 'There was an accident. Your father's youngest sister died.'

'Oh? How did she die?' Caroline felt a chill at the base of her spine. She had never even known that her father had had two sisters. 'What happened to her? Aunt Emily never mentioned her to me, and nor did Papa.'

'She was drowned in the lake,' Silas explained. 'It was tragic. She was reaching for a hat that had blown into the water and fell in. She could not swim and the weight of her clothes dragged her down; she drowned before anyone realised what had occurred.'

'That is terrible,' Caroline said, but was relieved that it had nothing to do with her dream. 'Was she young?'

'A little older than you are now,' he said. 'Henry could not bear the place after that, so he brought you and Helena here.'

Her father had never seemed a sentimental man to Caroline, but she realised that the accident to his sister could have changed him. It might even be the reason for his rather remote manner.

'Was my father very fond of his sister?'

'Yes, perhaps too fond,' Silas replied. 'He was never the same man after she died. I think Helena suffered for it.'

'I do not think he was always kind to her,' Caroline said.

'You noticed it, too?' Silas gave a snort. 'I was never sure . . .'

'What was her name – his sister?'

'Caroline. You were named for her.'

Once again Caroline felt the coldness stealing down her spine, but she was prevented from asking more questions by Sally's return, followed immediately by Mrs Lambert. Conversation became general over the teacups.

It was not until she was alone in her room later that Caroline had time to ponder her guardian's revelations. He had been reluctant to talk of it, but she was determined to learn more before he left.

Caroline continued to wonder about the aunt she had never known as she changed her gown for dinner that evening. It was odd that no one had ever mentioned it to her. She could understand such a tragic affair being kept from her as a child, but not when she grew up.

'Your Aunt Emily probably felt it would only upset you,' Sally said when she told her what she had learned. 'After all, you had lost both your parents in an accident.'

'Yes, I suppose so,' Caroline said, thoughtfully. 'My mother had a brother, you know – a Mr Edward Brockleton. He wrote to me once after my mother's death to say that he was unable to offer me a home because he was a bachelor. Since then he has sent me an occasional Christmas gift but I've never seen him either. Don't you think it all seems a little odd? I

136

mean, why wasn't he appointed my guardian instead
of Mr Taverner?'

'Your father obviously trusted Mr Taverner to look
after your interests. And he has done so rather well,
hasn't he?'

'Yes, yes, he has,' Caroline admitted. 'What do you
think of him, Sally? Do you like him?'

'I think so. On the whole.'

Sally's reply was less than enthusiastic. 'You aren't
sure – why?'

'I don't know.' Sally hesitated, her expression rueful. 'My first impression was favourable, but I confess
I should not feel comfortable leaving you alone in the
house if he were to stay longer than planned.'

So Caroline had not imagined that look in his eyes!

'He will be leaving before you do,' she reassured
Sally. 'There is no need to delay your own plans for
my sake.'

'No, I suppose not.' Sally was still doubtful.

'I will admit to some unease myself,' Caroline said.
'But I may have misjudged him. Besides, you are
here, and I have Mrs Lambert.'

'Do you think it was all those years in India?' Sally
mused. 'He was born a gentleman, of course, but
there is something not quite civilised beneath the surface, don't you feel?'

'I think we should not keep our guest waiting for
dinner, Caroline laughed. 'For shame, Sally! The poor
man has done nothing to deserve this. We are allowing our imaginations to run wild.'

'So you see,' Silas said, after dinner was over and they
had retired to the drawing room. 'I feel it would be
better to make some adjustments to your investments
before you marry.'

137

'Of course, I trust your judgement,' Caroline replied. 'But I hardly feel it is necessary to change things at once. Why don't we leave it to our lawyers to settle between them?'

'I think I have more experience than any lawyer.'

His annoyance was palpable, but Caroline was not inclined to do as he asked and sign papers that would give him even greater control over her fortune than her father's Will had previously.

'I think that since I am to be married so soon I would prefer to leave things as they are.'

'I have not yet given my permission, Miss Manners.'

She stared at him in surprise. 'But what possible objection could you have? It is an excellent match and I am past twenty – quite old enough to be married, sir.'

'Yes, of course. I did not say I would refuse.'

'Within six months I may marry whom I choose without requiring permission from anyone.' Caroline looked at him hard. 'I do not imagine my father intended you to block such an advantageous match when he made you my guardian, Mr Taverner.'

'Of course you have my permission,' he muttered, perceiving his error. 'I just wish you would change your mind about these papers – it is for your protection.'

'Are you suggesting that Lord Carlton's lawyers would seek to cheat me?'

'No . . . certainly not.' He gave a sigh of exasperation. 'I simply wish to see that your investments are placed to your best advantage before they pass out of my hands. I would not care for anyone to think I had been careless in my stewardship.'

'I'm sure no one could think that, sir.'

Her conciliatory words did not mollify him. He looked at her with flinty eyes. 'Perhaps I may ask once more that you consider my proposals?'

'Leave them with me,' Caroline said. 'I shall give it a little more thought and you shall have my answer in the the morning.'

'Very well.' Silas was tight-lipped, as though keeping his temper in check. 'I have business in Portsmouth and must leave after breakfast. I hope my trip will not have been in vain.' He bowed his head to her. 'Excuse me, I must retire early in order to get a good start tomorrow.'

'He was not best pleased with you, my love,' Sally remarked after they had said farewell to Caroline's guardian the next morning. 'Don't you think you were a little stubborn? After all, he did come a long way and he has been a good steward of your fortune.'

'That does not give him the right to bully me,' Caroline said. 'If he hadn't threatened to withhold his permission for my marriage I might have been more inclined to listen, but that unsettled me. He has hardly seen me for years, then he presumes to question my decision . . .'

'No, I am sure he did not,' Sally soothed her ruffled feathers. 'You have been used to having your own way, Caroline. He could have made things difficult for you had he wished.'

'For a few months perhaps.' Caroline felt her skin prickle with goose bumps. 'I cannot help it, Sally – he just made me want to rebel. I expect his suggestions were all sound ones, but I had a feeling that something . . .' She shrugged, dismissing her disquiet. 'It was very foolish of me to annoy him, I suppose, but I did not take to him.'

'No . . . well, he has gone now and I doubt he will bother with you again. He will no doubt be relieved to wash his hands of you.'

'Yes. It is very ungrateful of me, but I do hope he does.'

'You are not afraid of him, are you?' Sally looked at her anxiously.

'Afraid? No, of course not,' Caroline denied. 'I am engaged to Lord Carlton, and will soon be his wife – what possible harm could Mr Taverner do to me?'

Chapter Fourteen

Silas was furious as he commenced his journey to Portsmouth – to be outfaced by a chit of a girl! It was frustrating and inconvenient, but there was little he could do about it. He could hardly force her to sign the papers he had so carefully prepared. The trouble was he had thought of her as a young girl and she had grown up. Inevitably.

He would have to sell the wine for the best price possible and tell her the house had fetched only a trifling sum. It was going to be a delicate business if she insisted on handing everything over to Carlton's lawyers before he'd had time to muddy the waters a little. Why had he ever sat down at that card table? Why had he ever come back to this Godforsaken country at all? He felt cold and his bones ached, and it all seemed too much trouble.

Closing his eyes, Silas tried to block the other reason for his frustration out of his mind. His first sight of Caroline Manners had taken his breath away. She was far more lovely than he had expected, making an impression on him the way no other woman had since Helena . . . Helena, the only woman he had ever truly loved.

It was all so long ago, but the wound of her rejection had never quite healed. He had been young then, and vulnerable in matters of the heart; it had hurt his pride, too, when she had chosen Henry Manners – a cold fish, if you like! – instead of him.

'Why, Helena?' he murmured as a picture of her fair beauty came into his mind. 'I've never understood why.'

He was fairly sure she had regretted her choice. He had never been able to prove Henry was mistreating her; had he done so, he might have killed the man. It was for Helena's sake that he had stayed close to Henry, especially after that odd business with his sister. It had almost paid off too. She had decided to leave Henry, and asked for his help.

'Of course,' he had promised, without hesitation. 'I'll do anything you ask of me.'

'I must bring Caroline. I couldn't leave her alone with him. You do understand, Silas?'

He would have promised the earth for the chance to be with her, even though he knew she did not truly love him. Everything was arranged, passages booked for all three of them on a ship bound for America, and then, only a few days before they were due to leave, Henry's carriage overturned killing both him and Helena. For a while after that Silas hadn't cared whether he lived or died. But he was a survivor.

He would survive this latest setback in his fortunes, too. Perhaps the Portugese wine would fetch a better price than he'd hoped. He would get the money somehow, damn it! Not that it would take away the sickness inside him, this longing to touch Caroline's white skin, to hold her close to him and inhale her perfume. The smell of it had inflamed his senses and it had been all he could do to keep his hands off her. It was just as well her companion had been present to remind him that this was England, and there were rules governing a gentleman's conduct.

'Damned fool,' he muttered to himself. 'She would not look at the likes of you, Silas Taverner. Too high in the instep by half!' And why should she when she had one of the richest aristocrats in the country eager for her hand.

Silas scowled at his own lustful thoughts. This wasn't like him, but he was still smarting over her rejection. She would come down a few pegs if he told her what he knew, though. A smile of pure malice touched his mouth as he remembered Caroline's haughty pride. He'd promised Brockleton he would never reveal the secret Helena had entrusted to him a few days before she died; it would have caused a sensation at the time and even now, many years later, would raise a few eyebrows amongst certain circles. It might even make Lord Carlton think twice about marrying her.

No, he could not do that to her! He wasn't such a scoundrel as to use blackmail to get his own way. He'd fallen a long way, but he wasn't that evil or that desperate. Not yet.

Chapter Fifteen

The pain in his leg had brought on one of his feverish attacks again. Lying in the huge, lonely bed, Fitz was aware of his valet's cool hands bathing his forehead. It soothed him.

'Thank you,' he murmured gratefully and opened his eyes. They widened in surprise as he looked into the face of the person bending over him. No valet, she. And she was even more beautiful than he had remembered. 'Julia . . . Julia, my love. You have come to me.'

'I shall always come when you really need me,' she said and bent to kiss his mouth.

Her lips were warm and sweet, just as they had been in life. He reached out to touch her, running his fingers through the silken strands of her golden hair, caressing the smooth flesh of her cheek. She was real, tangible, not a vision. He could feel her, touch her, see her – smell her own special perfume.

'Am I mad?' he asked in bewilderment. 'Or have I died and gone to Heaven?'

'Do not question it, my love,' Julia whispered close to his ear, her hands stroking his face. 'If you believe in me I am here. We can touch, kiss, make love . . .'

'Oh, Julia,' he breathed and reached out for her. 'Come to me! my dearest love.'

How often he had dreamed of her in his arms like

this, to be able to kiss and caress her lovely body, to know it fully as he never had in life. It was a dream of course, a fevered hallucination, but nothing could have been more real or precious to him than the sweet coolness of her flesh pressed against his, drawing out the heat that had kept him raging for three nights in a row; the melding of two desires, two hearts, two souls defying death itself to meet in an earthly passion.

Fitz knew an intense happiness as he possessed his love. He had never experienced such exquisite delight in the arms of the whores he had taken to drive out the devil of despair from his mind. It was sensation beyond all earthly passion, beyond the compass of a human mind. To know the sweet fulfillment of desire, the ecstasy of having his Julia in his arms again, was more than he had ever believed possible.

'I could die happily now,' he murmured as he gazed into her eyes as she lay beside him. 'To be with you through all eternity.'

'Not yet, my love,' she whispered. 'Be patient. Our time is coming. Be patient . . .'

Now she was slipping from his arms, retreating, no longer the flesh and blood lover he had held close to his heart but a creature of light and air, dissolving with the dawn.

'Julia,' he cried, stretching out his hands to her. 'Come back to me. Please don't leave me . . .'

'Soon . . . soon . . .' Her voice grew fainter. 'Be patient, my love. There are things you must do. Be patient.'

'Julia – don't leave me.'

His cheeks were wet as he woke. Such a bitter sweet dream. 'To have had her in his arms, to know such happiness.

It was the fever, of course. Fitz realised that it had

broken at last; his mind was clear and the pain in his leg was better. He would get up today. He reached for the bell to summon his valet to shave him.

Had Julia really come to him or had his imagination conjured her up? All right and reason said it must have been a dream, and yet she had felt so real in his arms. They had spent the night making love: there was that lazy, satiated heaviness in his limbs he had always associated with a night of passion. Yet how could it be true? He was so damnably lonely! Will was right – he needed a wife.

The sooner Caroline returned to Pendlesham the better.

Chapter Sixteen

'Are you sure you won't be lonely?' Sally asked as she kissed Caroline's cheek. 'I feel as if I am deserting you – especially as Mrs Lambert has let you down.'

'She could not help it,' Caroline said. 'Her daughter has been ordered to bed by the doctor, and there are all those children to be looked after. In the circumstances I could hardly refuse to let her go a week early, could I?'

'But it means you have only Rosa and Mary in the house with you.' Even on the point of departure, Sally was still doubtful. 'Perhaps I should stay with you until you go up to town?'

'You will do no such thing,' Caroline said firmly. 'I have decided to leave the day after tomorrow myself. As soon as the house is ready to be closed we shall go. There is not the slightest need for you to worry, Sally. Besides, I have the coachman and my groom, as well as my maids. What can possibly happen to me in two days?'

'Nothing, I suppose.' Sally laughed self-consciously. 'If you are sure, I ought to leave now. The poor coachman has kept his horses standing for at least a quarter of an hour.'

Caroline's own coachman was to take her into Norwich to catch the stage and then return the next morning, ready to rest the horses before setting off for London the next day.

'Off with you.' Caroline gave her a little push. 'I shall write to you as soon as I arrive in town.'

'I'll write back, care of your London house,' Sally promised, getting into the coach. 'Be safe, my love.'

Caroline smiled and waved as her friend was driven away. Not for the world would she have confessed that she hated the idea of Sally leaving her, for that would have been selfish. Besides, she would soon be in town, and after that the time would fly.

Walking back into the house, Caroline stared at the narrow staircase. It reminded her of the one in her dream – the recurring dream that came so often these days. Why had it begun to haunt her again?

'Will you be wanting your dinner served in the dining parlour, Miss Manners?'

Caroline was startled out of her reverie. 'No, I think not, Rosa. Just some tea and a little bread and butter in the parlour. You and Mary have your hands full with the packing.'

Caroline sighed as the girl left. She wished that she might share their work rather than sit here alone with a book she did not really wish to read, and the uncomfortable thoughts that would not let her be easy.

The house seemed so empty without Sally. She began to play with a pack of cards, then frowned as she realised she was attempting to tell her own fortune: there it was again, the knave of clubs in adversity to the queen of hearts. What could it mean?

The rattle of carriage wheels outside made her jump up. Surely Sally had not returned. That would be so like her! Caroline's spirits revived, but then as she heard a man's deep voice in the hall, she was chilled.

'It's Mr Taverner, Miss Manners,' Rosa announced.

'Sir!' Caroline stared in surprise as he entered, still heavily cloaked against the bitter wind. 'I had not expected to see you so soon. Indeed I am shortly to return to town.'

Rosa backed out, closing the doors.

'Perhaps we may travel together?' Silas suggested. 'I was on my way there when I thought of returning here.'

'I have not changed my mind about my investments, sir,' she cautioned him.

'The papers are no longer my first concern. I have been tortured for too long, but my conscience will not permit that I remain silent. There is something you should know – something that may make you pause for consideration before you marry.'

Caroline was astonished. 'What can you mean? Pray speak plainly, sir, for I do not understand you.'

'I had hoped to spare you.' He was clearly agitated. 'If there was any other way . . .'

He looked desperate, *was* desperate if she had but known, but she could know nothing of a ship sunk in stormy seas with all its crew and cargo of fine wines. Taking with it this man's last chance of saving himself from ruin. She knew nothing of his agony, of restless nights and the bitter regret that had brought him to this moment. Yet she could sense that something important was about to happen and it frightened her.

'Pray tell me what is on your mind, sir.'

'I know you have taken a dislike to me, Caroline, but believe me, this gives me no pleasure. I would not hurt you willingly.'

His look was that of a tormented soul, his eyes red-rimmed and wild, as though he had not slept.

'Whatever it is, I would know it.'

'You asked about your father's sister . . .'

'You told me she died in the lake?' She felt suddenly fearful, certain that what she was about to hear would not be to her liking.

'That much was true but it is not all. Your aunt took her own life after a terrible quarrel with her brother. He had threatened to send her to an institution of correction for wilful girls.'

'You mean a mental institution, don't you?'

It was the dream. She had witnessed the scene, seen her young and lovely aunt begging for forgiveness . . . seen her dragged away screaming!

'Why? Why did he want to send her to such a terrible place?'

'Because she would not give up her lover. She had disgraced her family and her name by consorting with a person of low birth – a groom your father had dismissed.'

'She had a lover?' Caroline was trembling. 'Tell me, sir, did she also have a child?'

'Yes.' Silas seemed almost disappointed. 'How could you know? Henry wished it kept secret. Did Helena tell you?'

'Tell me what?' Caroline's head was spinning. 'What ought I to know?'

'That you were not Helena's child.' His voice seemed to come from a great distance. 'She could not bear a child of her own – so when it was discovered that Henry's sister was with child, it was decided that the birth would take place in secret and Helena would claim you as her own.'

Caroline half fell into an armchair, her head spinning with shock.

'No, no, I do not believe you!'

Her senses were slipping away. She was vaguely

aware of being lifted and carried to the sofa, of his voice calling for assistance, of his tending to her as she lay in a swoon. She opened her eyes at last to find him bending over her, stroking her forehead.

'Forgive me,' he murmured. 'I would not have caused you so much pain for the world.'

Sitting up, she became aware that the neck of her gown had been loosened. She blushed, fastening the buttons and feeling the burn of his eyes on her as he retreated to the far side of the room.

'I have never fainted before.' But then she had never received such shocking news before. She born out of wedlock, a bastard! Yet could she believe this man she instinctively distrusted? 'Your words have shocked me, sir. If they are true . . .'

'Think not so ill of me,' he chided. 'Perhaps I was wrong to tell you, but it is the truth.'

'If so I should have been told years ago.' She closed her eyes as the pain swept over her. 'It explains much that has haunted me.' He looked puzzled, and she explained, 'I saw them struggling one night . . . it must have been the night she died. I see it now.'

'She fled into night as he tried to force her to his carriage,' Silas explained. 'He searched for her but when they found her it was too late. It broke him. He was never the same after they brought her body home.'

'He could not have loved her or he would not have treated her so ill.'

'And yet he did,' Silas demurred. 'In his own way he loved her very much, but he was a cold, hard man. She had disobeyed him and he wanted to punish her. I do not believe he meant to leave her in that place for long.'

'She could not know that. If she took her own life

151

rather than let him force her there, she must have thought he would never relent.'

Silas secretly agreed.

'Perhaps.'

No one could really know what had happened that fateful night: a frightened woman might have been driven to suicide or something even more evil might have occurred. Silas knew that Helena had believed it to have been murder not the action of a desperate woman, but there was no way of proving it either way after all these years.

'Are you feeling better now?' he asked as Caroline stood up.

'I have a headache. I think I shall go and lie down for a while.'

'Of course. You need time to reconcile your thoughts.'

She was suddenly afraid of being alone. 'You will not leave just yet? I should like to talk of this again.' Even Silas' company was better than none at all.

He took her hand, carrying it to his lips, eyes like burning coals. She wanted to wrench her hand away, yet felt strangely drawn to him, despite her earlier dislike. She needed someone to whom she could speak of this terrible thing that had turned her life upside down and only Silas knew the truth.

'Naturally I shall stay. I shall be here when you need me.'

Caroline would not have believed she could sleep, but she had. She woke at four in the afternoon, her neck aching and her face stiff with the salt of her tears. How could the man she had believed to be her father be so cruel to the sister he professed to love? It was as she had always thought – even when men spoke of love they could not be trusted.

Caroline bathed her face in cold water. She had been wise to accept Fitz's offer. Theirs would be a comfortable arrangement, with no burning passions to destroy it – as her mother had been destroyed.

The shock had been great, but she was coming to terms with it. After all, it was all in the past and the protagonists were all dead. She would always grieve for the mother she had never known. Poor frightened woman to take her life that way. Yet it had been preferable perhaps to incarceration in an institution for the deranged. How wicked Henry Manners had been to threaten his sister with something so vile!

She would never forgive him.

Need it change her plans to marry? Naturally, she must tell all to Fitz, because it could cause embarrassment if it were generally known. And yet the tragedy had been concealed for all these years – why should it become common knowledge now?

Caroline washed and changed into a fresh gown. Now that she was calmer she wondered just what Silas had hoped to gain by revealing the truth to her in that dramatic way. Did he imagine it would force her to withdraw from the marriage contract?

Her old unease had returned, and she now wished she had not asked him to stay. It would in any case be improper for him to stay without a chaperone in the house. Perhaps she could reasonably ask him to leave after supper?

Silas was by the parlour fire drinking brandy when she entered. He got up and came to her at once.

'I trust you are recovered now?'

'Thank you, yes.' She drew away as he attempted to touch her. 'You will stay for dinner?'

153

'I had hoped to break my journey here.'

'That would not be quite proper, sir. My companion is no longer with me, nor my housekeeper. For the sake of stilling gossiping tongues, I believe you should leave after we have dined: there is a tolerable inn in the village where you could stay.'

'If you wish it – but I am reluctant to leave you alone while you are in some distress.'

'I am much recovered now. I was shocked, I admit – but I think it can make very little difference.'

'You think Lord Carlton will not wish to withdraw?'

Caroline tossed her head, 'If you knew him, you would not think it. It *would* cause some embarrassment if it were generally known – but there is no reason for anyone else to be told.'

'Will you keep it from him then?'

'No, I must tell him the truth, but I am certain it will not matter to him. He is the kindest, gentlest of men.'

Silas remained poker-faced, though seething inside. 'I see. Then I am indeed happy for you.' My only regret is that I have caused you distress.'

'Not so. I believe you have done me a service, sir. I think I shall not be plagued again by the dream that has haunted me for far too long.'

'I would like to think I had been of service to you.'

Something in his husky voice drew her to him against her will, almost as though he had some strange power to control her mind. But, surely that was not possible.

They began to talk of other things: the weather, the King's health, which had been poor of late, books and politics. Then she asked him about India, and in listening to his fascinating tales, found her reserve melting once more. There was something about him that had the power to charm.

Silas had been drinking steadily all evening. When dinner was served he switched from brandy to wine, replenishing his glass again and again. He seemed to be drinking a great deal, but Caroline made no comment. All she desired was that he would leave her house as soon as he had supped his fill.

'I believe I shall retire now,' she said at last. 'Please let my servants know when you are ready to leave so that they may lock up for the night.'

Silas stood up, towering over her. 'I have decided to stay. I am your guardian after all. You can offer me a bed for the night, can't you?'

She hesitated uncertainly. 'I suppose . . .'

She broke off as he lurched towards her, eyes blazing with a strange light. 'I have wanted you from the moment I saw you,' he said thickly. 'I shall not let you marry Carlton: you are *mine*. I hoped you would see it was impossible and turn to me, but now I realise that you are stubborn. Yet I shall have you! Once I have possessed you, that blue-blooded fool will not take you back.'

Caroline recoiled in horror. 'You are drunk, sir. You know not what you say.'

'I have taken only enough wine to make me bold,' he said. 'But not enough to prevent me carrying out my threat. Unless you will see sense and understand that your future lies with me? I can make you happy, dearest girl. I can make your flesh sing with pleasure . . .'

She shook her head, backing away from him.

'No,' she whispered. 'Do not . . . I pray you, do not come near me.'

'Caroline . . . precious love . . .'

155

How could he have such a hold over her senses when her dislike of him was so intense? Perhaps it was some mysterious power acquired on his travels in the East? The touch of his hand on her shoulder made her shiver, but she resisted, breaking away and running from the room before he could seduce her further with his husky voice.

She did not stop until she reached her own room, hoping to lock herself in, but he caught the edge of the door before she could close it, forcing it back, and her to retreat into the room. His eyes fixed hers with a hypnotic gaze that seemed to drain her resistance.

'Do not be foolish. Do not resist me. You are mine. You cannot escape me.'

Caroline fended him off with a push of her hand.

'Come one step closer and I scream for the maids!'

'Your maids are sleeping. They were grateful for the wine I gave them for their supper – a harmless drug that will keep them from disturbing us.' He chortled. Your grooms are in like condition.'

'No! It shall not happen!'

He was close enough to touch her now. His eyes held hers and she could not look away. She was weakening, beginning even to question why she should deny him.

'You are a devil, sir. You shall not prevail!'

She had retreated until the bedpost was at her back; to her left, within reach, was the little table that held her books, flowers and candlestick. As Silas embraced her, his lips descending to her neck, her fingers touched the glass vase, then searched for the hardness of metal, the heavy candlestick that was her only weapon. She grasped the stem, drew back her arm and struck him on the temple with her full strength.

Silas gave a gasp of surprise and pain, His eyes

156

glazed over and he crumpled to the floor in a heap. Caroline froze momentarily, half expecting him to rise up and grab her, but he lay still at her feet. Had she killed him? She dare not feel for a pulse. Escape was all that mattered. She must get to Pendlesham! Fitz would protect her.

Glancing around the room, she saw only three things she wanted: her cloak, her riding whip and the box containing Will's locket. She scooped them up, stepped over the inert figure of her guardian even as he stirred, uttering a low groan. He was recovering his senses. She must leave immediately!

One glance at her sleeping servants in the kitchen told her it would be impossible to wake them. She did not dare to stay, even to write them a message; she would send for them when she was safe at Pendlesham.

Opening the back door, Caroline clutched her cloak to her as the wind snatched at it. It was a wild night. She struggled towards the stables, almost blown off her feet by the ferocity of the wind. Her only way of leaving was to ride one of the carriage horses; they were unbroken to a saddle and would not be easy to control, but she had no choice. If she left on foot Silas would soon catch her.

As she took a lantern from its hook outside the stables, she saw the groom and coachman snoring in the straw. More of her guardian's wickedness. The men continued to sleep soundly as she collected a bridle and slipped it over the head of the most docile-looking horse. It tossed its mane, snickering uneasily at the unfamiliar harness.

'Steady,' Caroline soothed. 'Careful now. I'm not going to hurt you.'

She had no saddle. In any case she doubted whether the horse would have let her put one on its back. Would it tolerate her at all? Sometimes her own grooms rode the carriage horses bare-backed about the yard, but this was not one of her own horses.

Leading it carefully into the yard, Caroline stroked its neck, gentling it as it shied and side-stepped nervously. She waited until it quietened, then used the mounting block to slide across its broad back. She was accustomed to riding side saddle, and it felt odd to sit astride the huge horse with her skirts over her knees.

'Steady, boy. Steady.'

It had begun to rain now and the wind seemed to be on the rise. Perhaps she would ride only as far as the nearest inn and there find help. She had a few guineas in her pocket, sufficient to purchase lodgings for the night and take her on to Pendlesham in the morning.

A door crashed behind her.

'Caroline – where are you?'

Silas! He had recovered faster than she expected.

As light streamed out of the open door, Caroline dug her heels in hard against the horse's flanks. It gave a snort of fright and took off in a panic, with her clinging desperately to the reins.

Beyond the house, the darkness seemed to close about her. The wind snatched her breath away as the horse plunged on crazily while she bent forward over its neck and prayed that she could stay on its back for long enough to escape the clutches of her evil guardian.

Chapter Seventeen

Will saw the carriage drawn up outside the house and caught his breath. Caroline was back!

Despite himself, all the problems and heartache her return would bring him, his heart quickened at the thought of seeing her. He walked more quickly, wanting to see her, to touch her hand. Would she be as lovely as the woman who had haunted his dreams these past weeks? Or had his imagination run away with him?

'Will – thank God you're here!'

Fitz's greeting sent a chill through him. Something was wrong! His eyes went to a thin-faced man standing in the hallway, instinctively on his guard, disliking and distrusting him for no good reason.

'Is it Caroline? Is she ill?'

'She has disappeared, I'm afraid,' the man said.

Pain lanced through Will, so sharp and bitter that he could scarce keep from crying out. 'Disappeared – how?' His eyes narrowed in suspicion as he regarded the stranger. 'Who is this person?'

'Silas Taverner,' Silas supplied, offering his hand. 'Miss Manners' guardian.'

He felt uncomfortable beneath Will's probing stare, as if *he* could read his mind and know that it was his fault Caroline had fled into the night.

Some days had passed since that wild night; his

local inquiries having come to nothing, he had been forced to seek out his ward's fiancé. It had taken courage to come here, knowing he might be denounced as a cheat and a seducer. For if it were known that he had tried to ruin his ward as a means of hiding his embezzlement of her property, he would be utterly cast out from all decent society – perhaps worse.

'What do you mean – she has disappeared?' barked Will. 'She was in her own house with a companion and servants. What happened?'

'I wish I knew, Silas replied, his expression bland. 'Her companion had left a day or so earlier, but there were servants in the house. I supped with her, left her happy and safe, and heard nothing until I was woken with the news the next morning.'

'Had her bed been slept in?'

'I believe not. A horse from the stable was found wandering the next day . . . a carriage horse.'

'Explain yourself, sir!'

'Will, Will,' Fitz remonstrated. 'Mr Taverner has had the whole village searching for days. He has done all he could, and now comes to us for help.'

'But why should she leave her house in the middle of the night?'

'That might be my fault.' Silas looked awkward. 'She asked me for information about her childhood and, unwisely, I told her the truth.'

'Speak plainly, sir!' Will's hands worked at his sides in frustration. If anything untoward had happened to Caroline, he would know who to blame. And he would answer for it! 'What did you tell her that so upset her she ran away?'

'At first I suspected kidnap,' Silas lied. 'However, having considered, I now believe she found the truth too terrible to bear. Caroline was the illegitimate child of Henry Manners' sister. He and his wife took her for their own to save Miss Manners from disgrace.'

'And you told her *that*?' Will itched to break the fool's neck. 'God curse you for a knave and a fool, sir! Did you not think what it might do to her?'

'She demanded the truth . . .' Silas retreated from Will's fury, turning sallow as he realised what his fate would be if Caroline should ever denounce him. This man would surely kill him!

'Steady, Will,' Fitz murmured. 'Mr Taverner meant no harm. Besides, I do not see why this should cause Caroline to run away.'

'Then you too are a fool!' Will rounded on him. 'Don't you know how proud she is? She probably believed you would withdraw if you knew she was bastard born.'

'I'm sure Caroline knows me better than that,' Fitz said, but he was shaken by the possibility.

'There was more, I'm afraid,' Silas said, ingratiatingly. 'Her father was a groom from Manners' stables, and her mother drowned herself in the lake some months after her child was born.'

His announcement caused a stunned silence. Will was the first to recover. He directed a curled lip at Silas, but said nothing.

'You say a carriage horse was found wandering?' Fitz said evenly. 'Why would she choose to ride such an unsuitable animal? What made her so desperate to escape?'

Silas swallowed hard. He had come only out of a need to discover if his ward was here, and now he wished himself a thousand miles hence.

'I did nothing to harm her,' he protested. 'Only what I have told you.'

'You have searched thoroughly for her in the district?' Fitz asked. 'And there is no sign of her?'

'None.' Silas looked grave. 'I would have continued the search – but I thought it best to inform you.'

'You were considerate,' Fitz said, nodding, smiling almost. 'Will you dine with us, sir?'

'You are good to ask me, my lord, but I have other urgent business. I must go to London and seek word of my ward there.'

'She would not have gone there without letting Fitz know.' Will glared at him. 'She has been kidnapped – or murdered.' His expression implied he believed her murderer to be close at hand.

'Will . . .' Fitz gave him a searching look. 'You are jumping to conclusions. We do not yet know that she has been harmed. She may have decided she needed time alone, to think about all this.' He turned his mild gaze on Silas. 'Has she any relatives whom she could visit? Any friends she might have sought out in her distress?'

'I have not seen my ward in years. Her companion could tell you much more, though I know she has no close family.'

'I recall she mentioned an uncle once,' Fitz said, 'but I may be wrong.'

'Helena Manners had a brother,' Silas was forced to admit. 'Edward Brockleton. We met only a few weeks ago. I doubt he could help you. They were not close.'

'Sally would know,' Will said. 'I have her sister-in-law's address. I think it best if I go down at once to see her.'

'As you wish,' Fitz agreed. 'I shall go down to Norfolk in the morning, to satisfy myself that everything possible has been done to trace her.' He smiled apologetically at Silas. 'Not that I doubt your word, sir.'

Silas bowed stiffly. 'If you will excuse me. I shall send word if I hear anything, of course.'

'Of course,' Fitz murmured silkily. 'We are indebted to you, Taverner.'

The cousins stood in silence as Silas walked away, his boots ringing on the marble floors, then Will turned to Fitz, eyes blazing.

'I do not trust that man. I'm sure there is more to this than he has told us.'

'I think I agree with you,' Fitz murmured. 'A most disagreeable man – and a liar to boot.'

'Has he harmed her, do you think?'

'I cannot be sure, though I am inclined to think not. I would not put it past him to have contrived the whole story for our benefit.'

'Then you think Caroline might be . . .' Will choked on his emotion.

Fitz shook his head, laying a calming hand on his cousin's arm. 'I do not think he has killed her. I believe he had more to do with her flight than he admits, but I do not think she is dead. He came here for a reason. If he knew her dead, I think he would flee the country while he could.'

'Then where can she be?' Will said, helplessly, unaware of the transparency of his emotions.

'I do not know,' Fitz said, mouth hardening. Gone was the softness Caroline had found so appealing; in its place the gritty determination of a battle-hardened soldier. 'But I promise you, Will – I promise you we shall find her.'

Chapter Eighteen

It was not until four days after the storm that Caroline finally became aware of her surroundings. She had heard voices previously but from a distance, muffled, the words making no sense. When at last her eyes opened she could not immediately focus, her lips parting in a moan as she felt the pain throbbing at her temples.

'It hurts,' she whispered. 'I'm so thirsty . . . water. Please, may I have some water?'

A gentle hand soothed her brow. She whimpered and a tear squeezed from the corner of her eye.

'You've been ill,' the voice said. 'Don't cry. You're safe here.'

The mist cleared a little and she saw two faces. One was a young girl's: brown-skinned and smudged with dirt, but pretty; fine, light brown curls of hair escaped from beneath a red scarf.

'Drink this,' another, older voice said, and a cup was thrust to her lips.

Caroline obeyed the command, her eyes searching the second face peering down at her – a weathered face that had known both sorrow and pain. She was allowed only a few sips of the water before the cup was removed.

'Too much and 'tis sick you'll be,' the woman said as she protested. 'You've been trouble enough to me as it is. Pity it is that Katya found you and that *he* brought you here.'

'Who brought me here?' Caroline plucked at the bedcovers, her face creasing in sudden anxiety. 'Who are you? Where am I?'

'You're safe,' Katya said. She had thought the woman might remember what had happened to her, but it was clear she did not. 'You hurt your head, but Cara has made you better.'

'It hurts,' Caroline tried to find the source of the pain, but her fingers encountered a rough bandage. 'What happened to me?'

Girl and old woman looked at one another. 'You fell from a horse,' Cara said at last. 'What does it matter? You will live now.'

Caroline felt that it did matter. Something was wrong, something was eluding her, but the faces and voices were sliding back into a mist.

'She's fainted,' Katya said, her fingers touching something in her pocket. Something she had concealed from everyone when she first found the woman lying unconscious on the ground the night after the storm.

'Nay, 'tis the sickness again,' muttered Cara. 'Mayhap 'tis for the best. Better if she knows nothing until that wound starts to heal.'

'We should tell Jake she woke up.'

Caroline was no longer listening. Now there was only the strange sensation of falling backwards into space, of everything rushing away from her. She tried to stop herself falling but there was nothing to hold on to.

'What is this place?' asked Caroline, when she opened her eyes to find the girl bending over her again. 'Are you from the village?'

'My name is Katya. Cara and I cared for you while you were ill.' The girl smiled. 'This is our caravan – our home.' She spoke with pride. 'Are you feeling better now? I think the fever has gone at last.'

Caroline plucked at her sleeve. 'What is my name?'

'Surely you know your own name?'

Caroline dragged herself up against the pillows, her eyes widening with fear. It had caught up with her at last, the shadow that had been hovering while she lay between life and death. She no longer knew who she was. She had no memory of anything before this moment.

'Please – you must tell me who I am!'

'But I . . .' Katya glanced over her shoulder, and jumped guiltily. 'Jake . . .'

A tall gypsy entered the caravan, his lips parted in a predatory grin.

'How are you feeling today, Sapphira?' he asked. 'Does your head hurt much?'

'Sapphira?' Caroline said wonderingly. 'Is that my name?'

'It's my name for you.' He shrugged. 'One name is as good as another. Would you like to be called something else?'

'I don't know,' she said, hands moving restlessly on the covers. 'Should I know you?'

'I am called Jake' he replied. 'We are travelling folk and you have been with us three weeks. You fell from your horse one stormy night and would have died if we had not cared for you.'

'Am I one of your people?' Caroline glanced at her hands; they were soft and white, very different from Katya's, which were rough and ingrained with dirt.

Jake hesitated, then shook his head. 'No, you are

not one of us, but you can stay until you are well again.'

She caught at his arm as he would have left. 'Do you know me? Why did you choose to call me Sapphira?'

'Because your eyes remind me of precious stones I once set into a necklace for an Indian princess,' he said. 'I am skilled in such arts and have travelled to many lands in search of beautiful things. You are beautiful, too, Sapphira.'

'Then my eyes must be blue.' Caroline frowned. How could she know that sapphires were blue and yet not know her own name? She reached up to touch her hair and gave a cry of surprise. 'What is wrong with my hair?'

'We cut it,' Cara muttered defensively. 'Your head was cut open. 'Twas the only way.'

'You were heavy handed,' Jake growled. 'But it will grow again. Kayta will help you tidy it when you are well enough.' He smiled at her. 'Your hair is the colour of liquid gold.'

Caroline gazed up at him. He was harsh featured, yet his eyes were kindly. She sensed that he liked her and somehow that made her feel better: she was amongst friends.

'I believe I have you to thank for my life. You, and Cara and Katya.'

'I brought you here,' he agreed. 'I gave orders that you be cared for. When you remember who you are, I shall return you to your home.'

'Shall I remember?' she asked, fearful once more. 'Why do I know some things and not others?'

'I doubt even the wise men of the East could answer that, and I've met men with great healing

167

skills on my travels. But I have heard tell of what ails you before this.'

Caroline leaned forward eagerly. 'Will my memory return?'

'I make no promises, but I believe it may in time.'

'Supposing I never remember who I am?'

'Then you are welcome to travel with us. We visit fairs, markets, race meetings all over the country. Perhaps one day you will meet someone who knows you.'

'And if not?'

'You will stay with us.' His eyes seemed to envelope her in warmth like a gentle balm. 'There is an ancient law amongst our people that says if you save a life it belongs to you. If by the end of one year you do not know yourself, you will belong to me.'

With a parting smile he turned and went out of the caravan.

'Does your head hurt again?' Katya asked, bending over her. 'I heard you cry out just now.'

She must have cried out in her sleep. She had been dreaming . . . a frightening dream in which she was trapped in a maze. She had been running from something . . . something that terrified her.

'Can I see myself? Do you have a mirror?'

Kayta shook her head. 'We are poor folk. 'Tis only gentry has such things.'

'Am I from the gentry?' Caroline thought hard. She knew there were all kinds of mirrors: large ones with gilt frames, free standing mirrors in polished mahogany for a lady's dressing table, and silver-backed hand mirrors with matching brushes and combs. 'I think I may have been,' she answered herself. Then, as an afterthought, 'Unless I was a ladies maid.' Again she looked at her hands, as if they held the answers.

For a moment panic almost overwhelmed her. She wanted to jump up and run away. But where would she run to? She did not even know where she was. She was lucky these people had taken her in. But for them, she might still be wandering, dazed, alone – or even lying untended on the ground until she died. No, she had no choice, she must stay here until she was well again.

She blinked away tears of self-pity. 'Does my hair look as awful as it feels?'

'I'll show you what it was like. I kept it.' Katya brought out a square of red cloth. 'See how pretty it is. 'Twas a shame to cut it.'

'It will grow,' Caroline sighed, touching the shining tresses. 'You could sell this to a wig-maker, Katya.'

'It belongs to you.'

'I have no use for it. You should sell it – buy something for yourself. Perhaps a small mirror. You are very pretty, did you know that?'

Katya turned away in confusion. Caroline watched as she hid the hair amongst her things. She seemed to have very little, just a few worn clothes and shoes. Looking about her, Caroline saw that the narrow interior of the caravan was sparsely furnished, with two narrow beds, a stool, pots and pans and a large wooden trunk that appeared to belong to Cara.

The old woman came in carrying bunches of dried herbs and grasses which she laid on top of the chest.

'Is Cara your grandmother?' Caroline asked the girl.

'No . . .' Katya shuffled her feet. 'She took me in because Jake asked her. I'm like you. I don't know . . .'

'Stop your chattering, girl,' Cara turned on her

angrily. 'There'll be no supper tonight unless you fetch me more wood.'

Katya looked at her with sorrowful eyes, then picked a shawl and went out without a word.

Caroline watched the old woman banging her pots and pans about.

'Why be angry with Katya? It is because of me, isn't it?'

Cara gave her a look of grudging respect. 'You see too much,' she muttered. 'You'll bring us bad luck. Your kind always does.'

'My kind?'

'Blood never mixes,' Cara mumbled. 'Jake is a fool.'

'Why are you frightened?'

The old woman stared at her. 'I know nothing. I see nothing. I hear nothing.' Her eyes glittered with anger. 'Return to your own kind and leave us in peace.'

'I would go if I could,' Caroline said. 'Can you tell me where to find my own kind, Cara?'

Cara seemed to hesitate, then shook her head. 'You came out of the storm,' she said. 'Jake brought you – and bad luck came with you, that's all I know.'

Chapter Nineteen

'Disappeared!' Sally looked as if she might faint. Will caught hold of her arm, to lead her to a chair by the fire. She gazed up at him in distress, her face pale. 'It's all my fault, Mr Carlton. I should never have left her alone.'

'You mustn't blame yourself,' Will said, though for a while he had been willing to blame her and everyone else for neglecting their duty. 'Caroline was not alone.'

'She had only those foolish girls to protect her,' Sally cried and fumbled for her kerchief. 'I would never have left her if I'd thought that man would return. Neither of us trusted him – and he was angry because she would not sign those wretched papers.'

'Papers?' He was suddenly alert. 'What paper?'

Will listened carefully as Sally repeated as much as Caroline had told her. 'I don't know exactly what they were, but she declared she wasn't prepared to give him more control over her fortune than he already had. She wanted to leave it all to the lawyers. Mr Taverner looked fit to do murder.' Sally's hand shook as she held her kerchief to her mouth. 'You don't think . . .'

Will's expression was implacable. 'I've wondered,' he admitted. 'Fitz won't hear of it, but I think

Taverner would be capable of anything. If only I could be sure . . . but we must hope for the best.'

'But where can she have gone?'

'We hoped you might be able to tell us.'

'She has no relatives – at least, there is an uncle she never sees. I can furnish you with his address and a list of her friends.' Sally got up and went over to a desk by the window, then glanced back at him. It is not like her at all, to run from unpleasantness. She is no coward . . .'

'Taverner told her something about her mother. He claims that upset her.'

Sally nodded. She hesitated for a moment, then dipped her pen in the ink and began to write. For several minutes there was no sound but the scratching of her nib. When the list was finished she blotted it and brought it to Will.

'I wondered if she might have changed her mind about marrying your cousin.'

'Why should she?' Will stared at her intently. 'She seemed quite certain of her own mind before she left Pendlesham.'

'If you don't know then perhaps I am wrong.' Sally twisted her kerchief between agitated fingers. 'It is not for me to say. I just thought she might prefer to marry someone else.' She raised quizzical eyes to his. 'Perhaps you would know more about that than I, Mr Carlton.'

'You mean . . . ?' Will turned away, his hands clenching. 'No – no, it cannot be that. She doesn't care for me.'

'You are wrong,' Sally said quietly. 'I believe she cares for you more than she will admit. Like you, sir, Caroline is very stubborn.'

Will received this in silence. He could not credit

that Caroline had disappeared because she did not wish to marry Carlton. She was too proud, too honest, to run away.

'No,' he said at last. 'Even if she had decided against it, she would have at least sent back his ring. She would never have chosen to disappear of her own free will. I am convinced of it.'

'So be it.' Sally gave a little sob. 'She must be ill or . . . or dead.'

'She could be lying injured somewhere,' Will agreed. 'If she fell from her horse – and remember it was a wild night. The horse might have bolted with her.'

'That devil Silas Taverner is at the back of this!'

'I am inclined to agree with you,' Will said. 'If I can prove it, he will pay. Assuredly, he will be punished for his crimes.'

He would kill Taverner with his bare hands if need be! Yet that would not bring her back. Will was filled with great anger and pain. A future without Caroline did not bear contemplating.

'Is there anything else I can do?' Sally asked, another sob escaping her. 'Please, please, you *must* find her!'

'My cousin has gone down to Norfolk to organise another search,' Will said soothingly. 'I shall contact every one of Caroline's friends personally. If she is alive, one of us will find her.'

'And if she isn't?' Sally asked, and her eyes were fearful.

'I shall discover the truth if it takes the rest of my life!'

Sally nodded. 'You love her,' she said softly. 'I've known that for some time.'

Will did not deny it. 'You did not tell her?'

'She would not have believed me.' Sally moved forward impulsively to touch his hand. 'If – when – you find her, tell her. Tell her how much she means to you, Mr Carlton. I believe you will discover that she cares for you a great deal.'

Will made a gesture of rebuttal, but the look in Sally's eyes was steadfast. Could she be right? If she were . . . Will groaned inwardly. If Caroline loved him, then all this might be his fault.

He would never forgive himself if she had come to harm because of him.

The ground was frozen hard and a few flakes of snow had begun to fall as Will dismounted and gave his horse into the hands of a groom. It was a relief to be back at Pendlesham after weeks of frustration. None of Caroline's friends had heard from her – not even Rachel Blackstone, who was expecting her as a wedding guest.

'I'm sure she would have written if she meant not to come,' Rachel said, close to tears. 'We were such good friends. Something terrible must have happened to her.'

Will nodded grimly. She was merely echoing his own fears. Caroline had definitely meant to attend the wedding; she had spoken of it. The certainty that she had not disappeared of her own volition was growing in his mind. As the days passed and there was still no news, it seemed that Caroline had simply ceased to exist. Fitz's last letter had confirmed that all his own efforts had come to nothing, and he too had decided to return to Pendlesham.

He was sitting by the fire in the library when Will walked in, but he got to his feet and poured a generous brandy for them both.

'Still no luck then?'

'None.' Will took the glass, draining it with a single gulp. 'It's bitter cold tonight. We'll have a foot of snow before morning.'

'Yes, I think you're right,' Fitz said, then as Will's face creased with pain: 'Do not fear she will die on that account. She's not out there, you know. I've had every inch of ground searched for miles around her home. We posted rewards for news of her at every inn for fifty miles. If her body had been found we should have heard by now.'

'Unless he's hidden it too well.'

'You still think Taverner is behind this then?'

'I'm sure of it.'

'He took a risk coming to us if he'd killed her.'

'I think he must have been desperate. I heard rumours in town that he is in some kind of financial difficulty.'

'Who inherits if . . . ?'

'Taverner. Unless she married or had reached her majority. I spoke to Brockleton. He endorsed Taverner's story about Caroline's mother. He was most put out that Taverner had broken his word not to speak of it.' Will drummed his fingers on the mantel. 'Seems there was some mystery about the way Manners' sister died – it might even have been murder. Brockleton claims his sister was about to leave her husband when they were both killed in a carriage accident. He thinks she may have been planning to run off with Taverner, and blames him for her death. It is even possible Manners found out and somehow caused the accident himself. Apparently, he was loath to speak out at the time because of the scandal, but he doesn't care much for Taverner, I can tell you.'

Fitz nodded, his face grave. 'If Caroline was told all this it might explain why she chose to disappear. We have to accept that possibility, Will.'

'I can't believe that. I'm not giving up, Fitz – are you?'

'No, of course not.' Fitz rubbed the bridge of his nose, looking thoughtful. 'I can't see that we can do much more for the moment, though. Unless . . .' He paused and sipped his brandy. 'When we were making inquiries in Norfolk someone said there were gypsies in the woods before the storm.'

'Gypsies!' Will stared at him. 'Do you think they might have taken her?'

'It's possible. I don't know.' Fitz sighed heavily. 'You will think me a fool but, well, Julia came to me again last night. She told me to look for Caroline amongst the dark people.'

Will refilled his glass. He sat down by the fire and swirled the brandy, warming it between his hands.

'Julia is dead,' he said wearily. 'If her spirit told you to look amongst the dark people, Caroline is dead, too.'

'At first I thought that,' Fitz agreed, 'but Julia urged me to find her before it was too late. She warned me there was danger.'

Will glanced up. Was Fitz going mad, with his visions of a ghost who came to give him warnings? Once he would have been certain of it; he would have laughed the idea to scorn, in his own mind if not openly. Surely death was the end; there could be nothing after it, no contact with those who had departed this life. He wanted to believe that such a bridge between life and death was possible, that Julia knew more than they did. He was so desperate to find

Caroline alive, he would have clutched at any hope, no matter how faint or unlikely.

'What do you mean?' He gazed up at his cousin. 'Danger for who? Are you sure it wasn't just a dream?'

'I know it's hard to believe,' Fitz said softly. 'Sometimes I don't believe it myself. I think I'm going mad, or simply imagining things but . . .' He turned as the door opened and his housekeeper entered. 'Yes, Mrs Brandon?'

'Lord Parfitt has called, sir. He asked for Mr Carlton or you.'

'I'll go,' Fitz said, and pushed Will back into his chair as he made to rise. 'Stay here and rest a while, Will. You look worn out.'

Will nodded. The brandy was beginning to do its work, and he was thawing out but he did feel tired. He refilled his glass and drank steadily, letting it numb the pain that had lived inside him since he'd first heard the news of Caroline's disappearance, wanting deliberately to deaden the unbearable sense of loss. Then he bent his head, burying his face between his hands, and when Fitz re-entered the room he was unaware of it.

'Caroline . . .' he muttered. 'Oh, my love, have I lost you?' A sob escaped him. 'How shall I live without you?'

The words and the depth of pain they revealed confirmed the vague suspicion that Will's recent conduct had aroused in Fitz. His face pale and set, he turned and left the room silent as a shadow.

Chapter Twenty

'How do you feel today?' Jake inquired, as Caroline walked towards where he sat, outside his caravan. He noticed the way the other gypsies looked at her, the distrust in their eyes, knowing they resented her presence here amongst them, but dared not speak of it to him. 'Have your headaches stopped?'

'They come less often now.' She was curious. 'What are you doing?'

He glanced up before answering. She was wearing an emerald green dirndl skirt, a white silk blouse that he had brought from Russia on one of his travels, and a crimson shawl. Around her head was a silk scarf that allowed a few strands of her pale hair to escape. As yet her full beauty was not quite restored, but her hair would grow.

'I'm engraving this silver bangle,' he said, holding it for her to see the design of flowers and leaves on the smooth metal. 'Do you like it?'

She took the bangle from him, turning it over in her hands. 'It is exquisite,' she said at last. 'I do not think I have ever seen such intricate work. You are clever, Jake. Katya told me you made jewellery, but I did not imagine something as fine as this.'

'These bangles are trinkets.' He took up a cloth and began to polish the silver, rubbing in a special liquid from a stone jar beside him, and then wiping it off. 'I prefer to use gold and precious stones, but I can only do that when rich customers pay me.'

'Where did you learn your trade?'

'From an Arab goldsmith,' Jake said. 'He taught me many things, but the skill was in my hands from the beginning.'

'Katya says your jewellery has magic powers.'

'Katya is a foolish child.' Jake laughed softly. 'She sells lucky pixies at the fairs for me. The magic is that people will pay far more than something is worth if they listen to her nonsense.'

'Won't you use your magic powers for me?' Caroline asked. 'Help me to remember who I am and where I came from?'

'Are you so unhappy with us?' he said with a frown.

'No,' she assured him quickly. 'It is not that. You've all been kind to me. I just wish I knew who I was.'

'You are Sapphira,' he said. 'Don't you like the name I chose for you?'

Jake watched the changing expressions on her face, guessing at the emotions that caused them. He wondered why this particular woman should stir him in a way that few others ever had. She was lovely, but there were other lovely women, so it was not her looks alone. He had had his share of empty-headed beauties, loving them and leaving them without a backward glance. Even his Malinka, the princess who had paid him to make her fabulous jewels while she took him to her bed of silk pillows every night. She had been skilled in the arts of love, teaching him much. He had loved her soft body and her husky voice. But his Sapphira was a lady, intelligent and cultured.

179

'It's a pretty name, but it isn't mine,' Caroline said. 'It doesn't sound right, Jake.'

'Then what shall I call you?'

She shook her head. 'I don't know. It doesn't matter. Sapphira will do for now.'

Jake finished polishing the bangle. It gleamed, reflecting the light from his fire in its smooth surface. He held it out to her. 'Take it. I made it for you.'

'But why?' Caroline hesitated. 'You gave me these clothes. I feel awkward – I have nothing to give in return.'

'I ask nothing in return.' Jake caught her arm and slipped the bangle over her hand. 'But you can earn your keep if you wish.'

'How?' Caroline asked. 'What can I do?'

'Next week we go to a fair in Bodmin. You can help Katya sell charms.'

'Possibly.' She looked dubious. 'Why don't I offer to tell fortunes?'

'Do you have the skill?' Jake eyed her speculatively. She had a surprised look on her face as if she had spoken without thinking. His gaze narrowed. 'Have you remembered something?'

'I once told someone's fortune,' Caroline said, her voice breathy with a mixture of fear and excitement. 'I saw death in her cards – and she died.'

'How do you know?' Jake was tense. Once she remembered who she was she would leave them. He had forbidden his people to tell her where she had been found. He hoped that, if she could keep her here long enough to win her love, she would stay with him. He wanted to keep her, to possess her, more than he had ever wanted anything in his life.

'I – I don't know.' Caroline looked upset. 'It was like a picture in my mind. I saw a girl's face and the

180

cards, then a voice told me she was dead. It came and went . . .' She frowned. 'Perhaps it wasn't true.'

'I shall give you some cards. Wait here.'

Jake got up and went into his caravan. He brought a pack of greasy, well-thumbed playing cards to Caroline and pushed them into her hands. She still looked dazed and not a little distressed.

'Show me.'

Caroline shuffled the cards, then she squatted down and began to deal them on the ground. She laid four cards in a circle, then placed four more face up.

'The king of spades is you,' she said. 'Your position is one of power. All the other cards are in sub-serviance to you.' She turned up the card at the top of the circle. 'The jack of diamonds is someone you respect. Recently, you were able to do him a service for which he repaid you handsomely.' She turned up the queen of hearts. 'There is a woman you like very much . . .' The next card was the knave of clubs followed by the queen of diamonds. Caroline was silent.

'What does that mean?'

She met his eyes steadily. 'There is another man between you and the woman you want – but there is another woman who loves you.'

Jake looked at her hard, then nodded. 'You will do very well at the fairs,' he remarked, then he picked up the knave of clubs and tore it to pieces, scattering them on the ground.

'Why did you do that? The pack is ruined now.'

'I shall give you a new one. Remember this, Sapphira – no man takes my woman from me.'

'No,' Caroline said. 'Not if she was yours by right. But supposing she chose not to be?'

'It would be her choice,' Jake said sullenly. 'Who can tell if it would be a wise one?'

'May I have these?' Caroline gathered up the cards and slipped them into her pocket without waiting for an answer. 'I must find some wood for Cara. Please excuse me now.'

Jake watched her walk away. Had she the true gift of telling the cards? Or had it all been a clever game?

Caroline had been with the gypsies six weeks now and learned that Jake's word was law; he was both respected and feared by his people. She had also learned that Katya loved him, despite the way he treated her.

It was his Sapphira Jake wanted. He hoped to keep her with him, Caroline had sensed it from the beginning. As yet he had not tried to make love to her, but she knew he would one day. She wondered if he would let her go if her memory returned?

How worried her family must be by now – if indeed she had a family. Was there a husband or lover out there searching for her? Sometimes she was so restless she could hardly bear it; she did not belong here, that much she was sure of.

Life amongst the travelling folk was hard. In winter it was difficult to find enough wood to keep the fires going, and if the fire went out there was no hot food, nor the mint and nettle tea that Cara sweetened for her with wild honey. At nights, she suffered greatly from the cold, despite the blankets Jake had provided. Katya had given up her bed to sleep on the floor beside her, like a faithful dog. She'd laughed when Caroline offered to change places.

'I'm used to it,' she claimed. 'Besides, Jake would beat me. 'Tis you he cares for.'

Caroline had seen the hurt in the girl's eyes. It had not taken her long to notice that the other gypsies were not kind to Katya. They kept their distance from Jake's Sapphira, watching her with resentful looks but outwardly accepting her right to be there as Jake's ward. Conversely, Katya was greeted with harsh words and even blows when she came in contact with the other women.

One day Caroline asked Cara why everyone treated the girl so badly.

'Keep a still tongue for your own sake,' Cara muttered. 'Blood will out. Bad luck he's brought on us. Like his father before him.'

Katya always laughed at the old woman's warnings.

'Her tongue is sharper than a nettle's sting,' she told Caroline. 'But her heart is true. No one but Cara has ever cared for me.'

And Cara was good to the girl in her own rough way. Caroline soon realised the grumbling was dross. Deep inside, Cara was a generous woman, sharing what she had without thought of repayment.

But one day she would repay them both.

For now all she could hope was that she might earn her keep at the fairs. She was convinced she had told fortunes in the past. The action of laying the cards had been familiar, and she had known what words to use by instinct. Could she have been a performer of some kind? Perhaps there was even something unsavoury in her past that she would have preferred to forget?

Was that why she had lost her memory – because there was something she wanted to forget?

The thoughts chased themselves endlessly like

whirling pools of deep water, murky and slightly threatening.

'You've been luckier than me.'

Katya's voice startled her. She glanced at her bundle of wood she had collected. 'Is this enough, do you think?'

"Tis more than I've found.' Katya's eyes went to the bangle. 'Jake gave you that,' she said, half accusing.

'Yes.' Caroline felt guilty as she saw the hurt in her eyes. She slipped it from her wrist. 'You can have it – for looking after me when I was ill.'

Katya stared at it longingly, then shook her head. 'Jake made it for you. He would be angry with us both if you gave it to me.'

'Yes, I suppose so. I'm sorry, Katya. It should have been yours.'

It was hardly surprising she should covet the bangle and Caroline wished she could give it to her. She would have liked to be able to help both her and Cara. Instinctively she felt that she had once been fortunate enough to own many lovely things.

If only she could remember who she was and where she came from.

'One day I shall give you something pretty,' she promised Katya. 'I am so grateful for the way you took care of me.'

Katya flushed. 'Don't want nuffing,' she muttered, and walked away.

Caroline called after her but she would not look back. She suspected Katya was beginning to resent her, which was sad. If Caroline knew her own true identity she would leave. That would not help Katya to win the man she loved – but at least she would not have to watch him fawn over another woman.

Something flashed into Caroline's mind. Not so

long ago someone else had given her a present . . . a present that she had treasured. In her mind she saw a velvet box, inside it, a gold locket. Instinctively, Caroline's hand went to her throat, though she was not wearing a necklace.

Something told her she had been angry about the gift. Why was that?

Tears of frustration stung her eyes, yet she felt a tingle of dawning excitement. These flashes of memory must mean something. Perhaps the curtain of mist in her mind was beginning to lift. If she were patient for a little longer her memory might yet return.

Chapter Twenty-One

Silas stared gloomily into his brandy glass. There was a huge fire burning in the grate but his bones still ached with the cold. England in winter was a miserable place, and he'd wished himself elsewhere a thousand times these past weeks. Sometimes he was tempted to collect what money and possessions he could and take ship for warmer climes, but something held him back.

His financial position was precarious. He had always been a man of substance and felt himself too old to start up again now. The very idea of having to perform menial tasks for his living was frightening. He was conversant with the conditions in the mills and factories where men and woman worked thirteen or fourteen hours a day, allowed little time for recreation. Worse still were the conditions for children, often forced into the mills or mines almost as soon as they could walk, by parents who had no choice but to condemn them to a life of slavery. Having been a mill owner himself, Silas knew there was no pity to be gained from the harsh men who ran them.

Yet he could see little prospect for the future, unless . . . he shuddered as the wicked thought entered his mind. If Caroline were dead he would inherit everything, and it seemed likely that she was. Silas knew that Carlton and his hot-tempered cousin had had no success in their search for her. Silas too, had made further inquiries of his own, but there was no trace of her. Only one possibility remained to be investigated – the gypsies.

If the story about gypsies being in the woods were true it might explain Caroline's disappearance, though people were always quick to blame the travelling folk in cases like these whether or not they were culpable. Caroline might have gone with them of her own free will. If she had been kidnapped, surely a ransom demand would have been presented by now?

Silas' only hope of inheriting her fortune was to find Caroline first and make sure she was dead. He drained his glass, suppressing a shudder at his own thoughts. He had never intended any of this. Everything had got out of hand, sending him spiralling down a slippery slope from which it seemed there was no return.

Getting up, he went to the sideboard and poured another glass of fine brandy. He was living in Caroline's house; there was no one to deny him, no one to challenge his authority. Even the lawyers had been prepared to do as he asked. Up to a point.

'I shall need money for rewards,' he'd told them in his role as anxious guardian. 'And perhaps a ransom if she has been kidnapped.'

'It's a terrible thing, Mr Taverner,' the solicitor replied. 'Of course everything must be done to discover Miss Manners' whereabouts.'

Once the money was his he would go abroad, Silas decided. Somewhere his bones did not ache – but first he had to find Caroline. Or the proof that she was dead.

If the gypsies had taken her, he would make certain they took the blame for her subsequent – and permanent – disappearance. It should be easy enough to convince the authorities that the gypsies had done the deed. Always providing that the Carltons did not interfere too much.

Mr William Carlton was the one to watch. He was inclined to rashness, and already suspicious. Silas had sensed his distrust at their first meeting. He had told too many lies. There was no way out for him now, except to find his ward and stop her tongue for good.

For the moment he was powerless to do anything but wait for news. His own agents were shadowing Lord Carlton's. Should they discover anything of value, the news would come directly to him.

It would be better if Caroline was already dead. Murder wasn't really his style, but he would resort to it, if it were the only way.

He finished his brandy and poured another, nursing it in his hands as his thoughts tumbled in confusion. He was too much of a coward to face his own ruin. Better to face the gallows.

Chapter Twenty-Two

So this was Bodmin fair! Caroline was captivated by the noise and bustle, the gaily coloured awnings over the booths, the tumblers and Morris Dancers performing for the amusement of the crowd. She could not recall ever attending anything quite like this before. Despite the bitter cold the streets were thronged with people, for it was also a great market and all kinds of trading was in progress around her. Cattle and sheep blared from holding pens; horses and carts clattered by; tooth-drawers, peddlers and stallholders called out continuously to attract customers.

'Hot cakes, two a penny!'

'Chestnuts. Roasted and sweet!'

'Buy a bunch of mistletoe, for to kiss your sweetheart!'

'Holly! Holly boughs for the festive season!'

The cries intrigued and amused Caroline. She wanted to see and sample everything, almost wishing she had not suggested the fortune-telling. It would have been fun to circulate amongst the great jostling crowd, selling lucky pixies with Katya, but Jake had arranged to set up a special booth for her. If she changed her mind now, his displeasure would be considerable.

That morning he had brought her a bottle containing an odd smelling lotion. He had watched as she sniffed the contents cautiously.

'Smear a little on your face and hands,' he'd said. 'We want you to look like a gypsy. Your skin is too fair.'

So that was it. It was part of her disguise. He had brought her an old mirror. It was cracked and grey, but she was able to see enough of herself to realise that what he said was true. She did not look in the least like a gypsy.

At first she had stared at herself in dismay, trying to reconcile what she saw with what she felt about herself. Who was this woman in the mirror? Her hair was spiky and barely long enough to cover her ears, though at the front it had begun to curl across her forehead. She pulled at it, wishing she could hurry its regrowth, then covered it quickly with one of the scarves Jake had provided. That was better: she felt a little less naked now.

The lotion darkened her skin several shades. It changed her in other subtle ways too, made her look foreign. Perhaps she *was* foreign? How could she be sure of anything?

Things continued to come back to her, little by little. Sometimes she saw pictures in her mind: a house or a street, so vivid, so detailed, that she felt she must once have lived there. She could not put a name to the places and there were still no people, no certainty, nothing she could grasp. Once she had dreamed of a woman with a soft voice, and her cheeks had been wet with tears when she woke, but the dream faded and afterwards she could not remember what the woman had looked like or who she was.

At other times, Caroline felt that she had never belonged anywhere else but with the gypsies. Katya and Cara were her friends. Why bother with the past? She was safe with them. Yet, inside her, she knew that she must remember: it was important. Something was lurking on the edge of her mind, something that frightened and upset her. Whatever it was, she was prepared to confront it.

'There you are, Sapphira.'

Jake's voice recalled her wandering thoughts. He was standing a few feet away from her, his legs astride, his shoulders thrown back in a dominant stance. She went to him, feeling a flutter of nerves in her stomach. Supposing she wasn't very good at telling fortunes! He might be angry with her if she didn't do much business.

He had set up her fortune-telling booth at the edge of the market square. Inside were two wooden stools and a table spread with a red cloth. A crystal ball stood on the table and there were two packs of new cards. Hangings depicting the moon, the stars and the earth were pinned to the walls of the tent, giving it an atmosphere of mystery and romance.

'What do you think?' Jane asked. 'Will it do, Madame Sapphira?'

'Madame Sapphira?' She laughed and nodded, her eyes brimming with amusement. 'It will do very well.'

'You must charge at least sixpence for reading the cards,' Jake said. 'And a shilling for both the cards and crystal ball.'

'Do you think I shall have many customers?'

'I see no reason why not.' He gave her an approving glance. 'You are still too fair, but you look a little more like one of us now. If your customer is rich, you should ask her to cross your palm with silver – get as much as you can from those who can afford it.'

Caroline nodded. She thought privately that only

young women with more money than brains would be prepared to spend so much on having their fortunes told.

Caroline had been surprised by the steady stream of young women who visited her tent throughout the morning. They were just ordinary girls: maidservants on their day off, farmers' daughters, and some who were probably no better than they should have been, with painted cheeks and wicked eyes. They usually came in twos and threes, giggling and urging each other on. Most paid their silver sixpences eagerly, but one or two produced a whole shilling.

Caroline told them about lovers and husbands, children and good fortune. She encouraged them to talk and they told her more about themselves than they realised, so that she was able to guess what they wanted to hear and they went away with their heads together, well pleased with Madame Sapphira's predictions.

Then, when it was almost noon, the tent flap was pulled hesitantly aside and a young woman came in alone. She was dressed more fashionably than the others and the bulge of a wedding ring showed beneath the fine leather of her gloves. She looked nervous and awkward and seemed ready to flee given the smallest encouragement.

Caroline felt a tingle at the nape of her neck as the woman sat down. Some sixth sense told her that this one was in trouble.

'Do you want me to tell your fortune?' she asked.

'Yes, please,' the woman replied. Her hat had a long, lacy veil that hid her face, but her eyes seemed to plead from behind it. 'Will you give me a full reading – whatever you do. I must know . . . I must . . .'

'Cross my palm with silver,' Caroline said, and held out her hand. She stared at the golden guinea that was deposited on her palm.

'Will that do? I haven't any silver.'

''Twill do,' Caroline said, mimicking Katya. 'Please remove your glove.' She took the woman's hand in her own and looked at the soft white skin. It was the hand of a woman who had never scrubbed a floor in her life. 'You are unhappy about something – is that not so?'

'Yes.' The woman's hand trembled in hers. 'I want to know if . . . if my husband will find out that I have been unfaithful to him.'

Caroline traced the delicate skin with the tip of her finger. It was odd, but her intuition told her the woman was facing impending tragedy.

'You are afraid of your husband, aren't you?'

'Yes.' The woman gave a little sob and pressed a hand to her face. 'He is so – so violent and cruel. Can you tell me what is in store for me?'

Caroline handed her the cards. 'Shuffle these please.'

She did so, and Caroline laid them out on the table in what had become a routine for her – four face up and the others in a circle. She indicated the cards that were turned up.

'You are the queen of hearts. The king is your husband.'

She turned up the first card in the circle: it was the ace of spades. The card of death. A shiver ran through Caroline and she hesitated before turning up the next card. It was the king of hearts; the next was the knave of clubs and the fourth the queen of hearts. She drew a breath of relief.

'What does that mean?' the woman asked.

'The knave of clubs is your lover,' Caroline whispered. Her face would have been pale but for the stain. 'He stands between you and your husband.'

'What does this card mean?' The woman picked up the ace of spades and turned it over in her restless fingers.

'That is the card of death.'

'Oh!' The card was dropped instantly. 'Who . . . who will die?'

'Not you,' Caroline said, and a chill trailed down her spine. 'I can't be sure, but I think it may be your lover.'

'No! Oh no.' The woman pressed trembling fingers to her mouth. 'That is what I feared. Jonathan said he would kill him if he discovered that we had . . .'

She jumped up, knocking over the stool in her haste to leave. Caroline stared after her in dismay. The other fortunes she'd predicted that morning had all been trivial, superficial. She had enjoyed playing her part; it had been like a game. But this one had been different. It made her feel sick and shaky inside.

'I'm sorry,' she whispered. 'I should not have. It's dangerous.'

The tent flap was pushed back again, and Katya entered. For a moment Caroline was too shaken to speak. She sat staring into space as the gypsy girl straightened the stool.

'Will you tell my fortune, Sapphira?'

Caroline blinked and looked at her, then shook her head. 'Not today, Katya. Not now.'

'We've done it lots of times afore,' Katya said. ''Tis fun. I can pay you sixpence for a reading.'

'I wouldn't charge you,' Caroline said and smiled as she gathered her scattered thoughts. 'I'm hungry –

shall we find something to eat? I should like some of those hot cakes, would not you?'

Katya's face brightened at the thought. 'Will you tell the cards for me tonight then?'

'Yes, all right,' Caroline promised, trying to shake off the creepy feeling, lingering from her last session. 'Let's go and buy the cakes.'

As they emerged from the booth, she said aloud: 'It's all nonsense. It's just a game, Sally. You know that.'

Katya gave her an odd sidelong look. 'You called me, Sally.'

'Did I?' Caroline shook her head. 'No . . .' she said slowly. 'Not you. I was thinking of someone else.'

Katya stared at her. 'Have you remembered who you are?'

'No . . . but I do remember I had a friend called Sally.' Caroline sighed and linked her arm with the gypsy girl in a gesture of affection. 'It's so peculiar, Katya. I keep remembering bits and pieces. It's like a puzzle. If I could find the missing parts I would have a whole picture.'

'When you do, you'll go,' Katya said. 'I shall miss you, Sapphira.'

'We shall always be friends.'

'You'll go back to your own kind.'

'You could come with me. Be my sister. I would give you a home. If I have one to give, that is.'

Katya's eyes filled with tears and she looked away. 'You're always so good to me. 'Taint right. I don't deserve it.'

'Of course you do.' Caroline squeezed her arm. 'You mustn't let the other women bully you so much. Learn to stand up for yourself. You're as good as they are, perhaps better. You have a right to be happy, Katya.'

'No one 'as ever bin' good to me, only you and Cara.' She brushed away her tears, leaving a smear of dirt on her cheek. 'You might not like me if you knew what I'd done.'

'Well, what have you done?' Caroline asked teasingly. 'I'll wager it was terribly wicked – did you lose one of Jake's pixies?'

'He'd half kill me,' Katya said with a watery grin. 'I gave someone a pixie for luck once and . . .' her words trailed away and she turned pale.

'Did Jake get cross?' Caroline noticed her odd expression. 'Is something wrong?'

'Nuffing,' Katya said and averted her eyes. 'I remembered somefing, that's all.' She tugged Caroline towards the stall selling hot cakes. 'Come on then! I'm starving.'

It was mid-afternoon when Caroline returned to her booth. She was still puzzling over Katya's behaviour but forgot it when she saw that Jake was waiting for her. She smiled and took a handful of coins from her pocket, holding them out to him.

'I was busy this morning,' she said. 'I bought some cakes for Katya and me. I hope you don't mind?'

'You earned the money,' he replied. 'Keep it.'

Caroline was surprised. She knew that he took a large commission on what Katya earned, leaving her only a few coins for herself.

'I would rather you took it,' she said. 'I did this for you – to repay you for your kindness.'

'I need no repayment,' he said, an angry glint in his eyes. 'You know I care for you, Sapphira. I've made

196

no secret of it. I want you to be independent. If you stay with us, it must be because you want to.'

He moved towards her, his eyes seeming to scorch her as he gazed down into her face. Caroline drew in a breath, her pulses racing. For a moment she thought he meant to take her in his arms to kiss her, and she was afraid. Jake was a physically powerful man. If he was so minded, he could do with her as he pleased.

'No,' he said, as she dropped her gaze in confusion. 'I won't force you, Sapphira. If you come to me it must be of your own choosing. Just remember in a year you will belong to me. Then I shall never let you go.'

Katya had had a good morning at the fair. She sold all the charms Jake had given her and he was so pleased that he gave her three silver sixpences for herself. For him, this was the height of generosity.

Katya had seen the distraught young woman run from Madame Sapphira's tent as she made her way through the busy market square. At the time, she was thinking of how she would spend her windfall and the look of shock on Caroline's face had surprised her as she entered the booth. She'd asked Sapphira to tell her fortune on impulse, but she was glad when she refused: the sixpences were too valuable to waste, and in any case Katya knew her own future. She would never be more than she was; she had accepted that long ago.

It was when they had been on their way to the cake stall that Katya suddenly remembered what had been puzzling her for weeks. Of course Sapphira looked familiar when she'd first seen her in the woods – she was the one who had given her a half-sovereign that day at Pendlesham!

So she *was* a lady of quality! Cara had been right all along. Katya remembered that Sapphira had given her her name that morning, but it had gone from her memory. She'd curtsied in confusion, and the lady had smiled modestly and said: 'I'm only Miss . . .'

Katya searched her memory once more, but it was no use. She had been so frightened that day, wishing only to escape. She thought guiltily of the gold locket hidden amongst her things. There was writing inside it. Katya couldn't read, but she knew Sapphira could. If she returned the locket Sapphira might discover who she really was. A true friend would give it back.

Katya felt torn in two. If she returned the locket to Sapphira she would never have anything as beautiful again. It might mean that Sapphira would go away. Katya would miss her and yet it hurt so much when she saw the way Jake looked at the other girl. If only he would look at her like that.

But perhaps the locket didn't belong to Sapphira. It might have been dropped by someone else.

Katya finished eating the cakes, licking every bit of the spicy stickiness from her fingers. She would wait a while longer. Sapphira might remember who she was without help, and then it wouldn't matter about the necklace. She could keep it forever.

'What are you thinking?' Sapphira asked her, with her familiar warm smile. 'Is something wrong?'

Katya shook her head, smothering her guilt. She would do anything else she could for her friend, but the locket was hers to keep.

It was soon after Sapphira had returned to her booth that Katya saw Jake come striding towards her. The look on his face told her that he was in one of his black moods, and she trembled inside. Had she done something to upset him?

Jake reached out and grabbed hold of her arm, pinching the skin, his eyes pinning hers with an angry glare. 'Has anyone been asking questions about Sapphira?' he demanded. 'Have you told anyone she is here?'

'No.' Katya stared at him with frightened eyes, quailing before his anger. 'No, I haven't said anyfing. No one's asked me anyfing.'

Jake's fingers bit deeper into her soft flesh, making her wince. 'If they do, you deny all knowledge of her. Do you hear me? If I discover you've whispered even one word about her, I'll thrash you black and blue.'

'I would not do nuffing like that,' Katya whimpered, rubbing her arm as he released her. 'You told me before I wasn't to say nuffing.'

'All right. Just you remember that.'

'Do you know her real name then?' Katya asked, and squeaked as he grabbed her again. 'I wus only askin'. I shan't say nuffing.'

'You had better not,' he said harshly. 'Remember you belong to me, Katya. You live with us because I say so. If you anger me I shall send you away.'

Chapter Twenty-Three

Christmas had come and gone. Life went on at Pendlesham just as it always had, but Will's heart was no longer in his work. It was more than three months since Caroline had disappeared. Sometimes Will felt sure she was dead, and at such times the pain was almost more than he could bear, but he refused to give up. The search must go on until they were certain one way or the other.

His thoughts were gloomy as he walked towards the house, no longer appreciating its beauty: neither the estate not the wealth and richness it represented meant anything to him at this moment. His thoughts were obsessed with Caroline. Fitz's agents had been busy, travelling the length and breadth of the land, but there were many gypsies wandering the countryside and so far none of them would admit to having any knowledge of her. Will frowned as he remembered the latest report they had received the previous evening from somewhere in the south west.

'I have heard rumours of a fair-skinned woman travelling with a band of gypsies,' the agent had written. 'I have not seen her myself but I managed to speak to their leader, a handsome brute by the name of Jake. He denied all knowledge of Miss Manners . . .'

Could it be a coincidence? Jake was a common enough name and yet it had stuck in Will's mind, nagging at him as he lay sleepless half the night. He remembered that Caroline had spoken to a young gypsy girl in the village some months before. She had felt sorry for the girl, and had wanted to help her – was it possible that she had gone off with her tribe, to escape the unpleasantness that Silas Taverner had inflicted on her? It would be easy to disappear that way if she chose to.

Supposing Sally was right? Supposing Caroline had decided she did not want to marry Fitz. No, no, she would have sent back his ring. She would have written or told Carlton to his face. Unless, of course, she was ashamed to confess to being the illegitimate child of a groom and an unmarried girl.

Will still could not believe that Caroline would run away because of an old scandal. She was far more likely to tell the world the truth and be damned to the gossips.

A smile touched his mouth as he recalled some of their past exchanges. She was more than capable of holding her own he thought ruefully. Yet there was a vulnerable side to her, a side she kept hidden. He had caught a glimpse of it in her eyes when he'd kissed her.

He was frowning as he entered the house. That report would bear a second reading. He turned towards the library but halted as Fitz called to him from the doorway of the green salon, his heart beginning to pump madly as it did whenever he had cause to hope.

'Have you news?' he inquired.

'Of a kind,' Fitz said. 'You recall that report from Bodmin?'

'Yes, I was about to read it again. Something has been bothering me. I can't get it out of my mind.'

'I too wondered,' Fitz agreed. 'You recall that Caroline was set on helping that gypsy girl.' He stroked the bridge of his nose with one finger. 'Today I received a new report of a fortune teller with fair hair who speaks like a lady.' His brows went up inquiringly. 'Does that not strike you as a little odd? Two separate reports mentioning such a woman?'

'If it is Caroline it might mean that she fully intended to start a new life.' Will said slowly.

'It might indeed. Yet, I believe we should investigate this report further. Who knows what we shall find? If it is not Caroline, no harm will have been done. Besides, we should not make hasty judgements, even if she did choose to run away, Will.'

'I shall never rest until we know the truth!'

'Nor I, my dear fellow,' Fitz murmured. 'As I understand it, this particular group of gypsies is due to visit a fair in Exeter next week, where our mysterious fortune teller will once more exercise her considerable skill.' Fitz took a gold watch from his waistcoat pocket and consulted it. 'Almost supper time. Perhaps we should continue this conversation later?'

'I shall go to Exeter myself,' Will said. 'I'll leave in the morning. You need not come until we are sure it is her – unless you wish?'

Fitz replaced his watch, his expression bland. 'I doubt it will be necessary. I shall come at once if you send for me, of course.'

'Of course,' Will replied stiffly. 'I was thinking it would save you the effort. You must be there if it is her, naturally.'

'I should prefer to be there when you speak to her,' Fitz said. 'I should not want Caroline to think I meant to slight her in any way.'

'It is your right. I have not forgotten she is to be your wife.'

'Was to be my wife,' Fitz corrected mildly. 'Caroline may have changed her mind.'

'Yes, that is a possibility,' Will said, not quite meeting his eyes. 'Or there may be another reason why she ran away – if she did.'

'We shall discover it in due course, if the lady in question turns out to be Caroline. It will not do to raise our hopes too much just yet, Will.'

'I pray to God it is her,' Will said. 'I don't care why she went or what she has done as long as she is alive!'

He turned on his heel and left the room, unaware of his cousin's cold gaze on his back. Nor did he hear Fitz's softly spoken words.

'I think I understand. Yes, Julia – I begin to understand . . .'

The weather was cold and crisp, making the roads easy to travel. White frosting hung like fronds from the bare branches of trees and the sky was overcast as Will set out the next morning, well wrapped in a greatcoat and mufflers against the bitter wind. He had chosen to ride rather than take the carriage, which would be too slow. He could not have borne to sit idly during the long journey to Exeter, and the physical act of managing his horse would help occupy his mind.

Please, God, let it be Caroline. Let her be alive. He could bear anything – even seeing her every day at Pendlesham as Fitz's wife – as long as she wasn't dead.

The fair was not due to take place for several more days but Will wasted no time on the journey. He would have to stop at an inn overnight, of course, but he intended to ride until darkness fell. Now that he knew there was a possibility of finding Caroline he was afire with impatience. He could not wait to see this fortune teller who spoke like a lady. The more he pondered it, the more he became convinced it must be her. Sally had spoken of Caroline's penchant for telling fortunes.

'She thinks of it as a game,' Sally had told him. 'But she has a genuine gift for it.'

The pieces fitted together so well. Perhaps too well.

It was very cold; cold enough to form a thin sheet of ice over a pond he had passed earlier, but at least the roads were hard instead of becoming the quagmire they could be in wet weather.

Will had been travelling for some hours before the odd prickling at the back of his neck began. Perhaps it was only his imagination, but he could swear he was being followed. It was a lonely road, with considerable distances between villages and sometimes he travelled for prolonged periods without sight of another human soul. He reined back and twisted in the saddle. Yes there he was – a horseman, too far away to identify. Now he too, stopped.

Will decided to stop at the next inn and wait until the other rider came by.

Then we'll see what you're about, my fine friend.' He pulled his muffler round his face to protect it from the bitter wind and resumed his journey.

Twenty minutes passed before he came upon the hostelry; it looked a poor place, though it boasted of being a posting inn and offered a change of horses. There was a strong odour of pigs, and cockerels strutted a yard thronged with farmers and yokels fresh from the near by market.

Will made his way across the muddy cobbles, which were unswept and littered with horse dung between the puddles. The groom who came to receive his horse seemed a cheerful lad and Will gave him a coin to take good care of the animal.

Inside, the inn smelt of stale ale, spilt fat and unwashed bodies – not the type of place he would have chosen to patronise. He ordered a meal of bread, cheese and ale, sitting by the window so as to have a clear view of the yard. A few minutes later, he saw another lone traveller dismount and speak briefly to a groom, before going into the taproom. This, he was sure, was the rider who had followed him all day. The newcomer asked for food, deliberately keeping his head averted.

'A bitter wind today,' Will said. 'We must be fools to travel on such a day – what say you?'

The man turned his head reluctantly. 'Indeed, sir. I would not venture so far, but my business is urgent.'

'Where are you headed? Perhaps we might ride on together?'

'I have no time to waste. I prefer to journey alone.'

Will nodded, accepting the brusque reply. Perhaps he was wrong and the man was simply on business as he'd said. Still, he felt instinctively that he had been shadowed for some time.

But who would want to follow him?

Of course – Silas Taverner! Caroline's guardian must know that he and Fitz were scouring the country for her. If Taverner had something to hide he would need to find her first.

Will was on his guard now. He had no intention of leading the stranger to Caroline. His fingers touched the pistol in his greatcoat pocket. He would use it if necessary, but there were other ways to rid himself of this shadow.

He smiled as he finished his ale and paid his reckoning. The challenge was stimulating. It would keep him from dwelling too much on what might await him in Exeter.

Chapter Twenty-Four

Caroline was restless. Her mind sought fresh diversions from story-telling – music, books and good company, for instance. Smothering a sigh, she climbed down the wooden steps of the caravan and stood looking around her. Although it was still January the weather had suddenly become milder overnight, and the birds had started to sing as if in anticipation of an early spring.

It might be quite pleasant to live as a gypsy in the summertime, Caroline mused. She had found it cold these past weeks and it was cramped in Cara's caravan with three women sharing the sleeping facilities. Such an arrangement could not go on indefinitely.

They were camped in a wood a few miles from Exeter, where a fair was to be held the next day. Caroline had played her part as Madame Sapphira a number of times now and there had been no repeat of the unpleasant incident at Bodmin. She confined herself to pure invention, invariably predicting good fortune for the empty-headed girls who came to be entertained and went away giggling.

It was harmless enough, but the incident with the woman who had sought her help haunted her. It had seemed amusing to play the part of a gypsy fortune teller, and it was satisfying to earn her own keep. She had been able to buy extra food and gifts for Katya and Cara.

Cara had accepted her gift with her usual grunt, but her eyes had gleamed when she felt the thickness of the new wool blanket. Caroline knew the old woman felt the cold and it was the best possible present she could have given her. For Katya she had chosen some pretty earrings that Jake had made from twisted silver wire and blue glass beads. He sold them to peddlers and market stallholders, preferring not to trade on the streets himself.

He was surprised by Caroline's request. 'For Katya, you say? 'Tis a waste of money to give them to her.'

Caroline looked at him intently, sensing the harsh words concealed a secret. 'What has she done that everyone should despise her?' she asked. 'Surely it is not necessary to be so unkind to her.'

'Do not question what you don't understand.'

Seeing the glint in his eyes, Caroline abandoned the subject. Jake was never surly with her, but he had a fierce temper when roused. She paid his price for the earrings and gave them to Katya that evening.

Caroline was remembering the girl's odd reaction as she walked through the camp, enjoying the weak wintry sunshine and the musky, mysterious smell of the woods. For a moment, as Katya took the earrings, Caroline thought the girl would burst into tears; then she'd turned away with mumbled thanks. Since then she had kept her distance, speaking only when spoken to.

'Where are you going?'

Jake's question broke into Caroline's thoughts. She had not seen him approach, and she blinked in surprise, wondering at his hostile attitude.

'I was going for a walk in the woods,' she replied. 'I thought I might find some firewood for Cara.'

'Katya can do that,' he said, his eyes narrowed to slits. He seized her wrist, turning up her hands to look at the palms. She had a rough patch where the skin had blistered and healed over. 'You will spoil your hands with rough work.'

'I thought you wanted me to be more like a gypsy?'

'I want you to be happy with us.' Jake stared at her long and hard, then laid his hand against her cheek, a sudden, uncharacteristic gesture that startled her. 'I want you for my woman,' he said softly. 'You know that, don't you?'

'Yes.' Caroline's heart was beating so fast she could hardly breathe. 'Yes. I knew it from the beginning.'

'I would be good to you,' he said. 'I am not a poor man, Sapphira. I live this way by choice.' His voice grew husky with desire. 'There is a Greek island that belongs to someone I once knew. It lies basking in the sun for most days of the year, surrounded by a sea nearly as blue as your eyes. I have a home there – a villa set on the cliffs overlooking the sea. If you wished it, we could go there.' His hands moved to grip her shoulders and his eyes burned into hers. 'At other times we could wander the world together. There is much I could show you, Sapphira, many wonderful things to gladden your heart. I could make you happy, so happy you would never want to leave me.'

Caroline dropped her eyes. His voice was soft and persuasive. The picture he painted was attractive and she felt drawn to him against her will.

'Please,' she whispered. 'Give me time. I need time to remember who and what I am.'

'But then you will leave me.'

'Perhaps.' Tears sparkled on her lashes. 'I'm sorry, Jake. I cannot give you the answer you want. Not yet.'

'Then I shall wait,' he said and his expression hardened. 'For a year and a day from when you first came to us. Remember, after that, you are mine by right.'

Caroline watched him walk away from her. What was she to do? Her memory seemed to be returning little by little. But just suppose it was never completely restored. Jake would claim her if she could not go back to her old life. Was she prepared to be his woman? Did she have a choice?

Caroline met Katya as she was returning to the caravan. She smiled at the girl, but Katya turned her head aside.

'What is it, Katya,' Caroline asked, hurt. 'Have I done something to upset you?'

Katya's expression became remote. She shook her head. ''Tis not you,' she muttered. 'I can't tell you. I can't!'

'Are you in trouble with Jake?'

'No.' Katya rubbed a hand across her eyes. 'Leave me alone, just leave me alone.'

Caroline stared after the girl as she ran away, at a loss to understand the change in her behaviour.

As she approached the caravan, Cara came out. She stood on the step swaying slightly. Concerned, Caroline moved swiftly to support her. She helped the old woman inside, sat her on her stool and crouched beside her, watching over her anxiously as the colour gradually returned to her cheeks.

'You're not well,' Caroline said. 'Shall I call Katya for you?'

'No, 'tis not worth the bother,' Cara muttered. 'I shall be better in a moment.'

'Has this happened before?'

'Mebbe.' Cara glanced up. 'You'll tell no one. I'm old. My time is coming. I shall die soon enough, 'tis natural.'

'What will Katya do without you?'

'She should leave us,' Cara said harshly. 'She should go with you – back to her own kind.'

'What do you mean? I thought Katya was a gypsy?'

Cara stared at her in silence for several seconds then sighed. 'You are her friend. I should tell you the truth before 'tis too late.' Her skinny fingers tightened on Caroline's arm. 'Take her with you when you leave, but tell her nothing until then – swear it! You must swear it on your own life.'

Caroline prised her fingers away, took the gnarled, bony hand in hers. 'I swear I shall not speak of this until the time is right.'

Cara studied her face, then nodded. 'Jake would kill me if he knew I'd told you this.'

'He will never know.'

'When I am dead you can speak.' Cara's eyes were distant, as though her thoughts were far away. 'Katya's father was a titled lordship.'

'What?' Caroline was so astonished she fell back on her bottom and sat there, on the floorboards, gaping. 'Do you know who he was?'

'Only Jake knows that.' Cara shook her head in sorrow. 'He was with Katya's mother just before she died. I had left her for a moment and I heard her cry out in pain. When I returned to her van she was dead and there was such a look on his face . . . such a look . . .' Cara shivered at the old memory.

'Katya's mother . . .'

'She was Jake's step-mother. A beautiful girl many years younger than her husband,' Cara said and her harsh features softened. 'Jake's father had three wives. Seven sons the first two gave him and Jake the seventh, but the third wife betrayed him. He loved her desperately with an old man's love and he died of a broken heart within a year of her passing: his dying curse has shadowed Katya all her life. Jake was only a child himself then. He blamed Katya for being a lord's bastard and for causing his father's death. He has never forgiven her.'

'Poor Katya,' Caroline said softly. 'To carry the burden of her mother's sins all these years. She knows nothing of all this, does she? Not even that her mother was Jake's step-mother?'

'No one has dared to tell her,' Cara said. 'Jake forbade it, and no one will disobey him.'

'I see.' Caroline looked at her thoughtfully. 'This explains so much – why everyone treats her so abominably.'

'I've tried to make up for it a little,' Cara said. 'I've cared for her as much as I was able.'

'Oh, I don't mean you,' Caroline said quickly. 'Katya says you've always been good to her. But the rest of them are so unkind.' She paused, then, 'Katya loves Jake. Do you think she would come with me were I to leave?'

'When you tell her the truth she will understand 'tis for the best. Jake thinks of her as a despised sister; she is his property to use as he sees fit but he will never love her. If she stays here she will never marry, never know happiness.'

'Poor Katya,' Caroline said again. Then stood up, nodding determinedly to herself. 'Yes, I shall take her with me when I leave.' She drew a shuddering breath. 'If only I knew who I was, I would go this instant and . . .'

'Hush,' Cara warned, a finger to her lips. 'Someone is coming. Remember your promise. Break it and my curse will be on you.'

'Rest easy,' Caroline assured her. 'I shall keep my promise.'

She could say no more then for Katya came into the van carrying a basket of fir cones she had gathered in the woods. There was a short silence and she glanced from one to the other suspiciously.

'What's wrong?' she asked. 'What have I done now?'

'You've done nothing,' Caroline said. 'Cara was telling me about the old days, that's all.'

Cara often told them stories in the long evenings. Katya smiled and put down her basket. She gave Caroline a timid look.

'I'm sorry I was cross earlier,' she said, head hanging. 'Will you tell my fortune, Sapphira?'

'Of course,' Caroline said. 'I want to try out the crystal ball, Katya. Only you must promise not to giggle when I'm conjuring up the pictures; it puts me off.'

Cara snorted her disapproval and the two younger women smiled at each other, amusement in their eyes as they shared a moment of perfect understanding. It seemed that they were friends again and Caroline felt a surge of relief. Perhaps Katya's odd behaviour was just a passing phase.

Katya moved amongst the Exeter crowd selling her lucky pixies. She had done well and most of the charms were already gone. Jake would be pleased with her. Her forehead creased in a frown as she remembered his threats to beat her and expel her from the tribe. They had played on her mind for days.

Ever since that man had asked her for news of Sapphira. Only he hadn't called her Sapphira – he had called her Miss Caroline Manners.

Katya knew Sapphira's real name now. It had been there at the back of her mind all along, and had required only for the man to say it to unlock her memory.

Sapphira had been so kind to her, buying her earrings and giving her cakes and meat pies when they visited the fairs together, it made Katya feel guilty to keep the knowledge to herself. At the very least she ought to give back the locket. Sapphira had a life and friends of her own; if she knew who she was she would go back to them. Jake had promised he would let her go, but he wouldn't do anything to ease her path, because he wanted her for himself. Katya suspected he had known her identity for a long time, perhaps even from the beginning.

Jake was not given to idle threats. If Katya helped Sapphira to find her true identity and Jake learned of it, she would be severely punished. She was not afraid of being beaten – it would not be for the first time! – but where could she go if she was forced out of the tribe?

Sapphira had said she could go with her. Would she keep her word? Or was it just one of those casual offers people make, not really meaning it?

Katya was torn between Jake and Sapphira. She had felt like crying when Sapphira gave her those earrings. As she remembered the gesture, her eyes stung with tears and for a moment she was blinded by them. Unseeing, she collided with someone, and gave a cry of pain as her foot was stepped on.

'I'm so sorry,' the tall, good-looking man

apologised instantly. 'I was not looking where I put my feet.'

Katya wiped her face, leaving a smear of dirt on her cheek. Her heart caught with fright as she looked up and found herself staring into the eyes of the man from Pendlesham; the one who looked after things for his lordship, the one who had been kind to her.

'It don't matter,' she whispered and turned away swiftly, but he caught her arm, preventing her from leaving. 'Please let me go.'

'Haven't I seen you somewhere before?' Will Carlton asked, frowning down at her. 'You were with Jake's people at Pendlesham, were you not?' His grip tightened. 'Yes, I'm sure it was you.'

Katya hung her head, her cheeks flushed beneath the dirt. She knew this man all too well. He had even shared his meal with her once, when she had met him by accident, while collecting berries in his woods.

'It *was* you, wasn't it?'

Katya stared at him in silence, then bobbed her head. Any second now, he was going to ask her about Sapphira. She knew it instinctively and she was sick with fright. If she told him the truth he would take Sapphira away and Jake would half kill her.

'Yes,' she whispered. 'You were kind to me.'

Will shook his head. 'I merely gave you some bread and cheese,' he said. 'But someone else was kind to you. She wanted to help you – do you remember her?'

'No.' Katya lied desperately. 'I don't know her. I don't know where she is. Let me go!'

She twisted free of his grasp, avoiding him as he tried to grab her again and speeding away through the crowd, her heart beating madly.

Chapter Twenty-Five

Caroline had been busy all the morning. The young women of Exeter were more than eager to hand over their sixpences in return for vague promises about lovers or good fortune, perhaps because their everyday lives were so hard. Conditions had worsened in the country since the end of the Napoleonic wars, with prices spiralling upwards and wages plummeting, a practice that had aroused much ill-feeling amongst the people and was the cause of many riots around the country. Hand-loom weavers who had once earned twenty-seven shillings a week now received less than fifteen, and that only if they were lucky enough to find employment. Caroline had discovered for herself how hard it was to buy enough food to survive, so she was constantly surprised that the young women queued to pay her their hard-earned money to learn what the future held in store. She assuaged her sense of guilt by donating the greater proportion of her income to her friends. Besides, the girls who came to her were in a holiday mood, and sought entertainment. She told them what they hoped to hear and they went away to gossip with their friends and thought the money well spent.

So many had crowded into her little tent that morning that Caroline began to run out of fresh ideas. Now there came a lull, and she wondered where Katya was. Mostly by this time of the day the girl had come in search of her, and they spent an hour or so exploring the towns and villages through which they passed.

As the tent flap was suddenly pulled back she looked up expectantly, then gave a hesitant smile as Jake entered, a worried frown creasing his forehead. 'I thought you might be Katya,' she said. Her smile faded when he reached for her. 'Is something wrong?'

'We're going now,' he said shortly, pulling her to her feet. 'I'm taking you back to the camp. Leave everything as it is. I'll send someone to pack up later.'

'But why?' She felt a tingling sensation at the nape of her neck. 'Something has happened – please tell me.'

'You are in danger.' Jake took hold of her arm, urging her towards the tent opening. 'Trust me, Sapphira. This is for your own good.'

'I don't understand – why am I in danger?' She hung back, reluctant to let him hustle her away.

He hesitated, a flicker of annoyance passing across his face, then drew in a hissing breath. 'Perhaps I should have told you, before but I did not want to upset or frighten you. I thought you might remember in time.' Jake paused, breath hissing through his teeth. 'When I first discovered you lying there in the woods you were conscious for a few minutes. You begged me to hide you from a man who would come searching for you. You were frightened for your life, hysterical, but you fainted again before you could tell me more.'

Caroline felt a chill of fear run through her. 'Is that why you wanted me to stain my face and hands, to look more like a gypsy – so that I would not be so recognisable?'

'Yes.' Jake's hand was urgent on her arm. 'That man is here now, looking for you. You must trust me. We have to leave at once.'

Caroline felt confused and uneasy. Perhaps later she might be angry with Jake for keeping this from her, but for the moment she would have to trust him.

His fingers closed about her arm as he rushed her from the tent. They paused for a moment outside, Caroline shivering in the bitter wind while Jake's eyes scanned the crowd, then he propelled her away, towards the edge of the market square.

Her heart was racing wildly. The wind tore at her hair and stung her eyes, but her mind seemed to have gone blank. Jake's behaviour was frightening her. Who was this man he was so afraid of for her sake?

Jake was thrusting her through the crowds, shouldering men and women aside ruthlessly, dragging her along with him like a baggage cart.

'Hurry!' he muttered. 'Damn! Damn him to hell!'

Caroline glanced back, wondering what had brought him to this state of near panic. All the faces looked the same to her, strangers who seemed to meld into a blur. Then she caught sight of a tall man with dark hair, though too far away for her to see his face, ploughing through the milling humanity in their wake.

'Caroline, stop! Wait for me . . . come back!' The cry reached her, rising above the hubbub, but meant nothing to her.

'Run!' Jake hissed at her. 'Go on ahead of me. We'll meet at camp. I'll try to block his way until you're out of sight – go!'

Jake's panic communicated itself to Caroline, and

she obeyed blindly. She did not know who the man was or why she should be afraid of him, but she was quite suddenly and unreasoningly terrified. Her heart was thumping madly against her ribs and she knew she had to hurry before he caught her.

She fled without a backward glance. Her pulses raced as the fear surged, her breath coming in tortured gulps as she ran and ran, faster and faster, away from the market square and the unknown, unseen menace, through the winding, cobbled streets of the old town. Houses, shops, inns, all faded into a blur as the terror possessed her mind, driving all else before it.

Night was falling when Caroline at last reached the gypsy camp. She had spent many hours wandering in the wood and fields, and was staggering with fatigue, her hands and feet numbed by the cold. The welcome warmth of Cara's fire drew her like a moth and she held out her aching fingers to the flame, sighing with relief. She was safe now, back with her friends. A hand grabbed her arm. For a moment the fear flared anew, and she swung round, her eyes wide.

'Jake!' she cried, relieved. 'You startled me.'

'Where have you been?' he demanded. 'I thought something must have happened to you.'

'I got lost,' she replied with a rueful twist of her lips. 'When you told me to run, I panicked. It took me many hours to find the right road again.'

'We're moving on at first light,' he said, his face granite hard in the firelight. 'It's not safe for you to continue your fortune telling, Sapphira.'

Caroline made no demur. She looked up at him, as it suddenly occurred to her that he must know her real identity.

'Who am I?' she asked.' Why was I running away from this man?'

'I don't know why you ran away,' Jake replied, his gaze intent on her face. He hesitated, then seemed to reach an important decision. 'So be it. I will tell you your real name.'

'Yes, oh yes,' she cried, reaching out to touch his hand. 'Who am I, Jake? Where do I come from?'

He flicked a stray ember into the fire with the toe of his boot.

'I found you in a wood some twenty odd miles from the little Norfolk village of Reepham,' he said finally. 'But where you came from I do not know. Only that your name is Miss Caroline Manners.'

Caroline – the name the man in the crowd had called even as she fled from him. She turned away, with a shudder, and covered her face with her hands. Now she felt more afraid than ever. All at once she felt Jake's arms go around her and his mouth touch her hair in a gentle kiss.

'Don't be frightened,' he said in a soft, husky voice. 'Sapphira or Caroline – you are still the same woman. The woman I love.'

She wanted to weep. She felt so alone, so vulnerable. Choked by disappointment. Knowing her own name had changed nothing. Her mind still refused to surrender its secrets; she knew no more of her past than she had before.

Jake turned her in his arms and she stared up at him, her eyes full of unconscious pleading. 'Sapphira,' he murmured, then bent his head to kiss her on the lips.

For a moment she stood passively. His mouth was warm and tender, his kiss persuasive. She swayed into his body, drawn by the comfort his strength offered. What was the use of resisting? She might never know more than her own name, and what would she discover if she did? Perhaps there was some reason why she could never return to her old life. Perhaps to be a gypsy woman was her destiny.

'Jake?' she said wonderingly, as his mouth released hers.

'Come with me,' he urged. 'Let me take you away to a place where you will be safe. Be my woman, Sapphira. Don't make me wait any longer – let me love you tonight.'

His words sent a thrill through her body. She hesitated, tempted to let him have his way. It would be so much easier not to resist. Jake was strong. He loved her, wanted her . . .

'Caroline – come back!'

The words were branded on her mind. She stepped back, shaking her head, as her instinct took over, bringing a new strength and courage from deep inside her. This was wrong. She could not lie with Jake; she could not subordinate her will to his. She had to know the truth.

'No, Jake,' she said, and her eyes were steady as she gazed up at him. 'You've been kind to me, but I must have more time. I need to know who and what I am.' She placed a finger across his lips, hushing his protest. 'You were right, a name means little. It's me – the person – I need to discover.'

Jake's eyes glinted with frustrated anger. 'You're mine,' he said fiercely. 'I found you. I saved your life. You belong to me.'

'Perhaps one day,' Caroline said. 'But not yet. Not yet, Jake.'

She turned and walked away from him, her head high.

Caroline woke with a cry as Katya shook her shoulder. She stared up at her in the light of the horn lantern, wondering what was wrong.

'You were crying in your sleep,' Katya said, putting a finger to her lips. 'I thought you might wake Cara.'

'I'm sorry.' She touched her cheek and found it wet. 'I must have been dreaming again.'

It was not the first time she had woken after disturbing dreams, to find herself weeping. But now her thoughts were for Cara rather than herself. She knew that Katya was worried and she shared her anxiety. For two days now Cara had taken to her bed, refusing to eat or drink anything she was offered.

'You rest now,' Caroline said. 'Let me watch over her for a while.'

'She's peaceful enough. Come outside so that we can talk.'

The sky was just beginning to lighten, birds calling to one another from the trees. A new day was dawning, a day that would likely be spent in travelling. Jake was restless, keeping them constantly on the move in the three weeks since they'd left Exeter.

'Cara needs to rest,' Katya said as she began to build a small fire. 'We should stay here for a while.'

Caroline agreed. They were camped on the outskirts of a village a few miles south of Salisbury, on land gypsies had used for centuries. She knew that Katya was not the only one who thought they should stay put for a while. Several dark looks had come her way, and she was sure the other gypsies blamed her for the upheaval.

Katya looked at her. 'Why were you calling out in your sleep? Were you dreaming?'

'I have the same dream over and over, but it tells

me nothing. Except that I think the woman who calls to me is my mother.'

'I never knew my mother.'

Caroline remembered her promise. It was not yet the moment to tell Katya the truth, but it was coming very soon.

'Have you remembered where you came from?' Katya asked.

'No – but sometimes I see a beautiful house and a park with gardens.' Caroline sighed. 'I don't know if I lived there or not.'

'If you went away – back to that place – would you take me with you?'

'Yes, if you wished. But we could not abandon Cara while she is unwell . . .' Caroline stared at her. 'Do you know something, Katya? If you do, please tell me.'

'I'm not sure,' Katya said warily. 'But you must promise not to tell Jake . . .' She broke off as a cry came from inside the caravan. ''Tis Cara. I must go to her.'

Caroline followed her inside. Katya was bending over the old woman, who was writhing and gasping. The girl turned to Caroline, pleadingly, face pale with shock as the rattle of death issued from Cara's throat.

'Don't let her die . . . please . . .'

Katya threw herself across the now still form on the bed.

'I'm sorry,' Caroline said gently, touching her shoulder. But perhaps it is for the best. She is not suffering now.'

'But I loved her,' Katya wept. 'She was my best friend.'

Caroline drew the girl into her arms, kissing her tangled hair. 'I know,' she said. 'She loved you too, but you are not alone. You have me. I shall always be your friend.'

Katya stared up at her with tear-drenched eyes. 'Do you mean it? Would you truly take me with you?'

'Yes,' Caroline promised. She held the girl as she wept. 'I shall not desert you. Ever.'

Caroline did not attend Cara's funeral, which had been carried out according to ancient rites: the body burnt along with all Cara's possessions. Only her horse passed on to Jake, to dispose of as he pleased.

Katya and Caroline now had a wagon of their own. They had more room to move about, but they missed Cara and her mutterings, mourning a woman they had both loved in their different ways.

Katya had been quiet since the old woman's death. She was clearly troubled by other things besides her grief, but Caroline had held back from questioning her.

She understood the girl needed peace, to come to terms with her new situation.

Soon it would be time for her and Katya to leave the gypsies. Caroline felt this instinctively. She would tell Katya the truth about herself, and then they would be gone. She at least *must* leave, because Jake was becoming too demanding, seeming to begrudge the year's grace he had accorded her before she surrendered herself to him. And something in her rebelled against his promises of an exciting life.

Two weeks had passed since Cara's death. There were signs of spring in the woods, though it was not yet March. Katya had brought her the first snowdrops a day or so earlier, presenting them with a shy smile.

Their relationship had grown stronger since Cara's death. Caroline sensed that Katya was making some kind of a decision and she had not tried to reopen the conversation they had begun just before Cara died. There was time enough for Katya to make up her own mind.

'Have you seen Katya?'

Caroline looked up in surprise from skinning the rabbit, as Jake approached the camp fire. She had thought it odd that Katya had gone out so early, and so silently that Caroline had not awakened.

'No, not since last night,' she replied. 'Perhaps she went to look for more wood.'

'That girl is more trouble than she's worth,' Jake muttered, and walked off scowling.

She watched him go. He was angry, and not only with Katya. Caroline knew he resented her reluctance to give in to his wiles, and sometimes she wondered if he would really wait for the year and a day he had promised her. If he were determined to have her, there was nothing to prevent him from taking her, even if she were unwilling.

Perhaps she would talk to Katya over their meal that evening. She glanced up at the sky; the afternoon was wearing on. It would soon be suppertime. Where *was* the girl? It was unlike her to go off without a word.

She stripped the skin from the rabbit and began to prepare it for the pot.

Katya crept out as Caroline slept. For a moment she stared down at her friend, wondering if she ought to wake her and tell her what she planned. If Jake were telling the truth, the man from Pendlesham was Caroline's enemy. Katya had worried over it for weeks, but in her heart she knew that Jake was lying. He had deliberately lied to Caroline to frighten her so that she would run away with him: he was set on keeping her for himself, and none would gainsay him.

Katya remembered the beautiful ring she had seen on Caroline's hand that day in the woods. She knew that among the gentry it was a sign that a woman was promised to a man – perhaps the man who had come searching for her.

Torn between loyalty to Caroline and the man she had once adored, she had told Jake nothing of the man. So gradually that she had scarcely been aware of it, her feelings for Jake had changed over the past weeks. Only in the last day or so had she begun to be sure of her own mind. She still loved Jake and believed she always would, but he was no longer the all-powerful god of her childhood.

Caroline had taught her self-respect and a kind of independence. She washed her hair and her body as often as she could these days and she was beginning to stand up for herself against the other women in the camp. It surprised her when they seemed to accept her new confidence and treat her more as an equal. Only Jake still treated her as if she had crawled from beneath a stone.

Katya picked up her shawl and left the caravan. Caroline had not stirred. Perhaps this was best. Since Cara's death Katya had known in her heart that the time was coming when Caroline would return to her old life. If she wanted Caroline's friendship, she must earn it.

There was very little light as Katya led her horse away from the silent camp. An owl hooted, making her jump. Jake would half kill her if he caught her, but her decision, once made, was irrevocable. She was going to Pendlesham to seek out Caroline's friend.

Chapter Twenty-Six

Silas awoke to a throbbing head, his mouth filled with a foul-tasting bitterness. He had sat drinking long into the night, tumbling into bed in a state of mindless inebriation, his last defence against the fear that constantly haunted him. His creditors were hounding him for money and Caroline's solicitors had refused to advance another penny until the matter of her disappearance was solved. He suspected Helena's brother had poked his nose in where it was not wanted, but if Brockleton tried to claim Caroline's fortune for himself he would come unstuck. It was his by right!

His resentful thoughts were interrupted by the chambermaid's knock at his door. 'Enter,' he shouted irritably, and glared at the round rosy face that peered around the door. 'What is it?'

'A man is asking for you, sir. He will not give his name, but says it's urgent.'

'I'll come down presently.'

He waved her away impatiently. If it was those damned lawyers again he would tell them where to go. He was sick of being pestered for accounts of the money he had spent in the search for his ward, and suspected that interfering cousin of Lord Carlton's was egging them on.

He dressed carelessly, his head aching as he went

down to the parlour. It was all Caroline's fault: a merry dance she had led them all!

His mood lifted slightly as he saw it was not her lawyers but one of his own agents.

'Have you found her?' he barked irritably.

'I think it is her, though she stays close to the camp and I've not been able to get close to her.'

'Where is this camp?' Silas demanded. 'Was anyone else watching it?'

'I've seen no sign of Mr Carlton or his agents.' The man grimaced. 'For all he was so clever giving me the slip on the way to Exeter, stealing off in the night the way he did, I believe he lost the trail weeks ago. I only discovered the camp by accident as I was on my way to visit my sister in Salisbury. This Jake is a clever devil; they've been moving on all the time, travelling in a circle to throw off the scent – but I'm up to him now.' He tapped the side of his nose with one finger.

'How do you know they won't have disappeared again during the time it took you to come here?'

'Because I've paid one of the men to keep me in touch. They'll do anything for money – even arrange little incidents if the price is right. Besides, they don't like this woman. They want her found so that they can return to their old ways.'

Silas nodded, eyes gleaming with excitement. Caroline was within his grasp at last. He studied the agent beneath hooded lids. For the present he needed the man, but he would become expendable just as soon as he had arranged a little accident for his troublesome ward!

Chapter Twenty-Seven

Will stared moodily into the fire as the logs crackled and popped before crumbling into a fine ash. In his own mind he was certain the woman he had glimpsed in the crowds at Exeter had been Caroline, yet though he had spent the next three days searching for her, he had been unable to find any sign of either her or the gypsies.

'You saw her only from a distance,' Fitz pointed out, mild mannered as ever. 'You cannot be certain it was her.'

'I should have done more. I was so close.'

Will could not explain why he was so sure. He was both angry and confused, torn between his desire to find Caroline and hurt at her seeming rejection. She must have seen him. Must have heard him call to her!

If so, that could only mean that she had chosen to disappear.

Sally refused to believe it. 'You don't know her or you would not say it,' she had admonished him. 'She would not make us all suffer like this. She is a sweet, compassionate girl. It would be against her nature!'

Will was tortured by the thought that he had let her slip away. Since that day a nagging fear had begun to haunt his sleep – a fear that she was in peril, that if he did not find her soon it might be too late.

He had stolen away in the dark of night on that

journey to Exeter, giving Taverner's careless agent the slip and feeling well pleased with himself for it, riding hell for leather across country so that the fellow could not come up on him again.

His inquiries in the taverns of Exeter had seemed to indicate that his hopes of finding Caroline were close to realisation – a woman calling herself Madame Sapphira had set up a fortune telling booth in the square that very day.

He frowned as he tossed a log on to the fire. If he had not tarried to question the girl . . . Damnation! It was useless to speculate. Yet the fear in the gypsy's eyes when he had spoken of Caroline, was not a product of his imagination.

Why did no one else believe Caroline was with the gypsies? Sally could only weep and reproach him, while Fitz was withdrawing more and more into a world of his own. He felt a flicker of guilt as he realised he had neglected his cousin of late. He must pull himself together, remember his duty to Fitz and the estate.

He turned as his cousin came into the library, sensing his air of excitement. 'Has something happened?' he asked, his voice taut with emotion. 'Is it Caroline?'

'Not in person,' Fitz said and smiled. 'But news of her. Good news, Will. We have a visitor, a friend of hers.'

Will looked beyond him but saw nothing.

'She is in the kitchen being cared for by our good Mrs Brandon. She has travelled a long way and is chilled to the bone – hungry, too.'

'The gypsy girl! Caroline is with them. I *knew* it!'

Will felt a surge of elation. Now they would know the truth. He could hardly contain himself. He wanted to run on ahead but forced his pace to match Fitz's limping step.

They entered the kitchen where the girl was wolfing down bread and soup. She looked nervous as they entered, putting down her spoon and rising to her feet, intimidated by their rank and presence.

'Where is she?' Will demanded. 'Where is Caroline?'

'Steady, cousin,' Fitz laid a calming hand on his arm. He smiled at Katya, to put her at ease. 'Finish your meal, child. We can wait a moment.'

Katya wiped her mouth on her sleeve. 'Why do you want to find her? You won't hurt her, will you?'

'Hurt her?' Will echoed. 'Why should we hurt her? We are worried sick about her.'

'Caroline is to be my wife,' Fitz explained to Katya. 'What is your name, child? Do not be frightened. We shall not harm either you or your people. We are Caroline's friends. We love her and want only what is best for her.'

Katya gazed into his face, and saw only kindness. She nodded. 'I am called Katya. Cara and I saved Caroline's life when she fell from her horse.'

'Was she badly hurt?' Will asked hoarsely.

'At first we thought she might die, 'twas the fever, see. Cara tended her poor head where it was laid open her cures ceased the fever. Sapphira . . . Caroline would surely have died but for us.'

'We are grateful for all you did,' said Fitz. 'But why did no one tell us she was ill? We posted rewards for information and sent agents to scour the country for her.'

'Caroline does not know who she is or where she came from. We were not sure what to do.'

'What?' Will's cry startled her. 'Are you saying she has lost her memory?'

Katya cringed, her fear returning.

'How did you know where to come?' Fitz asked, in a soothing tone.

'She was kind to me once – when I came to tell you about the poacher. I knew her, but not her name – not until Mr Carlton asked for her at the fair.'

'But you knew, that day at Exeter,' Will had recovered his composure. 'Why run away? Why wait so long to tell us?'

Katya looked anxiously towards Fitz for reassurance. 'I was afraid. Jake forbade it. He said someone wanted to harm her – that she was running from someone when she fell that night.'

'Taverner!' Will growled.

'So it would seem,' Fitz agreed. He looked at Katya. 'Does Caroline know you have come to us?'

'No, 'twas my own idea. Did I do right, sir?'

'Yes, Katya.' Fitz reached out and patted her arm. 'We are deeply in your debt. You shall be well rewarded for your trouble.'

'Caroline is my friend. 'Twas for her I came.'

'You will take us to her?' Will asked urgently. 'Is it far? How soon can we be there?'

'Gently, cousin. I know you are anxious, but Katya needs to rest. We shall leave in the morning. One night can make no difference after all this time.'

Will nodded, a nerve flicking in his cheek. How could Fitz be so calm? He would not rest until Caroline was back at Pendlesham. Yet Fitz was right: one night could make no difference and the girl did look too exhausted to be dragged off in search of the encampment.

He followed his cousin from the kitchen. Only now

232

was it beginning to sink in: Caroline was *alive*. She had not run away, gone into hiding. She did not hate him after all.

'Thank God,' he choked. 'Thank *God* for restoring her to us.'

It was worrying that she had been ill and lost her memory, but they would bring her home and make her well again, and then . . .

Will's jaw hardened as he remembered that nothing had really changed. Caroline was promised to his cousin. Once she had recovered from her adventures, she would wed Fitz and in the name of honour he would have to quit Pendelsham for ever.

Chapter Twenty-Eight

Katya's disappearance was a mystery. When she did not return the first evening Jake swore furiously, then dispatched some of the men out to search for her in the woods and fields. Caroline was torn between a desire to help in the search and staying where she was in case Katya should return. In the end she remained behind, knowing that the girl would need someone to warn her of Jake's displeasure.

Jake's rage grew as the evening progressed. It disturbed her to hear his shouts and curses and she knew then that she had been right to resist his advances. She could never love such a man. He was handsome and intelligent, even decent according to his own lights. But there was a harshness and brutality in him, too. Such men were not for her. She needed kindness and tenderness. For a moment she came close to conjuring up a face in her mind, but then it slipped away again.

'Are you sure Katya didn't tell you where she was going?' Jake's sharp voice made her start. 'Is this a conspiracy between you?'

'A conspiracy – about what?'

Jake glared at her, his eyes glittering like black ice in the firelight. There was a fierce, hawklike quality about him then that made Caroline tremble inwardly, but she lifted her chin and met his gaze without flinching. He looked as if he wanted to hit her, his hands clenching and unclenching. Then he turned abruptly and strode away without another word. She gazed after him, wondering why Katya's disappearance enraged him so. What was he afraid of?

Katya had been missing for three nights now. Caroline was convinced she must be injured or dead.

'Won't you search for her again?' she begged Jake. She could not bear to think of the girl in pain and alone. She had come to love Katya as a sister.

'I'll waste no more time on her,' Jake muttered. 'We'll wait one more day then we go, with or without her.'

He stalked off, his body stiff with anger – directed, she believed, as much at her as Katya. It helped her to make up her mind. She must leave the gypsies and fend for herself. In any case, if Katya did not return, she would be friendless and at Jake's mercy, with no one to take her side.

She would hate to desert the girl. Perhaps she would walk as far as the nearest village herself and make enquiries.

Her crimson shawl was lying on the narrow cot. She picked it up and draped it around her shoulders, pausing to look at herself in the old mirror Jake had given her. The stain had worn off her skin at last, and her hair was growing, clustering around her face in little tendrils. She no longer needed to cover it with a scarf and soon she would be able to brush it back behind her ears as she had once as a child, when they'd cut it after a bout of scarlet fever.

When she was a child? How did she know that she had had scarlet fever as a young girl?

'It will soon grow, Caroline darling,' she remembered her mother saying, to soothe her tears. 'You were so ill we had to cut it short.'

There was a garden where she had played while her mother had tea on the lawns with her friends. Sunlit, happy days, before her mother died. The pictures were suddenly as clear as the certainty that her mother had died when she was still quite young. Tears trickled from the corners of her eyes. Her memory was returning!

Caroline felt strange. It was somehow frightening. More and more pictures of her childhood crowded into her consciousness. She wanted to remember everything and yet at the back of her mind was the shadow of fear that had hung over her during her first days with the gypsies.

She left the caravan, pausing for a moment to absorb the scene about her. Women talking, children playing, dogs barking and the smell of woodsmoke. Perhaps this was the last time she would see it, for she knew that once her memory returned it would all change. She would become Caroline Manners again, possibly a lady of substance.

She walked quickly out of the camp, away down the lane leading to the village. The sun had made its first appearance for days and was warm on her face. Trees were bursting their buds, green leaves starting to unfurl, and there was a hint of spring in the air. It had rained during the night; she could smell the freshness of wet grass as she crushed it beneath her feet, the scent seeming to stir memories.

Her mother and father had been killed in an accident. It had been raining then, too. Caroline could remember their faces: her aunt crying, dabbing at her eyes with a lace handkerchief that smelt strongly of lavender water. Afterwards she had gone to live with her aunt – but where? In Bath, of course! Those odd steep streets that she had seen in disjointed visions, were in the city of Bath. She had lived there until . . .

The clop of a horse's hooves intruded on her nascent reminiscences and she glanced back, more in curiosity than in trepidation. The horse was a big grey beast and even as she took in the face of its rider, he reined in alongside her, dragging his mount back on its haunches.

The rider, a thin sallow-featured man in a shabby greatcoat, dismounted. The horse immediately lowered its head to graze.

'Hello, Caroline,' the horseman said, his voice unctuous.

She stood very still then. A chill of fear snaked down her spine.

'Who . . . who are you, sir?'

'Don't pretend you don't know me,' the man said, moving closer.

'Know you? I . . . I . . .'

The floodgates that held her memories in check crashed open and suddenly she remembered it all: she knew who she was and what she was and how she had come to be riding home on the night of the storm. She saw a picture in her mind of the tree crashing down in front of her, her horse rearing in fright, a sensation of falling and the final blow to her head . . .

And above all she remembered *why* these things had happened.

'You!' she hissed.

'Yes,' said Silas Taverner. 'Did you doubt that one day our paths would cross again?'

She backed away, fearful but not yet cowed.

'Don't come near me. I have friends close at hand.'

'Don't rely on your gypsy colleagues to rush to

237

your aid,' he sneered. 'You forget, perhaps, that you are still my ward.'

'You're despicable!' Her eyes flashed with scorn. 'You betrayed a sacred trust.'

'Such passion,' Silas said, his voice thickening. 'Such fire! Would that it were mine. Why did you reject me, Caroline? I would treat you well, I swear it.'

'You knew I did not care for you, yet you tried to impose your will on me.'

'And why not? You are a beautiful woman, and I a normal man, with a healthy appetite.'

As he advanced, step by step, she retreated, her pulse racing. So many memories were rushing in on her that she was confused and bewildered, incapable of dealing with this new threat.

'Will . . .' she whispered, and her heart caught with pain. 'Sally . . . Fitz . . .'

Her eyes went to her left hand. Where was her ring? Had she been wearing it? Of course, she must have been. Her locket! That too was missing.

She covered her face with her hands as emotion overwhelmed her. It was all too much to grasp: Katya. The gypsies. Her accident . . . how worried her friends must have been not knowing where she was. So many months had passed. That must have been Will looking for her at Exeter fair. No wonder his cry had haunted her dreams ever since. How could she not have known him!

'I must go,' she cried aloud as the pain and frustration twisted inside her, her fear of Silas Taverner forgotten. 'I must get to Pendlesham.'

'I can't let you do that.' His voice was dull, resigned.

In her desire to see her loved ones again, she had not wondered why Silas was here, on this lonely road. Now she stared at him, uncomprehending, noticing the changes in his appearance. He was carelessly dressed, his cravat loosely tied and his clothes crumpled as though he had slept in them. His eyes were red-rimmed, his skin yellow in hue; he looked a sick man.

He advanced on her, a snarl twisting his mouth.

'Stay back,' she cried, holding out her hand to ward him off. 'If you come near me I shall scream.'

'And who will hear you?'

He grinned triumphantly, as if he sensed her fear. Caroline knew he was right. They were too far from the camp to be heard. Besides, who was there who would care? Jake was angry with her and Katya had disappeared: the others had always hated her.

Seeing the feverish gleam in his eyes, she backed away from Silas.

'I'm ruined,' he growled. 'I was always a gambler, that's why I left England after Henry died. I couldn't stand a debtors prison; the cold and damp would kill me. You should have signed those papers, Caroline. I would have gone away and left you alone.'

'I'll give you money,' she promised. 'We'll forget what happened. Just let me go. Please?'

She would have promised anything, but she could see that he was beyond reasoning. The wild look in his eyes warned her of the danger. He meant to kill her!

He was almost within reach of her now. She stepped back, then turned and fled, knowing her only chance was to reach the village. If she could attract attention she might yet escape; surely he would not dare harm her before witnesses. He was close behind her; so close she could hear the rasp of his breath. She gave a despairing scream as she felt his fingers pluck at her sleeve. Now she was struggling, yelling and kicking as he tried to pin her arms. With a tremendous effort she wrenched free of him and ran on, faster now, gasping and panting in her terror as he pursued her relentlessly. A hard push in her back sent her flying. She went down beneath him, skirts flying, the weight of his body crushing hers so that for a moment she could not breathe.

His face was close up against hers. She could smell cheap wine on his breath. Then his mouth was on hers, bruising her, his tongue invading her mouth. She gagged and struck out at him with her fingers, jabbing fiercely. He yelled in pain and slapped her hard across the face with the back of his hand.

'Little bitch! I'll show you who is master here.'

His hands were round her throat, his fingers tightening, restricting the flow of air. She choked as she fought for breath, tearing at his hands and trying to throw off his weight. He was too strong for her, and too heavy; his weight pinned her to the ground while his hands slowly squeezed the breath from her body. The scudding clouds above began to haze over, and a blackness closed in around her.

From somewhere close by came a terrible yell of anger. Caroline heard it as from a distance, not understanding its purport. She was slipping away – away into the depths of an endless night . . .

Will had ridden beside the carriage carrying Katya and his cousin for most of the journey, but as they approached the village beyond which the gypsies were camped he could bear it no longer. Something gnawed at his guts, telling him to hurry.

'I'm going on ahead,' he called to his cousin

through the carriage window, and pointed down the track.

He skirted the village, praying that the camp had not moved on since Katya had come to them. Even if it had, the girl had told them she would know how to follow the signs her people always left as they travelled. He was so close – so close! Surely nothing could stand between them now . . .

The screams, when they came, galvanised him into action, trusting the instinct that had led him here. Ahead of him the lane opened out on to common land and it was there that he saw the woman fighting for her life. Although he was not close enough to see her face he knew instantly that it was Caroline.

'Stop!' he bellowed, leaping from his horse. She was on the ground now, the man on top of her, his hands around her throat. She had ceased to struggle. 'Damn you!' He dragged the man off her, was unsurprised when it proved to be Silas Taverner. 'If she's dead, I'll kill you!'

He was too late. He saw her lying like a broken doll and felt despair sweep over him. A terrible rage filled him as Silas sprawled on his back, fear and bewilderment passing across his face.

'This is none of your business, sir!'

He tried to fend Will off, but Will's strength went beyond that of any normal man. He set about him, loosing a blow to the jaw of such ferocity that Silas' head felt as if it had been torn from his shoulders. He fell back, dazed, while Will bent over Caroline.

'Speak to me, my love,' he cried, helpless in his anguish.

Caroline had not moved. The certainty of her death was like a stone in his breast.

In tending to her he had taken his eye from Silas,

who reared up and stabbed at him with a knife, its blade ripping through his sleeve and scoring his arm. He leapt back, avoiding the second deadly thrust and grabbing hold of Silas's wrist.

Silas was still strong despite the way he had punished his body with too much heavy drinking this last winter, and the contest between them became desperate as they wrestled for possession of the knife. Will's fingers tightened about the other man's wrist, managing at last to break his grip on the shaft. The knife fell to the ground and was kicked away in the continuing tussle, but then Silas went for Will's throat. Will retaliated by thrusting his hand in Silas's face, forcing his head back; then he brought his knee up in his groin. Silas gave a groan of agony and twisted sideways, catching his breath before coming back at Will with a heavy punch to his chin. They exchanged several more fierce blows, circling each other warily, panting for breath.

The sound of voices made Will glance over his shoulder. Katya was running across the fields towards them; Fitz limped after her, followed by a score of gypsies. Silas took advantage of his distraction to land a hefty punch to the solar plexus, which sent Will down on his knees, but he lurched sideways, grabbing Silas's leg and pulling him down too. They struggled on the ground for a few seconds, then scrambled to their feet once more, glaring at each other.

'You'll hang,' Will muttered. 'If I don't kill you first, you'll hang.'

Hearing a shout of warning, Will glanced round again. Fitz had stopped and was aiming a pistol. The report and plume of black smoke were followed by a yelp from Silas. He was not hit, for the shot was only a warning, that immediately brought him to his senses. He threw a look of hatred at Will, before running towards his horse, grazing unconcernedly a few yards off.

About to set off in pursuit, Will heard a faint moan behind him. Caroline! A sudden surge of hope wiped Silas from his mind, and he started towards her. Katya was there before him. She dropped to her knees in the grass, bending over Caroline and lifting her gently in her arms to support her shoulders.

'Is she badly hurt?' croaked Will. 'I was sure she was dead.'

''Tis but a faint,' Katya said, without looking up. 'She is coming round now.'

Even as she spoke, Caroline's lashes fluttered against her cheeks. She gave another little moan. As Fitz came limping up to them, Will turned, fists balling at his sides as he fought for control.

'He tried to kill her,' he muttered. 'I thought she was dead, Fitz. I really thought he had killed her.'

'It's thanks to you she isn't.'

'We must go after that scoundrel!'

Fitz glanced after the galloping horse, now a quarter mile or more distant.

'You'll never catch him now. Leave him to the hangman.' He touched Will's arm. 'He'll be brought to justice never fear. Caroline is safe now, that is what matters.'

A cry of distress made them both look at Caroline. Her eyes were now fully open and she was clinging to Katya, weeping.

Fitz moved towards her. Caroline became aware of him – and beyond him Will, who stood scowling, apart from the little group.

'Please help me, Fitz,' Caroline whispered. 'I don't

243

think I can get up.' Fitz gave her his hand, assisting her to rise, his arm going comfortingly about her waist. She caught at his arm to steady herself as a wave of dizziness hit her. 'Thank you for coming.'

'Do you know me. Caroline?' he asked, looking into her face. 'Do you know who I am?'

'Yes.' She gave him a tremulous smile. 'It all came back with the shock of seeing Silas Taverner. He – he tried to seduce me the night I ran away. There was a terrible storm and I fell from my horse.' She attempted to take a step forward and cried out in pain. 'My ankle! I think I must have sprained it.'

'You must not try to walk.' Fitz turned as Will came forward. 'Will, you carry her?'

'Willingly. To your carriage?'

'No,' Katya cut in. 'We must tend her ankle first. Let us go to our camp. 'Tis but a short way.'

'Put your arm about my neck,' Will said to Caroline. 'Trust me. I shall not hurt you.'

'Thank you.'

She closed her eyes, her head resting against his shoulder, cheeks slightly flushed. Will's expression stared straight ahead as he walked ahead of Fitz and Katya, towards the camp, now visible through a line of trees. A knot of gypsies silently watched as they entered the camp. Fleetingly, Will's eyes met Jake's; the gypsy dropped his gaze. Will's chin jutted: the man had some explaining to do.

It was exquisite agony to hold Caroline like this, and yet be unable to tell her of his feelings.

Following Katya into the caravan, he laid Caroline tenderly on one of the narrow beds, then watched for a moment as the gypsy girl arranged pillows behind her. Fitz sat on the other bed, glad to rest his injured leg.

'Thank you,' Caroline whispered, looking up at Will and then quickly away. 'It was good of you to come with Fitz.'

Will nodded. In front of Fitz he could not look her in the eyes, anymore than she could him. Their feeling for each other was too transparent.

'While Katya puts a compress on your ankle, I will speak to Jake,' Fitz said. 'Then we shall take you home to Pendlesham, if that is what you want?'

'Yes. Yes, please.' Caroline caught Katya's hand. 'You are coming with us – aren't you, Katya?'

'If you want me,' the girl said shyly. 'I brought your friends – 'twas what you wanted?'

'Oh yes, indeed.' Caroline held her hand tighter. 'Why didn't you tell me where you were going? I was so worried, thinking you might be hurt.'

Katya glanced at Will nervously.

'You need to rest,' he said. 'I'll leave you together.'

His thoughts were confused as he left the caravan and stood watching Fitz speaking to the gypsies. He seemed to be in close conversation with Jake, and Will did not wish to intrude. He kicked moodily at the ground. His feelings had gone from deep despair when he thought Caroline dead, to soaring joy when he realised she was still alive. Now his despair was returning. He felt unsure of anything but the frustrated longing inside him. Caroline was not his: she belonged to Fitz. That was the end of the matter.

His cousin came up to him, his leg dragging a little on the rough ground.

'What did Jake have to say?' Will demanded. 'Did he explain why he sent us no news of her?'

'He says he was protecting her from an evil man who had harmed her. Apparently she told him something of Taverner before she lost her memory.' Fitz

245

took the engagement ring he had given her from his pocket. 'He returned this to me. He claims he took care of it so that it should not be stolen from her.'

Will scowled. 'He meant to keep that and her if you ask me.'

'Perhaps.' Fitz laid a hand on his arm. 'We have her back – and the ring. Does anything else matter?'

Will didn't answer. It still rankled that Silas Taverner had been allowed to escape. He would not be satisfied until the scoundrel was apprehended. At this moment, it would have given him great pleasure to vent his frustration on Jake.

'Revenge is never as sweet as one thinks,' Fitz said. 'Excuse me, I must see how Caroline is faring.'

Will stood aside. Perhaps Fitz was right. Caroline had been restored to them, that was enough for now.

Chapter Twenty-Nine

Caroline awoke to the softness of a feather mattress. She sighed and stretched, relishing the unaccustomed luxury. How good it was to be home again – for she felt that Pendlesham was her home now. She had no desire to go back to the house in Norfolk; besides, Fitz had been so kind and considerate to her that she could never hurt him. She glanced at the ring on her finger and frowned. Jake had kept it hidden until Fitz noticed it's absence, when he had promptly produced it. But what of the locket Will had given her? She was sure she had had it with her that night.

She supposed she had lost it on her wild ride, which was hardly to be wondered at. Even now the memory was enough to make her go cold with fear. If Jake had not found her when he did, she might have died there in the woods.

She had asked to see Jake before they left the gypsy camp.

'I want to thank you for saving my life,' she said when he came to the waggon and they were alone.

'It was nothing,' he replied. 'Anyone would have done the same.'

'I'm not sure that's true.' She smiled and held out her hand to him. 'Forgive me, Jake. I would like to think that we parted as friends.'

For a moment he hesitated, then he reached out to take her hand, pressing it briefly to his lips. 'I loved you,' he said, in a gruff tone that betrayed his emotion. 'I would have done anything to keep you with me. I lied to you when your friends came looking for you, Sapphira. You were unconscious from the start, but I knew that someone was looking for you from the very next day. I could have taken a reward then and let you go, but I wanted you for myself.'

'If you had taken the money I might be dead now. It was Silas Taverner who was looking for me then, not Lord Carlton.'

'Perhaps I truly saved your life then.'

'I'm sure you did. I am very grateful.'

'It was not gratitude I wanted from you.'

She spread her hands. 'I could give you nothing else. You must have known that from the start – when you took my ring.'

'To keep it safe for you,' he protested.

'Of course.'

It might be true, it might not. The ring was not so important. Carlton would have given her another.

A rueful grin twisted his mouth. 'You're to marry his lordship soon?'

'Yes.' Caroline's gaze dropped. 'Yes, we are to be married.'

'I shall not see you again.'

'You will not come back to Pendlesham for a visit one day?'

'No. Goodbye, Sapphira. I wish you happiness.'

He turned to leave.

'Before you go, Jake,' she said, and he stopped, looking back over his shoulder. 'Won't you tell me about Katya?'

'So . . .' His eyes narrowed. 'Cara told you as much

248

as she knew?' He nodded as she confirmed it. 'I thought she might.'

'She said that you might know who Katya's father was.'

'Yes, I know. But I swore on oath never to tell.'

'For her sake – please! She ought to know the truth.'

He shook his head, his eyes proud and cold. 'Not even for yours,' he said and went out.

Caroline stared after him. Why was he so determined to keep the secret? It could not possibly matter now.

Katya had come back to her a short time later. There was a bruise on her cheek and she had been crying.

'Who did that – Jake?'

The girl nodded. 'To punish me for fetching your friends. He warned me he would beat me if I told anyone.'

'Oh, Katya, I'm so sorry,' Caroline cried. 'I should have asked Will to take care of you.'

''Tis nothing,' Katya said and wiped her face with grimy fingers, smearing dirt on her cheek. 'His lordship made Jake stop hitting me. ''Twould have been worse if 'twere not for him.' She gave Caroline a shy smile. 'He's a kind gentleman. I like him. I'm glad you're to wed with him, milady.'

'Katya!' Caroline wagged a finger at her. 'If you address me as milady again I shall beat you myself. I am Caroline, and you are my dear friend, not my servant. We have been as sisters these past weeks and I intend that it shall stay that way.'

Katya sniffed and rubbed her sleeve beneath her nose.

'Shall I have to learn to talk proper then?'

'Only if you want to,' Caroline replied and reached out to squeeze her arm. 'Would you like to become a fine lady, Katya?'

'Me – a lady? 'Tis as likely as pigs flying!'

'Well, we'll see,' Caroline said. 'When we get to Pendlesham I'll find you some pretty dresses to wear. You would like that, would you not?'

Katya had agreed that it would be rather pleasant to wear finery.

Caroline smiled as she thought of their arrival at Pendlesham the previous evening. Mrs Brandon had taken one horrified look and ordered hot baths for them both. Katya had been suspicious about the whole business but once she discovered how agreeable it was to lie in the scented water she had refused to get out until it turned cold.

It was going to be fun helping Katya discover how different life could be among the aristocracy, Caroline thought and then yawned sleepily. There came a tap at her door, and she turned her head as a maid entered carrying a tray of rolls, strawberry jam and hot chocolate. She sat up, suddenly hungry.

'Good morning, Rosa.'

'Good morning, Miss Manners,' the maid replied. 'Will you be wanting to dress after breakfast? Only Mrs Brandon said you might want to stay in bed for a day or so, seeing as how you'd been ill and all.'

'I was ill for a time,' Caroline said, 'but I'm recovered now. Yes, I shall get up after breakfast.' She looked at the neat tray with its embroidered white cloth and the delicate porcelain. 'How lovely this all looks. Thank you.'

'It's a pleasure, miss,' Rosa said and gave her a curious glance. Her mistress had never remarked on such things in the past.

'Is Katya still asleep?'

'Mrs Brandon said as the young person was up early asking if there was a job she could do, miss. I think Cook sent her out to pick some herbs from the kitchen garden.'

'Thank you,' Caroline said. 'When you see her, send her to me, will you?'

'Yes, miss.' Rosa hesitated, her mouth drooping at the corners. 'Is she to be your maid then, miss?'

'No, she is my friend,' Caroline said. 'You will continue to look after me as always, Rosa.' She touched her hair ruefully. 'I want you to do something with this later if you can.'

Rosa was all smiles again. 'I'll have my work cut out, miss. Still, I've always thought it would suit you a bit shorter. Curls are all the rage now. You'll set a new fashion, I'll be bound.'

Caroline laughed and sipped her chocolate. 'Don't forget to send Katya to me, will you? I want to find her some decent clothes to wear. You and Mary can alter some of mine for now, then we'll have new ones made in time for the wedding.'

'That reminds me, miss,' Rosa said. 'There's a visitor arrived this morning. Set the household all upside down she has.'

'A visitor?' Caroline was puzzled. 'Is it Mrs Croxley?'

She was expecting Sally, but not for at least another week.

'No, miss. Mr Carlton said she was his mother, and that she would have the blue room.'

'I thought she was in Italy,' Caroline murmured. 'Thank you, Rosa. You may go now. I'll ring when I need you.'

Caroline lay back against the pillows and sipped

251

her chocolate. Fitz had told her that Will's mother was married to an Italian count. Rosa had made no mention of the husband, so she must have come alone: it would be interesting to meet her. She wondered if the rift between her and Will that arose from her precipitate re-marriage, had been healed.

Caroline's thoughts were suspended as the door opened and Katya peeped round, looking a little apprehensive.

'Come in,' Caroline said, patting the bed. 'Sit beside me. Have you had your breakfast yet?'

'Long ago,' Katya said and laughed. 'In the kitchen with Mrs Bambury. She's his lordship's cook, you know. She's been here since she was a child, started out as a scullerymaid and worked her way up. She remembers his lordship and Mr Carlton when they were lads.' Katya's eyes sparkled with mischief. ' 'Tis more I know about them than you do. I've been drinking tea with her for ages.'

'Then you certainly will know much more than I do,' Caroline said. 'You can tell me everything while I eat. Then we'll find you some clothes to wear.' Caroline inspected the dress Katya was wearing. 'Where on earth did you get that?'

'It belonged to Mrs Bambury's niece. Don't you like it?'

The dress was a dull blue and had obviously seen better days. It was however, as a ballroom gown to sackcloth compared with most of the clothes Katya had owned.

'I think I can find you something nicer,' Caroline said and reached across the bed to take hold of Katya's hand. 'We're going to have such fun, Katya. I'm going to buy you pretty clothes and lots of presents.'

Katya's eyes sparkled with tears. 'I don't deserve it,' she whispered, and pulled her hand away from Caroline's. 'You don't know what I've done.'

'What do you mean?'

'I kept this from you.' Katya took something from her pocket and held it out. 'I never meant to steal it, but I wasn't sure it was yours at first. It was so pretty, I couldn't give it back.'

'My locket,' Caroline said and opened the box, touching the smooth, buttery surface of the gold reverently with her finger. 'I thought I had lost it. Thank you for taking care of it for me, Katya. It is very precious to me.'

'Did his lordship give it to you?'

'No . . .' Caroline's cheeks were pink as she closed the box and slipped it beneath her pillow. 'It was a present from someone else.'

'Are you angry with me for not giving it to you before?'

'No.' Caroline sighed. 'Had I known I might have been. Perhaps it was just as well.'

'What do you mean?'

Caroline shook her head. 'It matters not.' She reached for a box on the table beside the bed and opened it, taking out a pretty gold and pearl pendant with a fancy chain that she had bought for herself in London. 'This is for you, Katya, to thank you for being my good friend.'

Katya hesitated. 'I would rather have the bracelet Jake made for you,' she said awkwardly. 'If you don't mind?'

'Have them both,' Caroline said. 'Yes, please do, Katya. I have bracelets enough. I would like you to have them. I would have given you Jake's bracelet long ago if I could.'

'Yes, I know.' Katya slipped the bracelet onto her wrist then turned so that Caroline could fasten the clasp of the pendant. She kissed Caroline on the cheek. 'Cara said you would bring bad luck when I found you, but she was wrong, you've brought good fortune to me.'

'I want you to be happy with us,' Caroline said. 'You won't miss Jake too much, will you?'

'A little,' Katya admitted, a wistful look in her eyes. 'I've always loved him, but he doesn't care about me – he never has.'

Caroline wondered if she ought to tell her the reason Jake and the others had been so unkind, but decided against it. It would be pointless to raise false hopes in the girl. She knew that Katya's father had been an aristocrat but Jake had refused to divulge the secret that only he knew. There was no way that Caroline could help her to find her family. Besides, they might prefer not to know her. No, it was best to let her remain in ignorance, at least for the moment.

''Tis hurtful to love someone who loves you not in return,' Katya said. ''Tis best to forget. Don't you think?'

'Yes,' Caroline said and her eyes closed briefly. 'Much the best – if you can.'

For a moment the pain swept over her. She slid her hand beneath the pillow, touching the box with Will's locket inside.

'Much better not to think about it. We'll find lots of exciting things to do, Katya. Neither of us will have time to be sad.' She stretched and yawned. 'This will not do! I must get up. We have a guest . . . someone I very much want to meet.'

*   *   *

254

The woman was sitting in a chair by the small parlour window. Her head was half turned away and Caroline could only see her profile. Then she turned towards Caroline and it was apparent that she must once have been a woman of great beauty. Her skin was still soft, her mouth gentle, but there were lines about her eyes and she had an air of weariness.

'No, please don't get up,' Caroline said. 'I thought you might be here. You're Will's mother aren't you?'

'And you are Caroline – may I call you that? I am Margaret.'

She was dressed completely in black. Caroline guessed what had brought her back to Pendlesham.

'Of course, Margaret. I hope we shall be friends?'

'I hope so, too. Won't you sit with me for a while?' The Countess Santini waved her hand towards a chair. 'I believe I may have made things difficult for you, my dear. I should not have come if I had realised you and Fitz were about to be married. Perhaps I should go away so as not to spoil your wedding arrangements.'

'We shall not be married for a few weeks yet,' Caroline replied. 'Besides, you must think of this as your home. You will always be welcome here, and you need not attend any parties or other social gatherings, unless it is your wish. I'm sure Fitz would agree with me.'

'Fitz would never be other than kind.' The countess sighed deeply. 'Did Will tell you about my husband?'

'No. I supposed that you had suffered a bereavement,' Caroline replied. 'Was it recent?'

Her sigh was profound.

'Two months since he died. But he had been ill for a long time. I stayed in Italy until everything was settled, then I came back. I have independent means,

255

you understand. Giorgio left me well provided for. He was always so good to me, so thoughtful. I shall miss him terribly.' She blinked hard and dabbed at her eyes with a handkerchief. 'So foolish, to be crying at my age! But we were in love, you see. After all these years.'

'You were very lucky then,' Caroline said. 'Love like that is rare, I think?'

'Oh yes, quite exceptional,' Margaret replied with her sad smile. 'I was less fortunate in my first marriage.'

'You were not happy with Mr Carlton?' Caroline looked at her in surprise.

'No, I was not happy. I never loved him, you see. One should never marry for any other reason, my dear. But of course, I have no need to tell you that. No one could fail to love Fitz. He is such a darling.'

'Yes . . . yes, he is.'

Caroline turned away, a lump forming in her throat.

'Is something wrong? Have I upset you?'

'No.' Caroline fought down her emotion. 'No, of course not. I – I have not been well. Excuse me. I must speak to Mrs Brandon.'

She walked quickly from the room before her emotions could shame her.

Caroline rose from her bed in the small hours, unable to sleep. She pulled on a silk wrapping gown and went over to the window, looking out at the gardens. It was not quite dawn.

What was she to do? She had tried to suppress her feelings, but it was impossible to shut them out any longer. She wasn't in love with Fitz, and never would be. He was kind, gentle, everything she had sought in a husband. And she was truly fond of him. But she was no longer sure that fondness and respect were solid enough foundations on which to build a marriage.

Once she had believed that romantic love was a myth; now she knew it was possible to love someone so much that the pain of it was almost physical. Or was it because her heart was being tugged one way while her sense of decency and loyalty tugged her another?

She had scarcely seen Will since her return to Pendlesham. She believed he was avoiding her deliberately, for the sake of decency.

Margaret on the other hand, suspected that he was staying out much of the time in order to avoid *her*.

'We don't get on as well as I should like,' she confided to Caroline, as they took tea together in the parlour. 'My fault of course. He will never forgive me for remarrying.'

'Surely he does not still censure you after all these years?'

'He was always a stubborn, sensitive boy,' his mother said, with an indulgent smile. 'I fear I hurt him badly.'

'Perhaps you should explain that your marriage to his father was not happy?' Caroline suggested.

'And hurt him more?' Margaret shook her head. 'He thinks of his father as a paragon. His memories of him are sacred and I would not destroy them for the world.'

On that note their conversation had ended.

Now, as Caroline gazed from her bedroom window, the figure of a man came into sight, pacing, hands clasped behind his back. In the half light his face was unrecognisable but the limp identified him. So Fitz, too, was restless.

It would be too cruel to break her promise to him now. But would it be fair to marry him, knowing she was in love with his cousin? Perhaps love would come with marriage, perhaps this feeling for Will would fade with the passing years. Sighing, Caroline returned to her bed.

It was a terrible tangle and she did not know what to do for the best. She could only wait and hope that somehow her dilemma would resolve itself.

Chapter Thirty

'Could I have a moment of your time, Caroline?' Will asked her one morning a few days later. Then, as she hesitated, 'I shall not keep you long.'

'Of course.' Caroline controlled her cowardly urge to run away, forcing herself to smile. 'I am in no hurry. I was simply going for a walk.'

She avoided looking directly at him, but as she followed him to the library she could not help but notice the strength and vitality that seemed to radiate from the man. He carried himself with such an air of authority, such power, that it struck her he would be a worthy custodian of a great estate like Pendlesham. Immediately she felt disloyal for comparing him with Fitz. It wasn't fair. Fitz had suffered so much, through war, it was not to be wondered at if sometimes he seemed as if he had lived his whole life during the first half of it, and only a husk remained of the warrior he once was.

In the library a log fire crackled and hissed and the shell of burning pine mingled with the fragrance of beeswax and dried rose petals from the previous summer. On the shining surface of a beautiful drum table several piles of documents were set out; it was to these that Will directed her attention.

'Carlton asked me to take charge of your affairs. I've been in touch with your lawyers. It seems that

Taverner gambled away your house in Norfolk. He had the power of attourney to sign the papers. I'm afraid that means we cannot recover the property.'

'It doesn't matter. I never liked the house. I would not want to return there even if . . .' She broke off mid-sentence. 'You look serious, Will. Is there more?'

'He has stolen some property from your London house: a painting and some silver, which have no doubt been sold. Also your lawyers advanced him five hundred guineas to employ agents to search for you.'

'So that he could use the information to kill me?' She gave a brittle laugh. 'That hardly seems a just return on my investment, does it?'

'Silas Taverner is deeply in debt,' Will said without looking at her. He seemed vexed and she wondered what troubled him, but his voice was without emotion as he went on, 'I think we must accept that the money cannot be recovered. However, I have made certain that he cannot interfere in your affairs again.'

'Thank you for that.' Caroline ran her hand along a line of handsome leather bound books and took one out. She flicked through it without reading a word. 'The money is not important – unless I am ruined?'

'Far from it. To be fair Silas Taverner had set your affairs in good order before he left for India. Whatever he has done since, he was a good steward of your fortune in earlier years.'

'I think he must be ill – or mad.' Caroline replaced the book and shivered as she suddenly felt cold. 'Someone just walked over my grave. I suppose he has not been caught yet?'

'No, not yet. We have people searching for him.' Will was silent for a moment, then, 'You need not fear him, Caroline. Fitz has given orders that his keepers are to be armed at all times. Wherever you go on the estate there will be someone to watch over you. If Taverner sets one foot on the estate he will be apprehended. I give you my word he will not harm you.'

'I am not afraid. Not here with Fitz – and you.' She turned a radiant smile on him. 'I have been told that it was you who saved me from Silas when he tried to kill me. I have not thanked you. I believe you also came to look for me in Exeter. I'm sorry I ran away. Jake told me that you meant to harm me, and I did not know it was you. Please forgive me for all the trouble I've caused you.'

'It was no trouble.' His manner was stiff, almost formal. 'Not to remember your own name – that must have been a terrible experience.'

'Yes, it was.'

For a moment Caroline relived the terror of that first awakening, the awful blankness, the fear that had swept over her when she realised she did not know her own name. She closed her eyes, clutching at the back of a chair.

'Caroline – are you faint?'

Will was standing beside her when she opened her eyes, his expression anxious. She drew a sharp breath, weak with longing to be in his arms. She ached for him to kiss her the way he had the morning they quarrelled in the garden. The same morning she had promised herself to Fitz.

'Caroline?'

She reached out her hand to touch him, inviting his embrace, then froze. No – she must not weaken again. It would be a betrayal of her promise to Fitz, a betrayal too of her own beliefs and standards.

'It's nothing,' she said weakly, and moved away to stand with her back deliberately towards him. 'I like

261

your mother. You should spend some time with her, Will. She tells me she intends to go away again soon.'

'She will do as she pleases, of course.'

He sounded stiff and awkward. Unable to maintain her aloofness, Caroline turned to face him.

'Will . . . I have no right to say this, but have you ever thought about why she married again so soon? Have you ever tried to see if from her point of view?'

'Because she wished it, I would imagine. She has always done as she pleased.'

'Don't you think your judgement is harsh?'

'Is it?' His manner was unrelenting. 'She could not have loved my father, or she would not have married again so soon. Do you not agree?'

'Her first marriage was arranged for her. She was very young, biddable, she obeyed her father. Was it so very wrong of her to take her chance of happiness when it came?'

Will was silent for a minute or more and Caroline wondered if she had gone too far, then he said: 'Are you concerned for her?'

'Not just for her,' Caroline said. 'If you could forgive her you might be able to forgive yourself.'

He did not answer. She could see that her words had caused him to reflect and perhaps those reflections would be painful and best done in solitude.

'Thank you for looking after my affairs,' she said in a soft voice. Now, if you will excuse me, I must find Katya.'

She walked from the room before he could answer.

She found Katya with Fitz in the music room. Caroline paused on the threshold, listening to them laughing together. She smiled at the happy sound: they had taken to one another at once, seeming like old friends after just a few days. The gypsy girl and the aristocrat. Such a contrast!

With her hair freshly washed, and wearing one of Caroline's gowns, Katya looked prettier than ever. She turned as Caroline entered, her face lighting up as she saw her.

'His lordship has been trying to teach me to play the flute,' she said, and put a little silver instrument to her lips. The resulting notes were far from musical.

'I see I have been wasting my time,' Fitz said with a quizzical lift of his brows. He stood up. 'Caroline, my dear . . . have you come to rescue me from this imp?'

'Only if you wish to be rescued,' Caroline replied. 'I have been thinking that when Sally arrives we might go up to town. Katya might enjoy it, and I would like to buy some new clothes for us both.'

'We shall all go,' Fitz agreed at once. 'I could not allow you to go alone, not until Taverner has been apprehended.'

'Surely he will not attempt to harm me again? He has no money, no credit, nowhere to live even, now that my house is barred to him.'

'Desperate men may try desperate things, but we shall not dwell upon that.' Fitz smiled at her. 'Of course you must buy some new clothes. And I shall provide this young lady with a suitable wardrobe.'

'Please may I go and visit Mrs Bambury, sir?' Katya pulled at his arm. 'Her nephew is bringing some kittens for her to rear.'

'Good mouse catchers, I trust,' Fitz murmured, his eyes crinkling with amusement. 'Away with you then, child, since you prefer the prospect of kittens to my music lessons.'

'I'll come back soon,' Katya promised, and ran away laughing.

'A charming child,' Fitz remarked after she had gone. 'I like your young friend very much, Caroline.'

'She must be sixteen or more,' Caroline replied. 'Not really a child. Though everyone alludes to her as one.'

'She has such an air of innocence.' He looked thoughtful. 'Remarkable after the life she's had, don't you think?'

'Yes, it is. But you have done wonders for her. I've never seen her as happy as she has been these past few days. I'm glad you like her, Fitz. I want to keep her with us. She has nowhere else to go. It would be unthinkable that she should return to the gypsies; they were unkind to her. I believe she was often beaten.'

'Be reassured, I would not dream of sending her away,' Fitz said, ofering her his arm. 'Shall we take a stroll in the gallery? The wind is rather cold out this morning.'

'I've seen you out on colder ones,' Caroline said. 'You go to the summerhouse very early sometimes, don't you?'

'Sometimes. When I can't sleep.'

'Does your leg still pain you a great deal?'

'Now and then.' He laughed ruefully. 'I fear it will be an accurate weather vane.'

'I'm sorry.'

He made a dismissive sound.

'Don't be. I manage very well.'

'Of course.'

He glanced at her face. 'Are you feeling better now, Caroline?'

'Yes – much – thank you.' She met his eyes and then glanced away. They had reached the long picture gallery now; the walls were lined with row upon row of portraits. 'Are these *all* your ancestors?'

'Yes, I'm very much afraid they are,' Fitz murmured, a note of amusement in his voice. 'Some of them are formidable, are they not?'

'A little,' Caroline admitted, staring up at a man with a fierce expression and eyebrows like two black slugs. 'Who was he?'

'The sixth Lord Carlton,' Fitz replied. 'And a tyrant by all accounts. They say his wife had a terrible time of it – this is she . . .'

Fitz's voice trailed away. He was staring fixedly at the portrait of a young woman. Caroline glanced up, wondering what had attracted his attention, then she gasped.

'She looks like Katya!' she exclaimed. 'Look at those eyes and the nose, her hair is somewhat different but their features are remarkably similar.'

'Yes, I am inclined to agree,' Fitz said thoughtfully. 'I felt I had seen Katya before when she came here the first time, but I could not place it in my mind. Now I realise the likeness is in the portrait. I always liked this particular one as a boy.'

Caroline bit her lip. It was not her place to speculate on the possibility of a common paternity between Fitz and Katya, yet what other explanation could there be?

'I've always known that my father had a good reason for allowing Jake's people to use the woods as they liked,' Fitz said. 'Now I think I begin to understand.'

Caroline almost laughed aloud. Fitz had arrived at the same conclusion unassisted by her.

'Cara believed that Katya's father was an aristocrat, though she did not know his name. Her mother was Jake's father's third wife. Cara told me the shock of her betrayal killed him and that is why Jake treated

265

Katya the way he did. He has never been able to forgive her for being born.'

'Then . . . then she must indeed be my half-sister.' There was a glint of anger in his eyes as he spoke. 'That she should have suffered as she did! All those years of beatings and deprivation . . . How could my father have allowed her to be brought up with gypsies?'

'Perhaps he expected them to treat her better.'

'If only I had known!'

Caroline squeezed his arm. 'You cannot blame yourself.'

'No.' Fitz glanced down at her. 'Thanks to you I have a chance to put things right. We shall take good care of her together, Caroline.'

'Yes.' She hesitated, then, 'Shall you tell her who she is?'

'Not yet. It might confuse her. I want her to learn how to behave as a lady, Caroline, grow accustomed to our way of life. But it will be difficult for her. She must be allowed to proceed at her own pace. Most of all, I want her to be happy.'

'You are such a good man, Fitz. I am so very fond of you.'

'Are you, my dear?' Fitz took her hand in his and raised it to his lips. 'That is indeed fortunate, for I am fond of you.'

There was such a melancholy look in his eyes that Caroline's heart jerked. She felt that he was waiting for her to open her heart to him; that he could see into her mind and know her true feelings.

'Fitz . . . ' she began. 'I . . . '

She was interrupted by the sound of running feet. Katya burst into the room, carrying a small ginger kitten, her eyes shining.

266

'Mrs Bambury says 'tis mine if I want it,' she cried. 'If you say I may keep it, sir.'

'It is yours,' Fitz said at once. 'But you must do something for me in return.'

'Oh yes,' she said. 'Anything you ask, milord.'

'You must call me Fitz when we are all private together,' he commanded. 'And you should properly say, "It is mine if I wish," Katya. A small thing, but pleasant to the ear.'

'Yes, sir. I know 'twud be proper to speak as you and Caroline do but 'tis very hard to remember.'

'You must try though,' Fitz said. 'To please me – if you will?'

'Yes, sir – Fitz. I shall try to please you, for you have been proper kind to me.'

Caroline held out a reassuring hand. 'You will learn in time,' she said kindly. 'Come with me now. I think you should learn to dance too. Would you like that?'

'I think so.' Katya screwed up her forehead doubtfully. 'Is it hard?'

'No, it's fun,' Caroline replied. 'Perhaps if we ask her nicely, the countess might play for us.'

They went out together. Caroline glanced back over her shoulder. Fitz was staring out of the window at the far end of the gallery, back in his private world – a world no outsider would ever be allowed to enter.

The knock came at Caroline's door as she was dressing for dinner.

'Enter,' she called out, thinking it must be Katya.

The door opened and the countess entered.

'Is it convenient, my dear? I wanted to speak to you alone if I may?'

'Of course. Please come in. I'm almost ready.' Caroline turned to Rosa. 'Thank you. I can manage now.' Then, when the maid had departed, she turned to the older woman. 'Would you help me with my pearls, please?'

'These are lovely,' Margaret said as she fastened the heavy gold clasp. 'Did Carlton give them to you?'

'They belonged to my mother; at least, to the woman I believed was my mother.'

'You must be fond of them then.'

She asked no more questions and Caroline was relieved. She had spoken of her true mother only once to Fitz, letting him know that she would understand if he wished to be relieved of his obligation to her. He had assured her that her illegitimacy was of no consequence. It was now a closed subject and Caroline preferred not to ponder it too often, though of course the dream still returned occasionally. At least she understood it now, and it no longer caused her distress. It was an old tragedy, long buried and best forgotten.

'I am indeed fond of the necklace,' she replied. 'But you wanted to speak to me?'

'My son and I have just talked at great length,' Margaret said. 'I believe we understand each other better now – and for that I think I have you to thank?'

Caroline kissed her cheek. 'If I helped I am pleased. I know it was not my place to speak. Nevertheless, I'm glad it has turned out so well.'

'My son thinks a great deal of you, Caroline.'

She blushed and turned away to pick up her fan. 'He thinks me a suitable wife for his cousin; as I shall try to be.'

'Are you sure that's what *you* want, my dear?'

Caroline's fingers tightened on the silver handle of

her fan. 'Why of course,' she said. 'Whatever can you mean?'

'Nothing. It was but a momentary fancy. Do forgive me.'

'There is nothing to forgive.' Caroline faced her, a smile on her lips. 'Perhaps we should go down now? We must not keep the others waiting.'

'Certainly,' the countess agreed. 'I understand you leave for London the day after tomorrow?'

'Yes. I was to have purchased my bride clothes months ago. We have decided to marry in June, and Fitz will have the banns called in May.'

'I may not be here when you return from town. I have decided to return to Italy. I prefer the climate there. In any case I came back only to make peace with my son.'

'But you must stay for my wedding,' protested Caroline. 'Please say you will?'

'If you really wish it?'

'Yes, of course I do.'

They left the room together and were joined by Katya, who was on her way downstairs. Her face was a little flushed and her eyes suspiciously red. Caroline suspected she had been crying and would have dearly liked to ask the reason. Instead, she smiled benevolently at the girl.

'You look pretty this evening,' she whispered, just before they entered the dining room. 'When Sally comes we are all going to London to buy you some new gowns of your own. You will enjoy that, I'm sure.'

Fitz came to take her in to dinner then and she missed the look of alarm in Katya's eyes. When she glanced back Will had his mother on one arm and Katya on the other.

How pleasant it all was, Caroline thought. They were already a family, everyone laughing and talking at once. Katya was smiling now. Whatever the reason for her tears it could not have been serious.

Chapter Thirty-One

It was early when Katya slipped out of the house. The dew was still on the grass and it was a bright, fresh morning. She bent down to slip off the little leather slippers Caroline had given her; it would be a shame to spoil them.

The wetness of the grass felt cool and refreshing on her feet. She wriggled her toes in sheer delight, then glanced back at the house nervously, wondering if she were being watched. Would they be angry with her? Everyone had been so kind to her, but she was beginning to feel stifled in that big house. There were so many rules, so many things to remember. Especially now that they all seemed to want her to become a lady.

Katya wasn't sure if that was what she really wanted. At first it had all seemed so wonderful, and it was pleasant to take warm baths at whim, even though she felt a twinge of guilt that the poor maids had to carry jug after jug of hot water up to her room to fill the porcelain hip bath. She had offered to take her bath in the kitchen, but that had caused cries of horror and dismay. Ladies did not bathe in the kitchen!

'I just thought 'twud save so much work,' she'd said to Caroline when they were alone. 'The servants have so much to do.'

'That's what servants are for,' Caroline explained. 'We pay them to look after us. Lord Carlton is very considerate of his people, but they are here to work.'

It seemed very strange to Katya to be waited on. She was not even allowed to put coal on the fire in case she made her hands dirty. Her hands had always been dirty when she lived with Jake's people. She had thought of it as natural, though it was true that cleanliness was preferable.

She sometimes thought she would have been more comfortable working in the kitchens with Mrs Bambury. She liked the cosy atmosphere and the appetising smells from the oven. It was fascinating watching Mrs Bambury at work, especially when she was preparing a special dinner. Katya had never encountered such exotic dishes: fish cooked whole and served up on a plate with toasted almonds and rich sauces; birds simmered in wine; meat baked in pastry shells with fancy twirls. And the desserts! All that cream and fruit and sugar: she had never tasted the likes of it.

'I should like to do what you do,' she had said once to the cook. 'Would you teach me?'

'It would be a pleasure,' Mrs Bambury replied, wiping her floury hands on a clean, damp cloth. 'But you must ask his lordship's permission first.'

Katya had run eagerly to the library. She had found his lordship there reading one of those books he seemed so fond of, and she had spilled out her desire to become a cook. To her disappointment he had looked at her in silence for a few minutes, then given a little shake of his head.

'I'm sorry, Katya,' he'd said. 'I could not permit it. It would be unseemly.'

Katya had not dared to argue, even though she was

not sure what 'unseemly' meant. His lordship's word was law. She both liked and respected him, and she did her best to please him, no matter what.

But it was so hard to behave like a lady when she had always been allowed to run wild.

It was only now that Katya realised how free her life had been. Oh, there had been blows and harsh words often enough, but no one expected anything of her. No one was ever disappointed, because no one cared. She did her chores for Cara and then she was free to roam wherever she wished, behave as she pleased.

She was going to the woods now. It was April and there would be violets and bluebells if you knew where to find them. She wanted to pick some for Caroline.

A little frown creased her forehead. Caroline's friend Mrs Croxley had arrived the previous day. She was an attractive, charming lady, but Katya felt there was disapproval in her eyes when they dwelt on her, as if she were wondering why Caroline had befriended an ignorant gypsy girl.

When they'd been in the gypsy caravan, Caroline and Katya had been like sisters; they had only each other's company and it had drawn them close. Things were so different now. Caroline was still as kind and generous as ever, but other people made demands on her. She had servants to look after her, and Rosa guarded that privilege jealously. Then there was the Countess Santini, his lordship, Mr Carlton and now Mrs Croxley. Katya could not help feeling a little left out, especially in the evenings, when they all discussed politics and talked about people like the Prince Regent as if they had actually met him. Katya knew nothing about the Corn Laws – which Caroline said were iniquitous and should be abolished – or of the rival Whig and Tory parties; she did not know who Lord Bryon was, nor could she understand why everyone so admired his verses, which sounded strange to her when Caroline read them aloud.

Not being able to follow these conversations made her ashamed of her ignorance. More and more lately she found herself wishing they were back in the gypsy camp.

Katya spent a long time gathering wild flowers, cones and mushrooms. She was feeling much more cheerful by the time her baskets were full. Being in the woods had healed her free spirit and she was ready to go back now.

It was only as she turned homewards that she was alerted by a twig cracking behind her. Her heart caught with fright and she glanced over her shoulder wondering if it was that terrible man who had tried to strangle Caroline.

'Who's there?' she cried. 'Come out so I can see you!'

For a moment nothing happened, then someone stepped out from behind a tree. Katya's skin prickled, then she drew a breath of relief.

'You,' she cried. 'You scared me. What are you doing here?'

'I've as much right here as you,' Jake declared, scowling at her temerity. 'You look different. What have you done to your hair?'

Katya touched her hair with a nervous gesture. 'I washed it and brushed it,' she said. 'Don't you like it?'

'It looks all right,' Jake admitted grudgingly. 'That's an expensive dress. I suppose *she* gave it to you?'

'Caroline has given me many things.'

Jake reached out and caught her wrist, touching the silver bangle. 'I made that for her.'

'She gave it to me. I didn't steal it – it's mine!'

For a moment his fingers tightened on the silver trinket as though he would snatch it from her arm, then he let her go. 'Keep it if you want,' he said. 'No doubt she'll give you better things.'

'Nothing could be better than this. Unless you made me one for myself.' Katya's cheeks were flushed and she did not dare to look at him.

'Why should I do that?' he said, his tone surly.

She stared at him defiantly. 'That's right, you never made anything for me because you never cared about me. I always loved you, always. But you treated me like the dirt beneath your feet.'

Jake's eyes narrowed. 'Did I? And why was that do you think?'

'I don't know.' Tears stung her eyes but she brushed them away. 'I've never known why you hate me.'

'Best you don't,' he said. 'You never belonged with us. Get back to them as want you.'

'I'm going,' Katya said with a sudden flash of fire. 'I wouldn't come back to you if you begged me.'

'I'm not like to do that. It's as well she took you. We're well rid of you.'

Katya recoiled from him. How could he be so cruel, even after she had declared her love for him?

'I don't know what I've done,' she hissed. 'But it could not be so bad that I deserve such words.'

And then she turned before he should see her crying.

'Katya!' he called after her. 'Katya, come back!'

She heard him . . . but heeded him not.

* * *

She sped across the lawns towards the rear of the house, sobbing. Her eyes blinded by tears, she didn't see Will crossing her path and they almost collided. At the last moment she tried to brush past him, but he caught hold of her arm.

'Tears, Katya?' he asked. 'What's wrong?'

'Nothing. Let me go. Please let me go.'

'Not until you tell me what has upset you. Come, child, surely you're not afraid of me? I would never hurt you.'

'I'm not a child,' she cried. 'Why does everyone call me a child? I'm eighteen – and I'm not afraid of you.'

'Eighteen? You look much younger.'

'It's because I'm too thin,' she said defensively. 'Cara said I had no womanly curves.'

'I would not agree with that.' Will smiled at her. 'You're a pretty girl, Katya, and I apologise for calling you child. Will you forgive me?'

He took out his handkerchief and gently wiped the tears from her cheeks, then handed it to her.

'All right,' she said, sniffing.

'Now – do you want to tell me why you were crying?'

She shook her head.

'Has someone hurt you?'

'No, sir.'

'My name is Will – remember? We are your friends, Katya.' He studied her damp features. 'You are happy here, aren't you?'

'Yes.' Katya blew her nose on his handkerchief. 'It was nothing – nothing that matters.'

'You don't want to tell me?'

Katya hung her head. She did not dare to tell him that she had seen Jake in the woods; he did not like

Jake on account of his keeping Caroline. He might even tell the keepers to send him away. For all her resentment towards Jake, it was a comfort to know he was close by.

'Caroline is taking me to London,' she said at last. 'I don't know how to be a lady: I can't understand politics or Lord Byron's poems. His lordship won't let me learn to be a cook. And Mrs Croxley doesn't like me. She thinks I'm a dirty gypsy.'

'What a catalogue of woes!' Will laughed suddenly. 'Now I'm sure Sally doesn't think anything of the sort. You spend so much time in the bath, you must be the cleanest person at Pendlesham.'

'It makes work for the maids,' Katya said, frowning. 'But they won't let me bath in the kitchen.'

'Oh, Katya!' Will bent his head to kiss her gently on the mouth. 'Don't let them change you too much. You are perfect as you are.'

'You don't mean that.' She blushed a fiery red. 'You're teasing me the way his lordship does.'

'No, I'm paying you a compliment,' Will said. 'When Caroline takes you to a dance in London a lot of men will say things like that to you.'

'They won't mean them either. I'm not perfect. I'm jealous and I don't talk proper and . . .'

'You are very human, honest and likeable,' Will said. 'I'm not perfect either, Katya.'

'Caroline is,' Katya said. 'I wish I was like her.'

'No . . .' Will smiled in an odd way. 'Caroline isn't quite perfect. But you mustn't tell her I said so.'

Katya tipped her head to one side, her eyes knowing as she looked at him. 'You love her, don't you?'

'What makes you think that?' The laughter died from Will's face.

'I just know,' Katya said simply. 'His lordship is

kind and good. But he doesn't love her the way you do.'

'You know nothing about these things.' Will's expression hardened. 'You would be wise to keep your opinions to yourself, young lady. Otherwise you might find yourself in trouble.'

'I'm sorry. I did not mean to upset you.' She dropped her eyes, gazing down at her feet which were still bare and filthy. 'I don't know how to behave as a lady. I don't know the right things to say. I try to please everyone, but I *can't*.'

'It doesn't matter. Don't cry again, Katya. I haven't got another handkerchief and I fear that one is ruined.'

She looked up, her eyes suspicious. 'Now you're teasing me.'

'Yes, I'm teasing you,' Will admitted. 'I wanted to make you smile. Please don't cry anymore. You'll have red eyes, and then Caroline will be cross with me for upsetting you.'

'I'm not crying.' She wiped her eyes. 'I'd better go now or my flowers will wilt.'

'That would never do!'

She gave him a watery smile. 'Goodbye then. And thank you for the handkerchief. I'll wash it and give it back to you.'

It was all so confusing, Katya thought as she padded on towards the house. She was sure that Will loved Caroline, and she was almost certain that Caroline loved him. So why was she engaged to marry his lordship?

To Katya it was very straightforward: if you loved someone you did not marry someone else.

Chapter Thirty-Two

Caroline observed the brief meeting between Katya and Will from the window of her boudoir. If she had not known that Katya was still hopelessly in love with Jake she might have been inclined to jealousy, but of course that would have been both selfish and ridiculous. In any case, Will's kiss was manifestly avuncular.

'You haven't heard a word I've said, have you? What are you looking at?'

Caroline gave a start and swung round to face Sally. She was holding up one of Caroline's gowns for inspection.

'I'm sorry. I was miles away.' She gave Sally a smile of apology. 'What did you say?'

'I was asking if you wished to take this gown, as you have often worn it before.'

'We'll leave it behind then.' Caroline smothered a sigh. 'Although it is one of my favourites. I am going to buy a new wardrobe – my trousseau.'

'You're still of the same mind then?'

'Yes, of course. Nothing has changed, Sally.'

'Will was out of his mind with worry when you went missing. I've never seen a man suffer as he did.'

'Please don't,' Caroline begged. 'You mustn't tell me these things. It isn't proper.'

'Don't you believe me? He was almost demented.'

'You exaggerate surely,' Caroline demured. 'Of course he was anxious for my safety. I am engaged to Fitz, and you know how attentive he is to his cousin's needs.'

'Stuff and nonsense! If ever a man was in love, it is him.'

Caroline turned away, pressing shaking fingers to her mouth. 'If I thought he really loved me . . .'

'He does. Believe me.'

'I'm not so sure. But even if he does it makes no difference, can't you see that? I've given my promise to Fitz. He's so good and so kind, I could never hurt him.'

'What about Will? Don't you think it will hurt him if you marry his cousin?'

'But he wanted me to. He practically arranged it.'

'Perhaps he did not realise he was in love with you himself until it was too late.'

'But it is too late, as you've just said yourself,' Caroline pointed out. 'How can I jilt Fitz now?'

'Just talk to him, Caroline. You would find him more understanding than you think. I am sure of it.

Caroline stared at her. She was right. Fitz would understand, of course. It was his nature. He would accept her decision in that quiet, gentle way of his though it would hurt him to the quick.

'You don't understand, Sally,' she said. 'Fitz needs me. He has told me so himself. And his sufferings have been considerable. I would never forgive myself if I did what you suggest. No, I have made up my mind. I shall keep my promise to marry him. Now, please may we talk of other matters?'

She was able to stop Sally talking about Will but she could not stop herself from thinking of him constantly. After yet another restless night she was glad when they finally left for London. At least for a while there would be shopping and sightseeing, and afternoon teas with her society friends, to keep her occupied.

Will had elected not to accompany them.

'I have neglected my duties to the estate of late,' he stated, when Fitz raised the subject. 'I have too much to do to visit town just at the moment.'

His eyes flicked towards Caroline for a brief moment, and she sensed that it was on her account that he had chosen to stay behind.

For her own part, she was somewhat relieved by his decision. It was becoming ever more difficult not to betray her feelings when they were together, and sometimes she thought that perhaps Sally was right. It might be kinder in the long run to break off her engagement to Fitz, and yet she still could not bring herself to hurt him, nor to break her word.

To stop herself dwelling on her own problems she resolved to devote herself to Katya's education. Fitz was determined that she should learn to be a gentlewoman so that she could take her place openly in society as his sister. In this at least Caroline could contribute, and she threw all her energies into teaching Katya how to sit, how to stand, walk, talk, eat . . . going over and over each little detail with infinite patience. As the days passed, her efforts began gradually to bear fruit.

The first two weeks in London were hectic, every day crammed full with shopping trips, fittings at the fashionable dress-makers, entertaining and sightseeing. What with visits to Vauxhall, the Pantheon, the opera, various museums, London Tower and the menagerie, the time seemed to fly by.

Katya had enjoyed the trip to the zoological garden most of all, and she pulled a long face when Caroline curtailed it to attend yet another fitting.

'Must we?' she asked, pleading for a little longer in the pleasure gardens. 'I'll never wear so many dresses. It's a waste of good money to buy them for me.'

'Fitz's money,' Caroline reminded her. 'He has more than enough. He wants you to dress and behave like a young lady, Katya. You would not want to disappoint him, would you?'

'No.' Katya sighed, then, 'When can we go home?'

'Don't you like it here?' Caroline enquired. 'She was a little put out by Katya's downcast manner. 'Aren't you enjoying yourself?'

'I liked the animals,' Katya replied. 'But I wish they weren't in cages; it seems so cruel to lock up a wild thing.'

'Just imagine what chaos they would cause let loose in the park!'

Katya laughed and Caroline was relieved. The girl had been very quiet of late, which made her wonder if she were uncomfortable in her new role. Caroline understood how strange and perplexing it must all seem to her, though she was trying very hard to learn how to speak and behave in company.

'We shall go back to Pendlesham soon,' she said. 'Do you like it better there, Katya?'

'Yes.' Katya bit her lip. 'I can walk in the woods sometimes when we are home. I feel more free.'

'Yes, I see.'

Caroline spoke no more of it, but that evening after Katya had gone up to bed, she confided her worries in Fitz.

'I believe she is pining for her old life,' she said.

'Perhaps you should tell her the truth now. She might find it easier then to understand why we all want her to change so much. It will also make her feel that her roots are here, not in the woods with a band of itinerants.'

'Katya does not care for London,' Fitz said, side-stepping Caroline's suggestion. 'To be candid I shall be glad to be home again myself.'

'We have ordered all the clothes we need and the dressmakers can send on what is not finished,' Caroline agreed. 'After Lady Blackstone's dance tomorrow evening there will be nothing to keep us here.'

'Then we shall leave the following day.' He smiled at her reassuringly. 'Do not worry about Katya, she will be happy again when we are back in the country. Before I tell her of her origins, I want her to get used to the idea of living with us.'

Caroline was not sure that the return to Pendlesham would necessarily restore Katya's smiles, but she would not argue. Fitz was determined that his half-sister should have all the things that had been denied her in the past, and she had promised to help him; it was not her place to interfere.

The Blackstones' dance would be Katya's launch into society. She had accompanied Caroline on afternoon visits and sat silently to one side when visitors called to take tea in the parlour, but this would be her first real foray into society at large. She was bound to be on tenterhooks, even though she had become a proficient dancer and could hold a simple conversation – providing she did not become self-conscious, when she would inevitably revert to her old style of speaking.

'I think I shall go and say goodnight to her, then retire,' Caroline said. 'Goodnight, Fitz.'

'Goodnight, my dear.' Fitz kissed her cheek. 'Do not be too anxious, Caroline. Remember she has nowhere else to go. If she is to live with us, she must adapt to our ways. It will be hard for a while, but it is for her own good.'

'Yes, I know.'

Caroline was thoughtful as she mounted the stairs. Perhaps Fitz was right, perhaps she was worrying too much. She knocked at Katya's door and went in. Katya was already in bed, her eyes closed. She looked peaceful and childlike with her hair spread out on the pillow. Caroline went over to the bed, bending to kiss her softly on the forehead.

'Sleep well,' she whispered. 'We all love you, dearest Katya. Remember that.'

As she turned and walked silently from the room, Katya's eyes opened and stared sightlessly at the canopy above her head.

'You look so pretty – doesn't she, Sally?' Caroline greeted Katya with a kiss as she came along the upstairs hall to join them; she was dressed in a simple pink silk gown, her hair wreathed in flowers. She wore Jake's bangle on her thin wrist and a pair of pearl drops, given to her by Fitz, dangled from her ears. 'You will be the belle of the ball this evening.'

Caroline was looking magnificent herself in a green striped silk gown with a square neckline and several flounces about the hem. Around her neck was a sparkling diamond collar, one of the many Carlton heirlooms she would inherit on her marriage. Matching eardrops and a bracelet completed the elegant ensemble.

She reached out to clasp the girl's hand. It was trembling, either with excitement or terror. She squeezed it and then tucked Katya's arm through her own, dropping her voice to a confidential whisper.

'You need not be nervous, dearest. Everyone is looking forward to meeting you. The Blackstones are my friends; they will be kind to you and so will everyone else.'

Katya repaid her with a tremulous smile.

'You look very nice,' Sally said with a nod of approval. 'Stay close to me this evening, Katya. I shall tell you who it will be proper for you to dance with and whom you should avoid at all costs.'

Katya nodded jerkily and she clung even more tightly to Caroline's hand.

'Sally will be your chaperone this evening,' Caroline told her. 'In fact, she is there to look after both of us.'

'But *you* don't need to be told these things,' Katya said in a small voice.

Caroline clucked. 'Now don't be silly. Just do whatever Sally tells you and you won't make a mistake.'

Katya's mouth turned down. Her face was paler than usual, and she did not speak again as they went out to the carriage, nor during the short journey to the Blackstones' London house.

Lady Blackstone greeted them with kisses and cries of delight.

'I am so glad you could come,' she said, patting Caroline's cheek with her gloved hand. 'Rachel is here with dear Captain Royston. She is glowing, my dear – positively glowing – and eager to see you. We were all so anxious when you had your little contretemps.' She turned her gaze on Katya. 'And this is your new friend. Delighted to meet you, I'm sure.'

Katya blushed and whispered that she was pleased to be invited.

'Caroline, you must come and talk to Lady Sarah . . .'

Caroline gave Katya a little push towards Sally and smiled meaningly at her as she herself was borne off by her hostess.

'Caroline – oh, Caroline!' Rachel came whirling across the room to greet her. They kissed and Rachel tucked her arm through Caroline's, shooing her mother away with a laugh and a pout.

'I want Caroline all to myself for a while,' she cried. 'I have so much to tell her.'

'How are you?' Caroline asked, smiling at her friend's elation. 'As if I needed to ask – you look wonderful.'

'I'm so happy,' Rachel said. 'Especially now that I know you are safe. You must tell me everything. I'm dying to hear your adventures. Did you really tell fortunes dressed up as a gypsy?'

'Yes,' Caroline replied, with a backward glance for Katya. She was sitting with Sally amongst the matrons, her eyes downcast, her face white as alabaster. 'I didn't know who I was, you see. If it wasn't for Katya I might not be here this evening.' She directed Rachel's attention towards the girl. 'Will you help me make sure she isn't neglected, Rachel? Can you get some of your gentlemen guests to ask her to dance?'

'Yes, of course,' Rachel said. 'I'm sure my cousins will oblige.'

Caroline's dance card had been filled within twenty minutes of her arrival. She prevailed upon those of her partners whose company she found agreeable to ask Katya for a dance, too, and the girl had stood up for more than half the early part of the evening.

Keeping a watchful eye on her Caroline had noticed that she had begun to smile a little when one or two of the young men talked to her.

'How is she coping?' she whispered to Sally between partners. 'Do you think she is enjoying herself?'

'She is a little shy, but the men seem to like that,' Sally replied. 'She is managing well enough.'

Caroline nodded and turned to her new partner. It was as he escorted her into the ballroom that she glimpsed Lady Blackstone greeting a new arrival. Her heart lurched. It was Will! She could not help staring and her step faltered.

'Is something wrong, Miss Manners?' her partner asked.

'No,' she said. 'Nothing is wrong, thank you.'

She found it difficult to concentrate as they began to waltz around the room. Why had Will decided to come up for the dance when he had been so set against leaving Pendleham?

A minute or two later she noticed him entering the ballroom with Katya on his arm. She was laughing up at him, her face transformed now that she was with a friend. She looked pretty, her eyes shining as Will swept her into the dance. They looked well together, Caroline thought, with a spurt of jealousy that she instantly suppressed. It was kind of Will to dance with Katya. She was certainly enjoying herself now.

The music ended. Caroline's partner led her back to Sally's side. She thanked him and pretended to watch him walk away. In reality she was surveying the twisting dancers for Will and Katya. Will had not returned Katya to her chaperone, and as Caroline was taken into the ballroom on the arm of a new partner she saw that they were still standing together. Will had procured champagne for them both, and Katya was giggling as the bubbles bounced up her nose.

When Caroline noticed them next they were dancing together. She saw that Katya's shyness had disappeared and she was now clearly gaining confidence. As the dance finished Caroline looked for Katya, but again they had left the floor. Many minutes passed before she saw them dancing once more.

Katya could not know how her behaviour would seem to others, of course, but Will must be aware that it would be taken as a sign of an agreement between them. Caroline herself was dancing again and could do nothing to warn Katya, but as soon as her partner released her she thanked him and walked to intercept the girl as she and Will moved to the edge of the floor.

Katya turned as Caroline came upon them, her eyes bright. 'Will is here,' she said. 'Isn't it a wonderful surprise?'

'Yes, indeed,' Caroline said, directing a cool glance at Will. 'Sally is looking for you, Katya. I think she wants you to go into supper with her.'

'I've had supper with Will,' Katya replied. 'I want to go on dancing with him, it's fun . . .'

'You may have one more dance with Will later,' Caroline said. 'For now I think you should go to Sally. You don't want people to stare at you, do you?'

Katya's cheeks turned a fiery red. 'I'm sorry,' she muttered. 'I didn't realise it was wrong.'

'It isn't wrong, but it might make people think you and Will have an understanding. You don't want that. Unless of course you do have an understanding?'

She was looking at Will as she spoke, and he frowned.

'Don't be ridiculous, Caroline. Katya and I are

288

friends, that's all. I asked her to dance several times because she is a little intimidated by Sally and all this.' He encompassed the ballroom with a sweep of his arm. 'Is there any harm in that?'

'You at least should know better. It was a foolish thing to do, unless you want people to gossip.' Caroline's tone was colder than she'd intended. She turned to Katya. 'I just want people to think well of you, Katya.'

'His lordship is beckoning to me,' Katya said in a subdued voice. 'May I go to him?'

'Yes, of course. Don't look so mortified. I'm not angry with you. Run along now and see what Fitz wants.'

'That was remarkably insensitive,' Will said as the girl walked away, head bent. 'I'm surprised at you, Caroline. Don't you know how terrified she is of upsetting you? She was feeling miserable, so I thought I would give her a little confidence. Now you've destroyed what little she had.'

'I did not mean to be harsh with her,' Caroline replied, stung by his criticism. 'She did not know what she was doing. But you must have realised it would set tongues wagging.'

'Does that really matter?' Will asked, his brows raised. 'I think both you and Fitz are being unfair to the girl. She has been raised as a gypsy. What makes you think she can become a lady overnight? Or that she would want to?'

'Perhaps we have been pushing her too fast,' Caroline said slowly. 'But it's what Fitz wants.'

'Why in God's name? Why not let her be in the kitchen with Mrs Bambury? She would be far more comfortable there. She enjoys cooking. She will feel at home there.'

'That isn't for me to decide,' Caroline replied. 'I think you should talk to Fitz. He may have something to tell you.'

'What do you mean?' Will stared at her, then his gaze narrowed. 'Good Lord! Do you mean she's the one! I knew my uncle had a child by a gypsy woman but . . .'

'You *knew* about it?'

Will nodded, looking thoughtful. 'Since you both know now I don't suppose I'm breaking any vows. My uncle wanted it kept a secret and I gave my word I would never tell anyone – not even Fitz.'

'Did neither of you consider what the child's life might be like? Have you any idea of how Katya has suffered?'

'It was my uncle's wish.'

'And of course that is all that counts,' Caroline flared. 'The fact that Fitz's half-sister has been beaten and half-starved for most of her life means nothing. You say we are unkind to her to try and teach her to become a lady, but I think you and your uncle behaved despicably!'

'You know nothing about it.' Will said in a resentful tone. 'You don't understand why my uncle did as he did.'

'I know all I need to know.' Caroline gave him a look of disgust. 'Excuse me, if you please. I must join Fitz and Katya.'

'Caroline . . .'

She pushed past him and walked away without a backward glance.

Chapter Thirty-Three

Caroline heard the muffled sobs as she paused outside Katya's room the next morning. She hesitated, then knocked.

'It's me – may I come in?'

There was a brief silence, then reluctantly, 'Yes, Caroline.'

Katya was sitting on her bed. As Caroline approached, she wiped her hand across her eyes. The thick velvet drapes were still pulled across the window. Caroline went to draw them, glancing out at the quiet street where a milkmaid was crying her wares, her back bent under the weight of the wooden yoke across her shoulders. In the gardens of the square a child in a sailor suit was playing with a hoop, and a dog was running after him, barking loudly. She confronted Katya, observing the redness around her eyes.

'Why were you crying?' Caroline asked. 'If it's because of what I said last night, I'm sorry. I was only thinking of you, and of what people might say. If you are to be accepted by our friends you have to be careful. Perhaps more careful than most.'

'Because I'm a gypsy?'

Caroline met her bright stare and felt ashamed. What were they trying to do to this girl, forcing her to behave in a way so foreign to her nature?

'You have no need to be ashamed of your past,' she said, sitting on the edge of the bed and taking hold of Katya's hand. It felt small and fragile: Katya was still thin, despite the prodigious amount of food she consumed. 'I was wrong to say anything last night. It's just that some very foolish people make rules, and we all think that we have to abide by them because everyone else does. Even me. You were simply enjoying yourself with a friend, there's nothing wicked in that, is there?'

'But I broke your rules,' Katya said. 'The truth is, I don't belong in your world, Caroline. I'm an ignorant gypsy girl and I can't be a lady however hard I try.'

'Perhaps you belong more than you think you do,' Caroline replied. 'I know it's hard for you to learn so many things, but one day you'll see it was worth it.'

Katya looked at her in silence, then, 'I don't want to make you ashamed of knowing me.'

'I could never be that,' Caroline said and kissed her cheek. 'Whatever happens in the future, I shall always care for you. You are my friend – my sister – and I love you.'

Katya's face cleared as if by magic and she flung her arms about Caroline, giving her a fierce hug.

'Will is just my friend,' she said earnestly. 'I like him and his lordship, but I would rather die than do anything to hurt you.'

'Katya . . .' Caroline breathed a sigh of relief that she appeared to have handled it right, without further upsetting the girl's sensitivities. 'Just remember you can always talk to me if you are worried about anything. And don't worry if you make mistakes. You have the rest of your life to learn. There's no hurry – really.'

'I will try,' Katya promised. 'I'll do whatever you want, Caroline.'

'Get up and wash your face then,' Caroline said in a rallying tone. 'We're leaving for Pendlesham within the hour.'

She smiled to herself as she saw the relief in the other girl's eyes. It was quite obvious Katya felt she was going home.

It was a lovely spring morning. Glancing out of the window, Caroline was amused to see Katya running towards the house, barefooted, her hair blowing free in the breeze. She looked like a wood nymph.

She had seemed much happier these past few days. The little upset in town was forgotten and she was relishing the freedom of the countryside. Caroline, too, was surprised at how glad she was to return. Pendlesham *was* her home now.

They had been back for just over a week and Sally was preparing to return to her sister-in-law's house. Caroline turned away from the window with the thought that they should do something special on their last day together. She glanced in her dressing mirror, patted her hair, then picked up a pretty blue glass scent bottle and dabbed a little of her favourite fragrance behind her ears. She left her apartments, intending to visit her friend's room, then paused in surprise as she heard raised voices along the corridor.

'I asked you where you had been, Katya. Mrs Brandon tells me your bed has not been slept in. Now I catch you creeping in looking as if you had been dragged through a hedge. Please explain your behaviour.'

The voice was Fitz's, the tone was – for him – harsh.

'I did nuffing wrong!' Katya cried defensively. 'Don't look at me like that. I telled yer . . .'

'You told me,' Fitz corrected sternly. 'But I am not sure I can trust your word. Where have you been?'

'What's going on?' Caroline asked, as she came up to them. 'Why are you angry, Fitz? What has Katya done?'

'Nuffing,' the girl cried, tears welling in her eyes. 'I only went to the woods.'

'You were out all night. It rained during the night, Katya.' Fitz's eyes had the shine of new forged steel. 'Please do not insult my intelligence by lying.'

'I'm not lying. I found a place to shelter.'

'Where? Who were you with?'

'Please don't bully her, Fitz,' Caroline said. 'I don't think she is lying.'

Fitz looked at her and he was not smiling. 'Please leave this to me, Caroline.' His gaze returned to Katya's flushed face. 'I have been informed that Jake is camping in the woods. Were you with him?'

Katya lowered her eyes and made no reply. She looked so downcast that Caroline's heart went out to her.

'Please answer me,' Fitz persisted.

Katya's head came up then, her expression becoming defiant. 'If I did see Jake, 'tis my affair, not yours.'

'That's where you are wrong. I will not have you slipping away to meet that gypsy. While you are under my roof you will behave decently.'

'I've done nuffing wrong.'

'You did nothing wrong,' Fitz corrected mechanically. 'I certainly hope not, Katya. I should be very disappointed in you if I thought you had. But you are not to meet him again. Do you understand me?'

'No.' Katya was trembling but defiant. 'I'm a gypsy,

too. I know you and Caroline want me to be a lady, but Jake is like me. I belong with him, not you.'

'Perhaps I should have told you this before . . .' Fitz began, but Caroline laid a hand on his arm.

'Fitz!' She gave him a warning glance. He ignored her.

'Your mother may have been a gypsy but your father certainly was not.' He paused, then, 'Your father and mine were the same, that's why I want you to learn how to behave, Katya.' He paused again, to let her absorb the shock. 'You are my half sister.'

Katya's cheeks drained of colour. She stared at him in stunned disbelief, then turned to Caroline. 'It's not true – is it?'

'I believe it to be so,' Caroline replied, her heart sinking. This was not how the news should have been broken to her. 'Cara told me your father was an aristocrat, and there is a picture in the portrait gallery that looks very like you. But Jake is the only one who could tell you for certain.'

'Why did you not tell me when Cara died?' Katya's eyes mirrored her sense of betrayal and her bewilderment.

'We wanted you to become accustomed to living here.' Caroline reached out to touch her hand, but she backed away, her manner one of distrust. 'Katya, please try to understand.'

'No! I trusted you and you lied to me.'

'No, that isn't so.' Caroline stared after the girl as she fled along the hall and down the stairs. 'I love you, Katya,' she called after her.

But Katya kept on running down the stairs. The slap of her bare feet on the floor faded. Somewhere in the house a door slammed.

'I suppose that means she is off to ask Jake for the

truth.' Fitz looked annoyed. 'I handled that badly. I only want what is best for her. You know that, Caroline.'

'Yes – but perhaps we have been blind, Fitz. Katya is unhappy. She may never settle here.'

'She cannot go back to those gypsies. I shall not permit it. You told me how ill they treated her.'

Caroline pursed her lips. 'Perhaps there is another way?'

'You mean let Katya go into service as a cook?'

'I don't know, Fitz. Perhaps we should let her do whatever she chooses.'

'She is my half-sister, and she is only eighteen. I have a duty towards her. In time she will forget all this nonsense and learn to be happy here.'

'Let me talk to her when she returns. Please, Fitz.' Caroline gave him a pleading look. 'She needs time. We have to be patient with her.'

He frowned, then nodded. 'As you wish. Excuse me now. I must speak to Will: I want that gypsy off my land.'

'No!' Caroline cried. 'You must not do that, Fitz. It would be a terrible mistake. Jake will move on soon, if left to his own devices.'

'As long as he stays here Katya will find a way to meet him,' Fitz said grimly. 'The sooner he goes the better.'

Caroline watched in dismay as he limped away, his back rigid with annoyance. Why could he not see how wrong he was to try and keep Katya like a caged bird. If Katya found out he had driven Jake off the estate she would only resent him more for his interference.

Will had warned her that Fitz had a temper when roused. This was a side of him she had not previously experienced: he was usually so mild mannered and agreeable. Left to himself, she feared he would frighten Katya away.

Katya did not return. When she did not come down for dinner that evening, Caroline went in search of her. She was not in her room, or any of the other nooks and crannies she had made her own.

Fitz was becoming impatient by the time she returned to the dining room.

'I cannot find her,' she said, and he frowned. 'I'm sure she will come back soon. No doubt she will apologise when she is ready.'

Fitz was not to be appeased so readily.

'She has been gone all day. This is not good enough, Caroline.'

Mrs Brandon was summoned. No one had seen Katya. Gradually, Fitz's anger turned to worry.

'She must be with that gypsy,' Fitz said aside to Will. 'I thought you told the keepers to report any sighting of him?'

'No one could find him,' Will replied. 'It's my opinion he has moved on. He will be miles away by now.'

'Taking Katya with him!'

'Perhaps.' Will looked thoughtful. 'She may just be hiding somewhere. She's a sensitive girl. If she thinks you are angry with her she may be too frightened to come back. Remember she has been beaten in the past.'

'She must know I would never lay a finger on her,' Fitz said indignantly. 'No, it's that damned gypsy. He has taken her with him. If he imagines that he can hold her to ransom he will rue the day.'

'Why should he?' Will asked. 'He never has. Your

297

father offered him money years ago, but he refused it. All he wanted was the right to come and go as he pleased.'

'And why was I never told any of this?' Fitz was clearly incensed that he had been kept in the dark. '*You* might have told me, even if my father did not. It could have done no harm after his death.'

'I made a promise and I kept it,' Will replied stiffly. 'Now, if you will excuse me, I must organise a search party for Katya. It's my belief we shall find her hiding somewhere in the woods.'

'Damn it . . . *Will!*'

Fitz swore beneath his breath as his cousin strode off.

Caroline had listened to the argument in dismay. It was the first time she had heard the cousins quarrel and it upset her. Fitz limped off after Will, without so much as a glance in her direction.

Left alone with Sally in the parlour, she confided her anxieties.

'I fear Fitz may be partly right,' she said. 'If Jake asked Katya to go with him, I think she would. She has always loved him and she pines for her old life.'

'It might have been wiser to tell Katya who she really is sooner, rather than spring it on her like that,' Sally said.

'Yes, I know. But Fitz insisted on waiting. He has behaved most oddly over this business. It isn't like him at all to lose his temper.'

'But understandable,' Sally murmured. 'I fancy there is more than a little pride involved. It must have been a shock to discover that he had a half-sister, and that she had been brought up as a gypsy.'

'Pride and guilt,' Caroline agreed. 'Fitz wants to

make up for all the years she was deprived of her birthright.'

'It is a worrying affair,' Sally said. 'Perhaps I should delay my departure for a while?'

Caroline shook her head firmly. 'No, you must go as planned. You can do no good by staying here, Sally. Besides, your sister-in-law will be expecting you.'

'If you need me . . .' Sally blinked hard. 'I deserted you once before – and look what happened.'

'Nothing will happen to me this time. I am quite safe. Not a word has been heard from my guardian and I doubt it will. If he has any sense, he will have left the country.' She squeezed Sally's waist. 'Silas Taverner is the least of my problems just now.'

'Yes, of course.' Sally smiled at her own foolishness. 'And I shall come back for your wedding.'

'Yes, we shall see each other again before long.'

They passed the remainder of the evening playing cards and talking, though both were uneasy, listening constantly for the sound of footsteps. Sally asked Caroline if she still told fortunes.

'No,' she said, with a rueful twist of her lips. 'It has ceased to be a game. I don't think I shall ever do that again, Sally.'

Fitz came in to the parlour just as Caroline had rung for the tea tray. She half rose from her chair, but he forestalled her with a little gesture of denial, and she sank back.

'There is no news,' he said. 'I came to apologise for my ill-temper earlier, and to say goodbye to Sally. I may not be around when she leaves in the morning.'

'You were not ill-tempered with me.'

'You are generous to say so.' He kissed her cheek

then turned to Sally with a smile. 'You will come to visit us again soon, I hope?'

'I shall be here for the wedding.'

'Indeed, I had forgotten.' He took her hand briefly. 'Excuse me now. Everyone is out looking for Katya. I came back only to say goodnight.'

'You should not tire yourself, Fitz,' Caroline said.

His eyes lingered momentarily on her face, then he nodded. 'Do not be concerned for me. Someone must remain here to co-ordinate the search parties, that is my task. And now I must leave you both. Forgive me.'

'Shall you retire now?' Sally asked when he had gone. 'You can do no good by sitting up.'

'You are right of course, but I don't think I could sleep just yet. Though you should go to bed, Sally. You have a long journey in the morning.'

'I am a little tired,' Sally admitted, 'but you must call me at once if you need me.'

They kissed and Sally went out. Caroline sat on alone. She shuffled the cards absent-mindedly, then found herself subconsciously placing them in the familiar formation. She turned up the first card in the circle: the ace of spaces – the death card! She hastily gathered the cards into a heap. She did not want to consult the future if it held unhappiness in store.

If anything had befallen Katya, an accident or worse, she would never forgive herself.

She jumped to her feet as she heard the ring of booted footsteps in the hall. The door was opened and Will came in still wearing his greatcoat. He stood staring at her for a moment in tight-lipped silence, then went over to the fire and warmed his hands.

'I thought you would have retired long ago, Caroline.' He spoke into the fire. 'There is nothing you can do by staying up. No need for you to lose sleep over this.'

'You must think me heartless,' she cried. 'Katya is my friend. She saved my life. I am anxious for her.' A sob broke from her. 'I feel responsible for her. I should never have let her run off like that.'

Suddenly the tears welled over and ran down her cheeks.

'It's all my fault. I brought her here . . .'

'Caroline don't – don't cry.' Will was at her side. 'Don't cry, my dearest. I can't bear it.'

She looked up at him, her eyes opening wide as he took out his handkerchief and wiped her face.

'You're always coming to the aid of damsels in distress,' she said, a tremulous smile on her lips. She was shaking inside, talking to hide her emotion. 'Like St George. Do you think Katya will return safe to us?'

'Perhaps she has gone to Jake,' he suggested, declining to answer with platitudes. 'I think she has met him several times since you returned from town. I've seen them together in the woods.'

'She loves him.'

'Yes, I gathered that. The question is – has she gone with him?'

'I think she would if he asked her.'

'Perhaps. Women do strange things for love.' Will touched her cheek with his fingertips. 'Or so my mother tells me. We talk to each other a great deal these days. She is teaching me tolerance Caroline.'

Caroline's heart was racing wildly. She gazed up into his face searching for a clue to his thoughts. What was he trying to say to her? What secret emotions were bursting to be exposed.

'Will?'

He looked down into her eyes for a moment longer,

301

then bent his head to kiss her. His lips were soft and gentle, touching hers lightly like a butterfly settling on a leaf, before he drew away.

'I've been a fool, Caroline,' he said. 'I was a child when my mother remarried and I've carried my hurt like a millstone around my neck. I blamed her for betraying my father's memory – and me. And because of that I allowed myself to become bitter. I dismissed love as a dream for fools and my own stupidity has cost me dear, but at least I now know I was wrong.'

'W-what are you saying?' Caroline stared up at him as her senses whirled. She felt faint and clutched at his arms for support. 'What do you mean?'

His expression was sad as he met her questing gaze. 'I think you know,' he said softly. 'But we both realise it cannot be, don't we?'

Caroline could not answer him. Her heart was thudding so fast she found it difficult to breathe and could only stare silently after him as he left the room. Only then did she recover her voice.

'Oh, Will,' she whispered to the empty room. 'Will, my love, my dearest love – what are we going to do?'

Unable to bear her unhappiness or the suffocating silence she ran upstairs and flung herself across the bed, sobbing as though her heart would break.

Chapter Thirty-Four

In the morning there was still no news. Caroline found the breakfast room empty when she went down, but there were signs that the men had been in and left again. Her face pale and puffy from lack of sleep, she helped herself to a little kedgeree from the silver entree dishes on the sideboard, but ate only a few mouthfuls before pushing away her plate. She went upstairs to Sally's room.

Sally had breakfasted in bed earlier and was dressed ready for her journey. She inquired anxiously after Katya. Caroline's headshake was answer enough.

'Are you sure you don't want me to stay on for a few days?'

'No, you must go,' Caroline insisted. 'I'm sure we shall find her eventually. I shall write and tell you as soon as I have news.'

The carriage was brought round and Caroline kissed her friend goodbye. As the brougham rattled down the long drive she waved until it disappeared from sight. Feeling restless and uneasy, she went into the house, there to find the countess arranging a vase of spring flowers in the sitting room she, like Caroline, favoured because of its pleasant outlook over the gardens.

'So Sally has gone then,' she said, glancing up. 'You will miss her, Caroline.'

'Yes, I shall.' Caroline touched one of the pale pink tulips. 'This is such a lovely colour, isn't it? I hope you are feeling better this morning?'

'Oh, much,' Margaret assured her. 'I understand there is no news of your other little friend?'

'Mrs Brandon says not. I haven't seen Fitz or Will this morning. Have you?'

'I did speak to Fitz for a few moments,' Margaret replied. 'He is greatly concerned for Katya. He feels it is his fault she ran away.'

'We are all concerned for her.'

'Of course. But you should remember that she is used to living in the woods. She could survive alone for much longer than you or I, even indefinitely.'

Caroline sighed. Will's mother was right. Katya was used to a harsh existence, and could undoubtedly live off the land. But that did not stop her worrying.

She left the countess arranging her flowers, and went upstairs. The house seemed deserted. Many of the servants had been sent to help in the search. Caroline felt she ought to be helping too, but knew she should remain in the house in case Katya returned.

She paced about her bedroom. Her nerves were on edge and she could not settle to anything.

Caroline's restless mood was not due only to Katya's disappearance. She was fast coming to the conclusion that she must after all speak to Fitz and seek release from her promise. Sally had been right all along – she could not wed Fitz, in the knowledge that she loved his cousin, and that Will loved her, too. Her marriage would be a sham.

It had taken her a long time to arrive at this decision. Far, far too long. Her one time belief that romantic love was no more than an idealistic notion, that the fondness she felt for Lord Carlton would deepen into love after they were married, was in tatters. The marriage might have worked, but only if she had not fallen deeply and irrevocably in love with Will.

There was no comparison between the warm affection she had for one man and the wild, sweet singing of her blood that the other's slightest touch could arouse in her. She could not, must not, marry Fitz – for all their sakes. So she would confess all and beg his forgiveness. That might mean that she must go away, leave Pendlesham for ever. That would sadden her, but it was the price she would have to pay for her folly, for her deception. For it had indeed been foolish and deceitful to resist what she had known in her heart for so long.

Caroline's thoughts were disturbed by the opening of the door. She paused in her pacing and turned.

'Katya!' she cried, in mixed relief and surprise, as she saw the girl framed in the doorway. Her feet were bare, the hem of her gown muddied and her hair was a wild tangle, but otherwise she appeared unharmed. Caroline rushed to hug her. 'You've come back. Thank goodness! We've all been so worried – where have you been?'

'In the woods.' Katya was like a block of wood in her arms, stiff and unyielding. 'I knew they were looking for me, but 'tis easy to hide from keepers – they don't know the woods like I do.'

'Have you been with Jake?'

'For a while.' Katya's lip trembled. 'He asked me to go with him, said that I would be his woman and that he would make me a necklace of sapphires and diamonds fit for a princess. But I said no.'

Caroline was stunned. 'Why? It's what you really want, isn't it?'

'If he truly loved me, I would be his slave,' Katya replied, and bit her lip. 'But he doesn't. He thinks I look prettier now, and it amused him because I spoke up for myself – but it's you he loves. He came back to see if you were happy, and now he's gone for good.'

'I'm sorry, Katya. You deserved his love.'

'It doesn't matter,' Katya said, and her face was proud. 'I know who I am now, and what I want to do with my life.'

'You are Lord Carlton's half-sister,' Caroline began but stopped as the girl shook her head. 'Cara told me . . .'

'Cara knew only half the story. My father's name was Carlton but he was *Will*'s father not his lordship's.'

'What?' Caroline, astonished, stepped away from the girl. 'How do you know this?'

'Jake told me. His lordship made him swear to keep the secret for Will's sake. His father had died and he was grieving. Later on when Will discovered there was a child, Lord Carlton let him believe it was his rather than destroy his faith in his own father. It seems Mr James Carlton was a bit of a lad, and caused his poor wife a deal of grief before he died. 'Twas no wonder she married again for love.'

'I see . . .' Caroline nodded. 'So Jake kept faith all this time?'

'Yes. He told no one. But he thought Will had somehow found out the last time they met.'

'I doubt that. I'm sure he still thinks you are his uncle's child.'

'You won't tell him, will you?' Katya said anxiously.

'No, but I must tell Fitz. He has to know, Katya.'

'That's why I came back, to tell you the truth. Then I'll go.'

Caroline reached instinctively to restrain her.

'What do you mean? I thought you had refused Jake's offer?'

'I have.' Katya's head went up, her eyes clear and determined. 'I'm going to learn to be a cook. Mrs Bambury has arranged a position for me with a friend of hers in a house in Devon. No one will know who I am. I shan't shame you.'

'Katya, please don't think that,' Caroline begged. 'All I have ever wanted was for you to be happy. If this will make you happy you have my blessing.'

Katya's eyes shone. 'Oh, Caroline, really?'

'Really.' Caroline moved to embrace her.

'You will write to me?' Katya said, as they hugged. 'I'll ask Cook to read the letters to me until I can read them for myself.'

Caroline drew back, gazing down into her face.

'I shall expect you to write back. Promise me you'll go on with your reading lessons.'

'I promise.' Katya took out a large handkerchief and blew her nose. 'You do understand, don't you? I could not go back to being what I was, but 'tis too much to be a lady like you, Caroline. I can't live by all your rules. I want to improve myself, I want to be like Mrs Bambury.'

'Then that's what you should do.'

'You won't stop being my friend?'

'We'll always be friends. I swear.'

They smiled at each other. 'Mrs Bambury will tell you where to write to me,' Katya said.

'But how will you get there? Let me at least give you money for the journey.'

'I've money enough. You've all been good to me.

307

I'll not forget that. I want to take the clothes you've given me – is that all right?'

Caroline made a disparaging noise. 'Of course. But won't you stay a little longer? We could have one last day together.'

'Mrs Bambury's nephew is to take me to the post-house in his waggon. The mail coach stops in the village this afternoon for five minutes and I can board it there. If I delay, 'tis another week before I can leave.'

It all seemed too rushed to Caroline.

'Won't you at least say goodbye to Fitz and Will?' she pleaded. 'You know how fond they are of you.'

'I can't.' Katya said firmly. 'They might try to stop me. I'm fond of them in my way, but you're the only one I really care about, Caroline. Will you forgive me for all the trouble I've caused?'

'But you haven't,' Caroline said, her throat tight with emotion. 'I may be leaving here myself soon. I should like to see you, make sure you're settled in your new life.'

'You've decided not to marry his lordship then?' Katya nodded. 'I knew 'twas Will you loved. I'm glad. He loves you.'

'I haven't told Fitz yet. It will hurt him deeply – as will your going. He only wanted to make up to you for all the years you had suffered, Katya. Please forgive him if he made you unhappy. He did not mean to.'

'I know. I like him, but I can't be what he wants me to be. He expects too much. I'm sorry, Caroline.'

'There's no need to be.' Caroline kissed her again. 'If ever you need anything – anything at all – you must send me a message.'

'I will,' Katya promised. 'Jed Bambury is waiting. I must go and pack my things.'

'You're sure you have enough money?'

'Jake gave me ten gold sovereigns,' Katya said. ''Twas a parting gift. Perhaps to say sorry for being unkind to me in the past.'

'You will take the pendant and the other things I gave you?'

'Yes.' Katya hugged her fiercely, then broke away. 'Tell his lordship I'm sorry. I'm going now, then I shall be gone. So let's say goodbye, now.'

They embraced once more.

'Goodbye. God bless and keep you.'

Then Katya was gone, the drum of her running feet in the corridor the only evidence of her presence, until that too faded. Caroline sank onto her dressing stool. She would miss Katya, but acknowledged that the girl must be free to live her own way. To try and stop her would be wrong.

She splashed her face with cold water from a jug on the washstand. She smoothed her hair, tidied her gown, took the sapphire ring from her finger and laid it down on the dressing table, then she fastened the gold locket Will had given her around her neck.

Now she must go downstairs and confront Fitz.

Fitz was warming his hands before the library when she entered. Although the weather was quite mild it was always a little cool in the house, perhaps because of the high ceilings and the thick stone walls.

'Mrs Brandon told me you had returned,' she said. 'You may call off your search and stop worrying now, Fitz. Katya is quite safe. She had been hiding in the woods, just as Will said.'

'You've seen her then?' he said, hoarse with excitement. 'Thank God for that! I shall speak to her later.'

'No, Fitz,' Caroline said. 'Katya is leaving us. As soon as she has packed she will be gone.' Fitz frowned.

'Gone? What do you mean? Is she taking up with that blasted gypsy? You should not have let her go to him. She won't be happy for long.'

'She isn't running off with Jake,' Caroline replied. She was surprised at his calmness. It was almost as if he were resigned to her leaving. 'She is going to learn to be a cook at a house in Devon.'

'Ah yes, I see.' He clasped his hands behind his back. 'I should have listened to her. It would have saved all this upset.'

'You don't mind . . . ?' Caroline stared at him, puzzled. 'I thought you would be furious.'

'Is that why she will not say goodbye?' Fitz shook his head sadly. 'I handled her badly, did I not? How cruel she must have thought me. I wanted to make her into the sister I never had, but I see now that was wrong of me. I ought to have been more tolerant, more understanding, as Will was.'

So woebegone was his expression, that Caroline's heart went out to him.

'You were not unkind, Fitz. You did what you thought best.'

'And the road to hell is paved with good intentions.' His mouth twisted ruefully. 'But I was wrong and Will was right. She should be allowed to do as she pleases. It is her life, after all.'

'Katya wants to make something of herself in her own way. Being a cook is not a bad life, Fitz. At least she will have a secure position and respect. She won't go back to being a gypsy. She has learned better now. Perhaps that is as much as we could hope for.'

'You did it, Caroline. Give me no credit, I deserve none.'

'You must not be too harsh with yourself.' Caroline hesitated, then, 'Now I must tell you something . . .'

'Yes, my dear?' Fitz turned his mild gaze on her. 'Something to do with Katya, or yourself?'

'Katya's father was your uncle. Your father allowed Will to believe he was responsible, but it was not so.'

'Did Katya tell you that?' Fitz asked, eyebrow cocked, then answered himself. 'Yes, Jake would have known, of course.'

'You already knew?' Caroline accused.

'Only since this morning. Margaret told me. She thought I should know, but she asked me to keep it from Will. She doesn't want him to know that Katya is . . .'

'Not to tell me what?'

The voice startled them. They turned as one, unable to conceal their guilt. Will came into the room.

Fitz was the first to recover.

'How much did you hear?'

'Enough.' Will's mouth hardened. 'My mother asked you not to tell me something – about Katya, I imagine?'

'Since you heard so much it seems pointless to try to conceal it.' Fitz shrugged. 'Katya is *your* half-sister, not mine. It appears that your mother and my father conspired to keep us in the dark.'

'My father's child?' Will looked thunderstruck. 'Then he betrayed my mother first.'

'Why talk of betrayal?' Fitz asked. 'These things happen. It hardly matters now.'

'To you perhaps not,' Will retorted angrily. 'You

311

thought otherwise when you believed Katya your sister.'

'I was wrong. I should have let her go her own way. But that is mended now. She has told Caroline what she intends.'

'She has *been* here?' Will exclaimed. 'And you did not think to tell me? Dammit, man, I have been searching all night and you did not think I would want to know she was safe? Where is she?'

'She is leaving,' Caroline said and began to explain, but Will scythed across her words.

'Did you do nothing to stop her? You let her go to that gypsy, who will beat and starve her? Damn you both! This is too much. I believe there are differences between us that cannot be reconciled. I shall leave Pendlesham at the earliest opportunity.'

'Don't be a fool, Will,' Fitz said, his brow furrowed in consternation.

'I may have been a fool, but I shall be one no more.'

'Will . . .'

But Will was in no mood to listen. He strode from the room, leaving Caroline staring after him in dismay.

'You can't let him go like that,' she said at last to Fitz. 'You can't let him walk out – Pendlesham is his life.'

'It is his decision,' Fitz pointed out equably. 'I can't keep him here against his inclination, any more than I can keep Katya or you.'

'What do you mean?' Caroline's heart jerked. 'Fitz . . .'

He smiled and his eyes twinkled with that slightly sardonic humour that was his hallmark. 'Do you really imagine that Will would leave Pendlesham because we had a few angry words? I can assure you

312

we have crossed swords many a time in the past.'

'I – I don't understand.'

'I think you do, Caroline. If Will has reached the end of his tether it is because of you, not me. Because he cannot bear the idea of our marriage. Because he loves you.' He reached out to stroke her soft cheek with one finger. 'As you love him, my dear.'

She gazed up into his face. 'You know? How long have you known?'

He chuckled softly. 'Since we rescued you from your unpleasant guardian. I had no idea before that. Nor did I realise my headstrong cousin reciprocated your love. He gave no sign of it until you disappeared. Then he was half demented with shock and grief. Transparently so.'

'Oh, Fitz, I'm so sorry. I had made up my mind to tell you, but I was afraid of hurting you.'

He held her to his chest. 'It would hurt me far more if you married me and I made you unhappy,' he murmured into her hair. 'I am very fond of you, my dear.'

'Oh, Fitz . . .' She clung to him, joyful yet sad. 'Please forgive me.'

'For what? I asked you to marry me knowing that I was not in love with you. I care for you as much as I am able.' His smile was slightly distant and she felt his thoughts were already somewhere else. 'I can never love anyone as I loved Julia. My heart was buried in her grave . . .'

'Don't.' She laid a hand on his arm, but he shook his head.

'Go and find my impulsive cousin before he does something he might regret.'

Caroline hesitated, then reached up to kiss his cheek. 'Thank you,' she whispered. 'Thank you for your understanding, dear Fitz.'

313

As she closed the door behind her she heard him whisper: 'Oh, Julia, my love . . . please come back . . .'

Caroline went into the little parlour. The countess was there, with a book of verses open on her lap, but she was not reading.

'Have you seen Will?' Caroline enquired.

'I believe he went out a few moments ago,' Margaret replied. 'Katya was here. Did you see her?'

Caroline thanked her and went outside. The sun was shining, and the birds had begun to nest in earnest now; she heard them calling to each other from the trees. There was no sign of Katya but she came upon Will, sitting on a stone bench by the pool, head in hands.

'Will?' she said falteringly.

His head came up. Despair was engraved in every line of his features.

'Did you see Katya?' she asked breathlessly.

'Yes,' he muttered. 'And she told me you asked her to say her goodbyes to me, and she had chosen to leave without a word.' He looked away. 'Please accept my apology for the harsh words I used.'

'Your reaction was understandable,' Caroline said, longing to touch him, comfort him.

'As for Katya . . .' He ran frustrated fingers through his dark hair, his eyes an ice blue in the late afternoon sunlight. 'You once accused me of not caring about her, but I never knew she had been mistreated. If I had . . .' His face twisted with grief. 'Good grief! What kind of a monster do you take me for?'

'That was wrong me me,' Caroline said. 'Please forgive me.'

'My uncle had promised she would be well cared for with her own kind. I discovered her existance just

314

before he died; it was too late to change things. Besides, I was sworn to secrecy for Fitz's sake.'

'And you were deceived in turn,' Caroline said.

'I would rather have known the truth.'

'The truth sometimes hurts,' Caroline countered. 'But it is best to know. Sometimes half-remembered truths can hurt even more.'

'Your mother . . .' Will's expression softened. 'Silas Taverner told us that she was Henry Manners' sister.'

'And my true father a groom, it seems.' Caroline smiled wryly. 'There was not so very much difference between Katya and I, except that I was luckier. Perhaps this affinity explains why we became so close.'

'She loves you dearly.'

His hand was gripping the edge of the bench, his knuckles showing white. Caroline rested hers on it.

'As I love her. You are not angry with her? Please don't be. In time she may choose to come back to you – to us.'

'I'm not angry with Katya. I never was.'

'Then you're angry with Fitz.' She gazed up at him, trying to read his mind. 'Will you really leave Pendlesham?'

He was silent, then, 'I think I must.'

She drew a deep breath. 'Then take me with you. Please?'

He stiffened; a nerve began to twitch in his throat. 'Caroline . . .'

'I'm not going to marry Fitz. It would be wrong. I don't love him. I thought I could learn to love him, that we could be comfortable together, but it would not work, I realise that now. I could never love him in the way I love you.'

She waited for his response, her pulses racing. His

315

face was impassive but the nerve kept jumping in his neck, betraying his emotion.

'Will?' she asked softly. 'Have you nothing to say to me? I thought perhaps you might care for me – just a little?'

'No,' he said at last, a smile breaking through the mask. 'No, I don't care for you a little.'

His words struck her like a douche of ice water. She recoiled, tears rushing to her eyes. So her avowal had been too late. If he had ever loved her she had killed that love. She got up to run away, to find a place to hide, to curl up and die from the shock of his denial. He caught her arm. She struggled to break free, hurting too deeply to look at him.

'Let me go,' she begged. 'Please . . .'

'No,' he said and his voice was stronger, firmer. 'No, I don't care for you a little, Caroline . . . I adore you, worship you, love every tiny part of you . . .'

She went limp from relief and almost fell to the ground. He spun her round, taking her into his arms and holding her as she clung to him, her fingers digging into his back. His lips brushed her hair as he whispered all the things she had longed to hear, his hands caressing her until she quietened and stood passively in the circle of his embrace.

'I realised I loved you too late,' he said. 'You were wearing my cousin's ring. I could not in all honour speak of my feelings. I loved you and yet I feared you.'

'Feared me?' Her eyes were quizzical. 'Why?'

'I thought all women faithless, remember?' He smiled at his own foolishness. 'I was afraid you wanted Fitz's title and wealth, that you would take my love and use it to amuse yourself, that you would . . . destroy me.'

She drew back a little, hurt by his bleak words. 'Did I seem so heartless to you?'

'You were proud and sometimes cold, my love – have you forgotten? You have changed since your return from the gypsies, but I loved you then and I love you more now. I think perhaps this Caroline was always there, but hidden.'

'Yes,' Caroline admitted. 'I have changed. I learned many things in that gypsy camp, and since. Our circumstances – yours and mine – were not unalike. My father was a cold, uncaring man who showed me no affection – with reason it seems. But I knew none of that. It hurt me that he never loved me, that he was often cruel to Helena. She was the mother I knew and loved – is still the only mother I remember.'

'You must have thought me like him. I was not kind to you.'

'At first I thought you unmannerly,' Caroline admitted. 'But then in a perverse way, I began to enjoy our sparring; I missed you when you were not there.'

'Oh, Caroline,' he breathed and drew her closer. 'My proud, beautiful Caroline. What fools we both were.'

She offered her lips willingly. He kissed her, gently at first and them with rising passion that stirred her blood so that she felt giddy with desire.

'I have wanted to do that so often,' Will said. 'Wanted you in my arms, in my bed; longed for you, hated and desired you. But even when I hated you I knew I would rather die than live without you.'

'I have only ever longed for you to kiss me. Even if I did not always admit as much.'

He ran the tip of his finger down her throat to the little hollow at the base. 'I've dreamt of you, Caroline,

317

almost every night. Hopeless dreams, feverish night-mares in which I held you only to see you slip away before I could make you mine: I won't let you slip away again.'

'My darling Will.' Her lovely face glowed as she reached up to touch his lips, almost wonderingly, unable to believe he was finally hers. 'I too am afraid I shall wake up and find it was just a dream.'

'We must be married soon. I could not bear to lose you again.'

He crushed her to him once more, his mouth moving feverishly against her white throat. She clung to him, moaning faintly, and she felt herself melting in the heat of his caresses. He kissed her, his tongue probing into her mouth as she opened to him like a flower. His hand plunged into her hair, caressing the delicate skin at the back of her neck. She gasped, swaying into him as she felt herself caught on the rushing tide of his desire.

'Must we wait?' she asked. 'Can we not be together now? As we shall be when we are wed . . .'

'Caroline?' He looked at her in disbelief, then as he saw she meant it his doubt turned to dawning delight. 'You are sure?'

'Completely sure,' she whispered. 'Make me yours, Will. Let us seal our love by the bonding of our hearts, minds – and bodies.'

'In the summerhouse,' he said huskily, his breath rasping against her ear. 'There are cushions and rugs.' A shudder ran through him as he touched her cheek in wonder. 'Caroline, my darling . . .'

She took the hand he offered and they walked across the lawns together, gazing rapt into each other's eyes.

Neither of them was aware of the figure at the

window, watching them, shoulders drooping under the weight of his sorrow.

'Soon now,' Fitz murmured, as they paused to embrace once more. 'Let it be soon now, Julia . . . please let it be soon.'

Chapter Thirty-Five

It was the day of the wedding. Caroline rose soon after dawn and sat looking out across the lawns to the summerhouse. She smiled and hugged herself as she relived that precious memory. Will had made love to her so tenderly, taking her with infinite care, bringing her to a gradual arousal; teaching her the true meaning of passion.

How well their bodies fitted together. He had slid into her welcoming warmth, filling and delighting her with an unimaginable joy. Afterwards, she snuggled into the firm haven of his muscular chest, secure in the certainty of his love. Cherished, loved, wanted as never before in her life.

They had not made love again since that day. The wedding had been arranged as soon as the banns would allow, and it was Will who had insisted they wait.'

'Once was natural and right after all we had suffered,' he said, between kisses. 'Neither of us could have stopped it happening, nor would we have wanted to. But next time it shall be in our marriage bed. We must do nothing to tarnish the brightness of our love. While we stay under Carlton's roof, we shall respect the hospitality.'

Caroline agreed that it was right and proper. They had sealed their love in the summerhouse, nothing could put it asunder now.

Fitz had been truly noble in the way he accepted their news. He insisted they should be married from Pendlesham.

'I want to hear no more nonsense about your leaving,' he lectured Will. 'This has always been your home. Besides, I could not manage without you. It will give me great pleasure to see you and Caroline married.' He laid a firm hand on Will's shoulder. 'Would you condemn me to an empty house and a life alone, old friend? For pride's sake? Stay with me – please? Let me be an uncle to your children, for I shall have none of my own.'

It would have taken a harder heart than either Caroline's or Will's to deny him.

At first they feared the news that Caroline was to marry Will and not Fitz would cause a terrible scandal, but as Lady Ross said when she called, 'I always felt it was Will you should marry. Everyone knows that poor dear Fitz is still in love with Julia. Besides, the servants have been laying odds on it for weeks – and servants always know what's going on before one does oneself.'

From their first meeting at Fitz's dinner party Caroline had known that in Lady Ross she had found a kindred spirit. She would have at least one confidente in the neighbourhood.

A few eyebrows were bound to be raised of course. Caroline was prepared for gossip and even to be cut by some of her neighbours, but she was too happy to care. Her true friends would understand, and the others were of no consequence. She was in love and loved: loved more deeply, more tenderly than she had ever dreamed possible.

Sighing contentedly, she went back to bed but not

to sleep. This would be the happiest day of her life, and tomorrow they would set out on their honeymoon.

As she was dressing, Sally came in, a garter of blue dangling from her finger.

'This is for you, dearest,' she said. 'Something borrowed, something blue . . .'

'Just what I am lacking,' Caroline said. 'For something old, Margaret has given me the lace kerchief she carried at her wedding to the count, and of course my dress is new.'

'So you are guaranteed good fortune,' Sally said and kissed her. 'You look radiant this morning, Caroline, and it is indeed a beautiful dress.'

'The lace came from Brussels,' Caroline informed her. 'It was embroidered with pearls and brilliants by a team of seven seamstresses no less.'

Sally made suitably impressed noises.

Around her neck, Caroline wore a collar of diamonds with a heart-shaped drop of pearls and diamonds that Will had given her. On her wrists were matching bracelets and she had dainty drops in her ears. Her headdress was a diamond tiara worn by countless Carlton brides. This had been pressed on her by Fitz as his personal wedding gift.

'There will be no other Carlton bride until your son marries,' he had said. 'I want you to have it, Caroline.'

'You are very generous, but you shall have it back when you take a bride yourself.'

'We both know that is unlikely,' he said, and kissed her hand. 'I am happy for you and Will, Caroline. Do not be sad for me. I have known a very precious love and I count myself a fortunate man.'

'Fitz gave me the headdress,' Caroline told Sally as

she turned in front of the mirror to inspect her veil from the rear. 'Was that not a generous gesture?'

'He is a generous man,' Sally agreed. 'But I'm glad you decided to marry Will. If you had gone through with your earlier intention, it would have been a disaster. Everyone would have been hurt in the end.'

Caroline bowed her head. 'Yes, I know you are right. I should have listened to you at the beginning.'

'And to your heart,' Sally squeezed her hand. 'I believe love is something you discover in your own time. It was perhaps more difficult for you than some.'

'I was blind and wilful,' Caroline confessed. 'And too proud for my own good. I learned a humility from living with the gypsies – a lesson I shall not forget.'

'It is a shame that Katya could not be here for the wedding.'

'She is settling into her new place, I am told. It is better this way, and we shall visit her when we are in Devon. We are going to spend part of our honeymoon there.'

There was a tap at the door then and the countess came in. She was laden with a bouquet of camelias, white irises and sweet smelling lily of the valley all bound together with trailing lace.

'Your bouquet has been sent up by the gardeners,' she said. 'How lovely the camelias are. Almost as pretty as the bride.'

'I shall go down now and wait for you,' Sally announced. 'It is almost time to leave for the church.'

As the door closed behind her, the countess handed Caroline the flowers and pressed cheeks.

'Will asked me if I would stay on at Pendlesham

323

after you are married,' she said, a suspicion of wetness in her eyes. 'I feel as if my son has come back to me, and I am sure it is on account of you.'

'Will has discovered his true self, just as I have,' Caroline replied, modestly. 'I, too, hope you will stay with us.'

'I shall think about it,' Margaret promised. 'And now it's time we went downstairs. Will and Fitz are already on their way to the church.'

They were to be married in the village church, so that all around could attend: friends, neighbours, Fitz's labourers were all invited. He had organised a splendid feast at the house for his people, fit to rival the wedding breakfast.

'It is a happy occasion,' he had said, when telling of his plans. 'I want everyone to share it.'

Caroline glanced towards the window. The sun had begun to shine, chasing away the clutter of grey clouds. It was the beginning of her perfect day.

Caroline stood facing down the aisle, on Lord Ross' arm. At the insistence of his Maudie he had offered to give her away, thereby implying approval of the marriage. It also meant that Fitz could stand up with Will as his best man. She smiled at her escort, then looked straight ahead towards the altar with its cross of shining brass, and began the walk, the last she would make as a single woman.

As she reached the side of her intended husband, Will turned to her with a smile of such tenderness that her heart swelled with love and joy.

'I love you,' he whispered. 'For always and ever.'

'I love you,' she whispered back, eyes shining.

The vicar cleared his throat and the marriage ceremony began.

'Dearly beloved, we are gathered together in the sight of God to join this man to this woman . . .'

How was it possible to contain such intense happiness? Caroline closed her eyes, trying to hold the moment. She wanted it to remain locked in her heart and mind for the rest of her life.

'If any man know of just cause or impediment, let him speak now or forever hold his peace . . .'

For a moment Caroline held her breath, but there was no ringing cry from the back of the church, no bolt from the skies to split them asunder. Then Will was slipping a wide gold ring on her finger, and it was all over. They kissed self-consciously and turned to leave the church to the sound of rejoicing bells.

It was as they stood outside the church listening to the bells and cheering voices when it happened. Afterwards, it would seem like a bad dream to Caroline, but in that moment of awful reality she saw it unfold under her gaze, sensed it before she understood, watched helplessly as the tragic events unfolded under her stricken gaze.

A child from the village had just presented her with a lucky horseshoe and retreated shyly to her parents. She became aware of Fitz, standing a little apart from a gathering of their more excited guests. His face wore a dazed expression and his lips were moving, as if they were intoning a prayer.

Caroline felt a prickle of concern and was about to draw Will's attention to his cousin when a man detached himself from the crowd of well-wishers. A man instantly recognisable, drawing a pistol from his coat pocket to point straight at the heart of her new husband.

'No!' she screamed as the shot rang out. 'Silas – no!'

Before the words were out of her mouth Fitz had

acted. He leapt in front of Will, pushing him sideways so that he cannoned into Caroline and they both fell to the ground. In the second before she was covered by her husband's body, she heard the crack of the pistol and Fitz's shout of pain, and knew that he had taken the ball meant for Will.

There was sudden pandemonium. Shouting and squealing as people tried to escape. Then a shrill, gurgling scream rising above the rest.

They told her long afterwards that a man had come swiftly behind Silas and slit his throat with the blade of a knife, disappearing as swiftly and silently as he came. No one remembered his face, though afterwards, a village woman swore he wore a gold ring in her ear. Caroline knew of only one man of that description who would have taken such sudden, violent and just retribution.

So Jake had come back this last time to see her wed.

But she heard and saw nothing after the dying scream of Silas, for she sank to the ground in a swoon.

When Caroline awoke it was to find herself lying in her own bed and Sally bending over her. She felt the coolness of cologne on her brow and sat up, passing a hand across her eyes.

'Where's Will? What happened to Fitz – is he badly hurt?'

'Lie back,' Sally commanded. 'You have had a terrible shock. You must rest.'

'Silas – has he been caught?'

'He will never trouble us again. You are quite safe, my darling.'

Caroline gave a glad cry and held out her hand as Will came into the room.

'Thank God you were not hurt,' she said. 'But

how is Fitz? I know he was shot. Please tell me the truth.'

Sally had slipped out without either of them noticing. Will sat down on the edge of the bed and reached for her hand.

'I fear he is gravely wounded,' he said, gloomily. 'The doctors are with him now. They have removed the ball from his chest but it was deeply embedded and he may not survive. He has not so far recovered consciousness.'

Caroline groaned. 'Oh, Will, it cannot be. He saved your life. If he had not acted so bravely Silas would have killed you.'

'I know this.' Will held her hand tightly. 'Just before he passed out Fitz spoke to me. Or rather, he spoke in my presence. He said "Now, Julia, now." '

'What did he mean?' Caroline recalled Fitz's curious behaviour immediately before the shooting. 'I saw him . . . he seemed to be talking to himself.'

'He often spoke to Julia when he was alone,' Will said, nodding. 'He believed she was a source of strength to him, that she helped him to get well again after Salamanca.'

'Then I pray she will come to him this time.'

'Amen to that.'

'We shall not be able to leave for our honeymoon tomorrow. We could not go while Fitz is ill.'

'It is not to be thought of.'

'Oh, Will,' Caroline cried, clutching his hand. 'Why did it have to happen? He was such a good man. That . . . that Taverner – I hope they hang him.'

'He is already dead. I told you – you have no need to fear him anymore.'

Her mouth opened in an O of surprise.

'What happened?'

'No one knows for sure, but someone took sudden retribution for what he did this morning.'

Caroline listened as he related to her the rumours and then she nodded. 'It was Jake, of course,' she said, with a cold smile of satisfaction. 'You know that, don't you?'

'I think it likely, but the matter is best not pursued, Caroline. For his sake.'

'No.' She looked up at him, understanding what was unspoken. 'Perhaps you are right, but I shall always believe that it was him.'

'And now you must stay in bed and rest,' Will said patting her hand. 'Our guests have all gone home. I cancelled the wedding breakfast, naturally.'

Caroline threw back the cover. 'I cannot lie here, useless. I could not rest knowing that Fitz is fighting for his life.'

'Nor I,' Will said, 'though there is little either of us can do for him. He is in the hands of the doctors now.'

'And God's. I shall pray that he lives, Will. If nothing else I can do that.'

Caroline spent an hour in the chapel in prayer for Fitz's recovery, but as she left and went back into the main part of the house she was met by Mrs Brandon and one look at the housekeeper's red eyes told her that his situation had not improved.

'I was about to fetch you, madam,' she said. 'His lordship has asked for you. Mr Carlton said would you please go up at once.'

'His lordship is worse?'

'The doctors say there is nothing they can do. He has lost too much blood.' Mrs Brandon burst into noisy sobs. 'Oh, Mrs Carlton, he must not die . . .'

'Do not upset yourself, Mrs Brandon,' Caroline said. 'While he lives there is still hope.'

Will met her at the door of Fitz's room.

'He wanted to speak to you alone, Caroline. He is very weak. You should go in at once.'

Caroline nodded, her heart too full to answer him and went in.

He was lying propped up against a pile of pillows, his eyes closed. As she approached he opened them, and a ghost of a smile tweaked his lips.

'Caroline . . . my dear. Do not . . . weep for me, I beg you.'

'Oh, Fitz,' she whispered, blinking away her tears. 'How can I not weep to see you like this?'

He held out his hand to her and she took it. 'It was my purpose in life to be there when Will needed me . . .' Fitz coughed and a trickle of blood escaped from the corner of his mouth. Caroline dabbed at it with her handkerchief. 'I want you to understand, Caroline. Don't let Will blame himself. It was my destiny. I was meant to live for this moment.'

'I don't understand. Why should you have to die now? It is too cruel. We love you . . .'

'And I love you both – you and Will,' Fitz said, with a weak smile. 'But now I am free . . . free to be with Julia.'

'Oh, Fitz.' Tears ran down Caroline's cheeks unheeded. 'Did you love her so much?'

'Yes. She was my heart, my life. I have not truly lived since she was taken from me.'

'And you believe that you will be with her?'

'Yes. I believe it, know it. I have waited for it.'

Caroline held his gaze. 'Then I shall not grieve for you, Fitz. I shall rejoice in your release.'

'I knew you would understand,' he murmured.

'Promise me you will not let Will take this on himself?'

'I promise,' she said. 'Dearest Fitz.' She bent to kiss his cheek.

His eyes were closed again. She sensed that his end was imminent and rose to summon Will.

'Goodbye, my dear,' Fitz murmured, and incredibly he was still smiling.

As she turned to leave she felt a sudden drop in temperature and it was as though something touched her cheek, like the softest of kisses. She could hear a faint sound . . . singing . . . high, sweet voices . . . like a choir of angels. At the door she looked back and for one brief moment she thought she discerned the form of a young woman bending over Fitz.

'Julia?' she said, uncertain yet unafraid.

The face that turned towards her was so lovely that Caroline understood why a man might die for love of her. She thought the woman smiled, then the vision was gone and she could not be sure her eyes had not deceived her.

She went outside to Will.

'You should say goodbye to him now,' she said. 'He is very peaceful. It will not be long now.'

Walking downstairs, Caroline let the tears slide freely down her face. Fitz would have his heart's desire at last, but Will would blame himself no matter what she said to comfort him.

Chapter Thirty-Six

Caroline awoke to find herself alone in her bed. She slid her hand across to where her husband had lain beside her and found the sheets cold. So it was a while since Will had left her to keep a vigil by his cousin's side in the chapel. She needed no one to tell her that was where he would be, for today was the day of the funeral of Lord Fitzgerald John Carlton. Fitz's coffin lay on a velvet covered bier in the family chapel, unsealed as yet so that anyone who cared to could pay their last respects to him. A steady stream of servants and people from the estate had passed through the chapel the previous day and Will had told Caroline of his intention to spend some time with his cousin at this quiet hour of the morning, when they could be alone together.

Her heart ached for him. As she had foreseen, he had taken Fitz's death hard and was blaming himself. She had seen the grief and guilt in his eyes, and the sudden flare of anger when one of the servants dared to address him as 'my lord'.

'My cousin is not buried yet,' he had replied coldly. 'Have the decency to wait until he is in his grave.'

His inheritance was unwelcome to him. He wanted no truck with Fitz's titles and wealth. That he was alive and married to the woman he loved whilst Fitz was dead filled him with shame.

Caroline had tried in vain to console him.

'Fitz was ready, even happy, to die,' she said. 'He is with Julia now, my love. Don't grieve so hard for him. He would not want it.'

'If I could believe that . . .' Will shook his head. 'I know you mean well, Caroline, but please leave me to settle this in my own way.'

Getting up from her bed, Caroline slipped on a silk wrapping robe and went over to gaze out of the window. The sky was just beginning to lighten.

She wanted to go to her husband, give him support and succour, but knew that he would not thank her.

His was a private suffering, to be borne by him alone.

In the chapel Will knelt with head bent and eyes closed. The burden of his guilt was almost unbearable. Fitz had died to save him, and the pain of that knowledge was as a dagger in his heart.

'How could you do this to me, Fitz?' he muttered.

Some subtle change in the timeless ambience of the chapel caused his head to jerk up. He felt a gossamer light touch on his cheek . . . a kiss or a breath of air, yet there was no air within the silent walls, just the smell of flowers and age. Generations of Carltons had worshipped here, many had been christened, buried or married within its walls.

A ray of light pierced the gloom and the coloured glass window gleamed like jewels: sapphire blue, brilliant green and blood red. Will's eyes were drawn towards the end of that rainbow of light as it fell on a silver cross on the altar. He froze, his blood turning to ice water in his veins. He rubbed his eyes, thinking it must be a trick of the light. That what he saw did not – could not – exist except in his imagination.

There before the altar, stood a man and a woman. The woman was dressed in a flowing dress of white like a bride, the man in a uniform of an officer of the Lancers. Will stared in stunned disbelief as the woman placed her hand in the man's and he heard her say, 'I am yours for always and ever.'

'Always and forever,' the man replied in a clear, strong tone.

Then he bent to lift her veil and kiss her gently on the lips.

'Fitz . . .' Will's voice was hoarse. 'Julia . . .'

They turned towards him but they did not see him. He was not there for them, for they were in a different time, a different place – a world that was theirs alone. They walked towards him and he saw that Fitz was younger and his limp was gone. A frisson of cold touched Will, then the phantom couple were past and he turned to watch as they proceeded down the aisle hand in hand from the chapel. He blinked as the light faded and they were no more.

It was not possible. Such things could not happen. The sane, worldly part of his mind denied it as an illusion, an hallucination borne of his grief and guilt. But he knew with an inner certainty that denied all reason and teaching that it had happened, that he had witnessed his cousin and Julia plight their troth to each other. With that certainty came an over-whelming sense of relief and joy.

Caroline had been right. He should not grieve too hard for Fitz. His cousin would be sorely missed, in the physical world, that was natural and right. But he need not rail against himself for the sacrifice Fitz had made. Fitz's body might lie in that coffin, but his spirit was with the woman he loved.

Always and Forever. Fitz and Julia had shared a

love so strong that even death could not deny them. They were together now for all eternity.

The new Lord Carlton walked from the chapel with a new resolve and a new purpose in his step. He understood now. He was the custodian of a great estate; it did not belong to him or any one man; it was his to cherish and safeguard and one day, inevitably, to bequeath to his sons and their sons after them. It was a weighty responsibility, but he would carry it with honour and with pride.

And he would do it with Caroline at his side. His lady. The woman he would love to the end of his life and perhaps to the end of time.

THE END